ASHES OF THE OLD

Paul McVay

Radically Poetic Press

The characters and events portrayed in this book are fictitious. Any similarity to real persons, living or dead, is coincidental and not intended by the author.

ISBN-13: 9781234567890
ISBN-10: 1477123456

Cover design by: Art Painter
Library of Congress Control Number: 2018675309
Printed in the United States of America

CONTENTS

Forward

Ashes was a book that took me a long time to put down on paper. Those of you that know me, know that it isn't that uncommon for me to get lost in my head from time to time but I did it. After all of these years I finally wrote a novel. A novel that I am proud of.

All you have to do is turn on the news, to truly appreciate how turbulent the world is. Often I wonder about how life would be if everything that I knew fell apart. Ashes is a raw and unfiltered vision of what I can imagine that life could become.

The people in this book, the good and the bad, are based off people that I have known in my life time. I wanted to explore the different cultures that I have been around in day to day life. The people that I interact with daily range so greatly that I have a strange incite into the divide in class.

Being a chef, one minute I can be hanging around the kitchen with people who have to fight everyday for everything that they have. In the next I can be standing tableside with someone who has millions in their bank account.

It's a strange cross section of people and I often wonder how they would react to each other in such an impossible situation. Ashes explores that conflict as I believe it would playout with good and bad on each side.

I'm going to keep this short and sweet. I hope that when you read this novel it makes you ponder how dark of future there could be. Also, I hope you can feel the underlying message, that love of your brothers and sisters in this human race is the greatest weapon that there is.

- To everyone out there that I havn't talked to or seen in a while, know I miss and love you.

CHAPTER 1

When the truck slammed to a stop, Emory's head bounced off the back window, and he caught Eugene as he slid into him. Dazed, Emory saw a ragged old man step out of the bushes, raise a shotgun and point it at them. Emory could barely make the man out. It looked like he was wearing threadbare old clothes that had been stained with blood and vomit. The man looked like hell and could barely walk a straight line. He was clearly intoxicated. That was not a good thing. Emory reached for his weapon, but his sister Emily put her hand on his and shook her head. Emily's wide eyes told Emory that with a matter of pumps that gun could put a lot of hurt on them.

Emory looked around at his friends and family in the truck. His sister Emily was holding her girlfriend Becky's hand. Becky had a look of fear on her face that no 19-year-old should ever be forced to express. Eugene, his eight-year-old younger brother, had taken refuge in Emory's girlfriend Margot's arms. Margot looked at Emory for an example of what to do. At 16 years old he didn't feel like he was qualified to be any kind of leader to the group.

In the cabin of the truck sat the two women that had saved their little family in their time of need. Jennifer sat with her hands glued to the wheel. Her mother Debbie sat with a double barrel shotgun across her sun dress. Debbie was a spry 65-year-old woman and Emory wondered how her daughter who was half of her age kept up with her. The silence was only a few seconds but to Emory it could have been a lifetime.

"Put yer guns on the ground and get out of the truck real calm-like and nobody is going to get hurt," a voice yelled from the front of the truck.

"Alright, mister. Just don't shoot us," Emily yelled back. Everyone threw the guns out of the truck, and they all got out with their hands held high.

"Everyone over here, on their knees. John, get your stinking ass up here. Keep your gun on them in case they try to get cute," the man said, laughing.

The two men were holding them hostage at gunpoint. The taller of the two men was thin and unshaven. He appeared to be their leader, as he was the one barking out orders. On the inside of the man's left forearm were Nazi tattoos of some sort. Things were going from bad to worse, Emory couldn't help but think as he looked at his sister's girlfriend, who was black. The woman he had fallen in love with sat on her knees next to him. She was Korean, and he didn't like the way this white-power fascist was looking at her.

They all did as they were told, lining up and getting on their knees. Emory studied the faces of the men. They looked old, beaten, and broken. They looked like they had nothing to lose. This was not good. Not good at all.

"If you want the truck and the gear, it's all yours; just let us go," Jennifer offered.

"Why in the hell would I do that? You all got something I need, and so many flavors to choose from. Which one should I taste first, Cecil?" He licked his lips and stared at the girls.

The man he had called Cecil was shorter. He was cranked out of his head on some kind of narcotic as he shook and shimmied all over the place, looking at the group. He wore a leather vest with no shirt on. The man's whole body was covered in Nazi and Nordic symbols. The man paced up and down and looked at the group while holding up his gun and pretending to shoot them.

"Damn, Hank. They all look pretty tasty to me. Maybe we

should try the two different flavors first. Then we can get rid of them and keep this little group pure and white the way God intended," he said, laughing and adjusting the crotch of his pants.

"Gross," Margot snickered.

"You're first then, buttercup," he said, picking her up by her hair and dragging her toward the bushes.

"Been a long while since I had some Chinese."

Emory jumped to his feet without even thinking. He rushed the man and delivered a low shoulder blow that took them both to the ground. He attacked like he was feral, and all thoughts left his head. He didn't even see the knife coming. Cecil sank the four-inch stag-handled knife from his belt into Emory's shoulder. Emory's adrenaline was pumping so hard he didn't even feel it. The assault didn't stop until the butt of Cecil's shotgun smashed into Emory's face, sending him flat on his back. Hank stood up and spit on Emory.

"I'm gonna kill your ass, but I'm going to make you watch me rape your girl first," he said with a sick smile as blood ran from his nose.

Hank got on his knees and started to rip off Margot's pants. Emory lay there in a fog, unable to move. Was this how it ended? It seemed like a cruel joke. He found love for the first time in his short sixteen years of life, and now it was being stripped away.

Was his sister next? Would it be her girlfriend? What were they going to do to his little brother? As the blood started to pool under him from his shoulder, he tried to will himself to move. Nothing. He looked over at his family. Emily was screaming something, but he couldn't make it out over the ringing in his ears. He turned his head in the mud and watched as the people he loved were about to be brutalized. He prayed for a miracle for the first time since his mother had passed. His sight was getting blurry, and it was hard to stay awake. Then came the darkness.

4 day earlier

The screeching blare of the alarm on Emory's phone shook him out of a night of restless sleep. Almost a year had passed since his mother had died, yet she haunted his dreams more often than not. It was always the same dream. The low light of the hospice wing gave him a headache as his eyes strained to adjust. He had watched for three months as the strong woman who had raised him shrank into a shadow of her former self. He could see her resolution to stay strong for his younger brother Eugene, who was only seven years old at the time. The fierce will to beat the sickness that plagued her burnt strongly in her eyes. But on this day, her last day, he saw something else. The sorrow that engulfed the room had infected her, and she couldn't hide it any longer.

His older sister Emily was hovering over her the way she always had. He watched as she adjusted the pillow and pulled the blanket up. At just nineteen years old, she had put it upon herself to be the surrogate mother for him and Eugene. She was perfect and proper in every way. She never lost control of her emotions, even when everyone around her was a cluster of emotions and tears. Her resolution was steadfast. Even though she didn't express her grief verbally, Emory could still see the sadness that filled her eyes. She was a strong woman. Much stronger than he was. He didn't have a filter on his feelings and wore his heart on his sleeve. As much as tried to be strong, he just couldn't be. It was all too much for him to handle, and he broke down on a regular basis. At fifteen years old, he couldn't process what was happening.

His mother's last request was to speak to everyone separately in order to say goodbye. This filled Emory with anxiety. He knew he was being selfish, but he didn't want to do this. He was last in line and the pressure was mounting. He felt like he was going to be sick, and his palms were sweating profusely. He couldn't help but sit, tapping his foot as he waited until his father stepped out of the room. His face was stricken with grief.

His dad had been a mess for months now. Growing up, Emory had never seen as much as a tear roll down the man's face; now he had seen a river. He knew how much his dad loved his mom. He had never even seen them fight. All his friends' parents were divorced, but his seemed to be as in love as the day they met. Emory's heart broke for his father. He knew what he was going through was hard. He couldn't imagine what it felt like to lose the love of your life. He looked up at his dad, whose eyes had tears welling.

"Your mother is ready to see you now, Emory," he muttered, tears rolling down his cheeks.

"I don't think I can do this, Dad," Emory said with shame, his eyes cast down to the floor.

"I know this is hard, son. This is one of the hardest things you will ever have to do. Look me in my eyes when I say this: there is no shame in tears. A broken heart breeds one of two things: strength or anger. You need to choose strength, or the anger and the hate will eat you up inside. I have seen what hate and anger can do to a man, and that is no way to live. Go in there and tell her how much you love her." With that, the tears rolled down both of their faces in a display of emotion that neither had the will or desire to contain.

Emory stood, and it took every ounce of control and strength in his body to keep his knees from buckling and collapsed into his father's embrace. That was where the dream always ended. Maybe the strength for what came next was not something that his mind possessed. Maybe it was the shame and guilt for his weakness that plagued his subconscious. Whatever the reason, it hurt him.

Her death had affected every aspect of his life. A deep crack of depression now ran through his brain. He no longer cared about school and saw it as just something that he had to do now. He had alienated most of his friends. He was quiet and brooded most of the time that he was there. He constantly wore headphones to keep people from talking to him. He lashed out at his family on a regular basis. With his mother gone, everything just felt pointless and bleak.

With that thought, he rose out of his bed and checked his phone: 6:30. Might as well get moving. He stared around his room in a foggy frame of mind as he sat up. There were still reminders of his mother everywhere he looked. He thought his bedroom was that of half a man and half a boy. There were the typical teenage things, such as a game console that was still humming from when he had forgotten to turn it off last night. There were also things like Lego sets and action figures displayed on his shelf that were gifts from his mother. These served as gentle reminders every day and all around. No matter where he was in this house, he had a reminder of the worst day of his life.

Emory picked up the picture of his family from the Christmas before his mother had gotten sick. They all looked so happy. Love permeated from the photo. It was one of the last times that his family had looked whole. Emory looked so much different then. So happy. The darkness had not taken control of him yet. He sat the photo frame back down and stumbled his way into the bathroom.

Junior year of high school had been good to Emory. He had lost most of his baby fat and grown five inches. He had been a husky kid before and endured bulling because of it. He now stood at six foot two and was tall and lean. Now most people left him alone. He looked into his green eyes, reflecting back at him in the mirror. His long, jet-black hair was disheveled, and he had the starting of a respectable beard. As he shaved his face, he heard his sister waking his brother from bed.

He could hear her singing a song to Eugene, but he

couldn't make out the melody. Emily was only a few years older than Emory but was far more mature than him. She was polite and cordial at all times. She was a petite girl who was always well-dressed and never even had as much as a hair out of place. She would wake up at the crack of dawn to meticulously get ready for the day before any of the rest of them thought about getting out of bed.

In Emory's whole life, as far back as when they were small children, he couldn't remember her so much as raising her voice at him (not even the times he deserved it). She had always spoken softly to him, explaining what he was doing wrong. If it weren't for her, he was sure his life would be taking an even uglier turn than it was. He was truly lucky to have such an amazing sister. Emily was a godsend for putting her life on hold in order to take care of three gruff men. As many times as her father begged her to go to college, she had refused him. She told their father that there would always be time for that later, but at the moment, she was going to keep her promise to her mother and help out. Emory loved her for it.

After shaving, he went to his dresser and pulled out some clothes. He typically always wore the same thing; Emory was a tee shirt and jeans kind of guy. He put on the black tee shirt and tightened his belt around his waist. Sitting on the edge of the bed, he put on his old, beat-up Chuck Taylors. They were one of the last things his mother had bought for him, and he wore them pretty much every day. He felt some sort of bond with the shoes. As time went on, they were falling apart and becoming less useful. It was exactly how he felt.

He walked over to his desk, shoved the books he needed for school into his bag, and slung the bag around his shoulder. He hadn't finished his homework last night and was going to have to do it before school started. The pitter patter of rain falling on the roof rang in Emory's ears and let out a sigh. They lived pretty close to the school but walking in the rain was not something he was looking forward to. He didn't have the motivation to get his driver's license. Emily had offered to teach him to drive, but he knew that meant long, awkward trips in the car. She would bombard him with questions about how he felt. It was easier to walk.

After getting dressed, he made his way downstairs to the kitchen. There, he found breakfast and the others waiting for him. Just like his bedroom, their kitchen also held a plethora of old memories: pictures of his mother on fridge, knick-knacks, embroidered dish towels... For such a small space, it held a ton of memories. Eugene, Emily, and Emily's girlfriend Becky all sat around the table, starting on a plate of eggs and bacon. Emily would make them breakfast every day and always made sure that they had enough to eat.

Becky was always around and all but official part of the family. For all his sister's grace and properness, Becky was the polar opposite. While Emily always wore skirts and dressed in pinks and pastels, Becks seem much more comfortable in jeans and a band tee shirt. Her long black dreadlocks went down past her shoulders and complemented the whole look. She wore thick black glasses and looked overall pretty hip. Being one of the few black people that lived in this town, she had also learned to deal with people's shit and didn't take flack from anybody. She was crass and had made Emory blush a few times. She would call him out on being a dick to his sister, telling him that she was only trying to help. She was the yin to Emily's yang. Emory had always enjoyed having Becks around.

"Hope you are hungry, pretty boy," Becky laughed.

"Hungry enough to eat a whole pig," Emory joked as he tussled his brother's hair.

"How could you eat a whole pig?" Eugene asked quickly, a look of bewilderment on his face.

"Got to start with the hooves. Everyone knows that," Becky mused, a sly smile creeping up her face.

"Stop it, both of you," interjected Emily. "You don't start with the hooves. The snout goes first." This roused laughter out of the collective group. "You heard from Dad? He didn't call last night."

"No, but sometimes he passes out after a long drive. Half the time his phone is dead, and after the hustle of getting to his hotel, he forgets to charge it. I'm sure we will hear from him soon. Not like anything exciting happens here anyway."

"It's not like him to not call."

"Meh. I'm sure he's fine. Anyway, you want to give me a ride to school? I really don't feel like hoofing it through the rain."

"Hoofing it?" Eugene said as he dropped his bacon back to the plate.

CHAPTER 2

School was only an eight-minute drive, but it felt like hours as Emory reflected on the past and stared at the trees of the subdivision whipping past his window. Their neighborhood was full of cookie-cutter houses that mostly all looked the same. Most of the people felt the same, too. All the times he had watched his parents interact with the neighbors were the same old talking points. Nobody ever did anything different or exciting. It was always a practice in the mundane. Take out the trash. Mow the yard. Watch football and drink beer. It was a boring existence to be a part of, and it dragged on him.

The worst part was when his mother died. Every single person around them brought flowers and food to the house. That was nice of them and didn't bother Emory. What bothered him were the constant questions. How are you doing? Are you okay? Eventually he had learned to wear his headphones when he heard the doorbell.

They had lived in this subdivision ever since he was a small child. He could remember how it used to seem so large and exciting, but now that he was practically grown, it seemed like a small prison to him. A small prison of conformity. It was the most boring place in the world, Emory often thought, as he dreamed of big adventures in cities like New York or Los Angeles. He just wanted to be somewhere else. Really any place but this.

"Having the dreams again?" Emily said in a soft, nurturing voice.

"Never stopped. Really don't feel like talking about this."

"Talking may help..."

"No."

Sometimes he hated the fact that she was so obsessed with his wellbeing. Her only desire was to help him. He wanted to be left alone. Her calmness drove him up a wall. She hurt too, even though she hid it. He could hear her crying in her room on some evenings. Thankfully she had Becky to lean on. The sadness that still lived behind that glowing smile of hers crept just below the surface. She just wanted to be motherly, but his mother she was not.

"Thanks," he managed to squeak out as he jumped as fast as his legs would carry him out of the car.

Monroe High School was a huge old building. It had been built in the 90's and had not been updated much since. The sidewalk up to the stairs was surrounded with trees, and a giant bee mascot statue stood in front of the entrance. It was a large school district, and Emory was one of five hundred kids in his class. Being in such a large social setting, it was easy for him to put in his headphones and get lost in the crowd.

As he climbed the stairs, his best friend Kenny was waiting for him at the top. Kenny and Emory had been friends since they were five years old. Kenny was a short and stout boy with cropped black hair and deep emerald-green eyes. He was one of the few black kids that attended the school and had faced bullying because of it. But through adversity, he had gained strength and was tough young man. He was hard and callous, and Emory was glad he was his friend and not his enemy. When Emory had alienated all his other friends, Kenny had refused to leave his side. As tough as he was, he had shed more than one tear while Emory's mother had been sick. He had been there for him through his mother's passing, and Emory couldn't imagine life without him.

"What up, duder? You hear about Sarah's party on Saturday night? I don't know about you, but I am ready to get tore up."

Kenny was always doing this to Emory. Trying to convince him to go and do things. Trying to break him out of the funk he was in. Kenny's intentions were good, but Emory didn't have the desire to do much of anything. He was content with hiding in his room with a book or playing video games. A few times he had given in and gone to parties with Kenny. He'd stood there, listening to the musings of his peers. He didn't feel like he could relate to any of the people that stood around telling stories and trying to climb an invisible ladder of popularity.

Most of the teen problems seemed mundane and tripe to him. He didn't care about who was dating who. He had been to a few dances with girls and even a couple dates, but he felt disconnected from them. He was shy and a little awkward around girls still. Before his transformation from a chubby boy into a fit man, no girls had really shown that much interest in him, so this new world of dating was hard for him to feel comfortable in. His mother had told him that fate would one day bring a girl in his path, and when they crossed it would be love at first sight. She was always a romantic like that. She was hopelessly optimistic about the good in the world and never focused on the bad. She just acknowledged it and moved on. She loved to tell the story of how she and his father had met. Emory hoped that someday he would find someone like that, but he wasn't holding his breath. He was used to being alone. It was safer, in his eyes, to be lonely then have his heart shattered again.

He didn't care about the clothes that people wore. Most days he could be caught in a pair of jeans and a tee shirt. Most importantly, he didn't care about who and what was considered cool. He had always done the things he liked, no matter how nerdy he might have seemed.

He froze in hesitation when Scott Ludlum appeared standing in the hallway with his two fellow football players, who followed him everywhere. They were like a pack of wolves. Scott was the alpha, but the other two could always smell a fresh kill and were quick to jump in. They had a superiority complex and were not afraid to flex it. They walked the halls of the school like they owned them. Nobody was safe from their merciless onslaught of insults and jeers. Emory had been on the receiving side of it on a handful of occasions.

Scott and Emory had been friends in elementary and middle school. That seemed like a lifetime ago. It was a simpler time, when everything seemed happier. Many weekends were spent playing *Call of Duty* and smashing copious amounts of pizza and washing it down with Monster. They would take turns spending the night at each other's houses. They were close, and besides Kenny, Scott was the closest thing that Emory ever had to a second brother. That was one of the things that made Scott so hard to handle now. He knew Emory's family and his secrets. Neither of which he was afraid to exploit.

That was the first time that Emory had learned nothing good ever lasted. Change always came and messed things up. That change occurred when Scott had tried out for football at his dad's behest. He made the team, and with that came new friends. Cool friends, who didn't want anything to do with a nerd like Emory. It was a hard thing for Emory to handle. He had tried to hold on to their friendship, but it slipped further and further away. until one day it was just gone. He hoped that he could pass without being noticed, but alas, Scott turned his head.

"What up, dyke boy?" This was not an uncommon jest thrown at Emory, because it was a well-known fact that his older sister was with a woman.

People assumed that his sister's relationship was a point of contention in his life. After all, Ohio wasn't the most forward-thinking place. It had never bothered Emory that his sister was with a woman. He was just happy that she could find someone that she could love and share her life with. He could see from the way that they looked at each other how deep their bond was. He hoped he was that lucky someday. When Scott said this, it stung a little more, since he had known her like a sister.

"What did you say to me?"

"Are you deaf? I said, 'what up, dyke boy?' How is that sexy little bitch? Bet if I got my hands on her and she had a real man she would be begging for it every day," he said with a sly smile as he flexed his arms.

Emory didn't know why this statement affected him so much more on this day. Maybe it was the smug smile on Scott's face. Maybe it was how proud of himself Scott was. Emory rarely got angry to the point of wanting to hit someone, but something about Scott's smugness on this day struck a deep nerve. He wanted to punch him in his face. He wanted to tear him apart.

"One day someone is going to knock your teeth out of the back of that thick head of yours. I hope I am there to see it," Emory said as he moved close enough to smell the Juicy Fruit that Scott chomped annoyingly.

"Who's that going to be? You? Your little homeboy over there?" Scott said, spitting his gum in Kenny's direction.

"Yeah, maybe," Emory blurted as his bravery started to waiver.

Emory had been through a growth spurt and had thinned out, but his physique was lean and slender. Scott had cannons for arms and a neck as thick as a tree trunk. As his fist started to ball up, ready for a fledgling attempt to defend himself, his phone started vibrating in his pocket. Who would be calling him now? His shaking hands retrieved the phone, and the name read *dad*. His dad had only called him during school one other day: his mother's last. Dread choked his throat as he briskly turned and started down the hallway.

"Dad? What's wrong? Is everything okay?"

"No, everything is not okay. Emory, you need to listen to what I am about tell you very closely. I don't know how much time we have. Things are about to become very dangerous. You need to get to Emily and take the family to your grandfather's house in Kentucky. Emily knows what to do. This next part is the most important thing I am going to say to you. Trust no one unless they are family. No cops, no soldiers, no..." He never finished that sentence. The phone when black, and for a split second Emory thought he saw it smoke before the lights went off, leaving him in darkness.

CHAPTER 3

The sunlight crept through the deteriorating bedsheet curtain of John's trailer like a rude reminder of another shit day to come. He had no idea what time it was. All he knew was that the whiskey from last night still permeated as the dominant taste in his mouth. He rolled over, and a bottle stuck him in the ribs hard enough to send him into a silent rage that was only expressed through a grunt. He sat up and grabbed his phone. Strangest thing was that it wouldn't turn on. "Piece of crap," he mumbled under his whisky breath as he slammed it back down on the table.

He reached into his jacket, which was still covered in little bits of vomit from his escapades the night before and pulled out an empty pack of Marlboro Reds. "Great," he thought as he flipped over his kitchen table, sending empty fast food wrappers and beer cans soaring across the trailer. He continued his assault of the putrid trash across the kitchen until he found the keys to his 1990 Ford Ranger. It may have been a piece of crap, but after all the abuse and drunken backing into cars, trees or whatever was in his way, it still fired up every morning.

When he slammed the front door shut on the way out, he didn't even bother to lock it. What was anyone going to steal? He piled himself into the front seat and turned the key in the ignition. Nothing. The stream of profanity and racial epitaphs he vomited out of his mouth were enough to make David Duke proud. The thought he had as he slammed his head over and over into the steering wheel was: why did this always have to happen to him?

CHAPTER 4

Emory tried to restart his phone five times. Nothing. The lights were still off, and most of the students lingered nervously in the halls, unsure of what to do. It was oddly quiet: just the low sound of hushed whispers. Everyone stood there, waiting for something to happen. Emory could almost taste the uneasiness floating over the crowd like a thick fog.

What had his father meant about not trusting anyone? Was he stuck in a dream right now? He had never met his grandpa. Hell, his father shut down every conversation he had tried to start about his dad's past. How messed up would things have to be for him to send them there? All Emory knew of his grandfather was that his mother had told them that his father and grandfather didn't get along. "At least it would be a new one," he thought, if this did turn out to be a dream. What the hell was going on? A voice over a megaphone broke his daze.

"Everyone to the gym in an orderly fashion. Come on, let's get moving, people. Nice and slow."

"We aren't going in that gym," Emory barked in an authoritative tone that took him and Kenny both by surprise.

"What? Why? I can't handle another detention," Kenny begged.

"Somehow, I don't think that detention is going to matter anymore," Emory said with a distant voice as he turned for the doors.

Emory had no idea what was going on, but he knew it wasn't good. His stomach tightened as he replayed the phone conversation over and over again in his head. What had his father meant? This made no sense to him. What was different about this power outage? Why wasn't his phone working? Panic started taking over his mind. He walked at a brisk pace to try to outrun his obsessed mind.

The rain had let up some as they walked down the stairs in awkward silence. The wind was brisk and cold as the slow rain seeped into their clothes. At least it was late summer and not fall, he thought to himself as he let out a shiver. Looking at the road, something started to feel funny. Nothing was moving. All the cars were parked. People stood outside of them, confused as they tried to figure out why their vehicles had stopped running. Then came the realization all the stoplights were out, too.

They passed one man standing outside of his Mercedes. He was wearing an expensive suit and had the hood open. He was trying to use his cell phone and letting out a stream of curse words. As they passed, he looked up and pointed at his car and shrugged. He asked them to use their phones and was very rude when they politely told him that theirs were dead as well. The last thing they saw as they walked away was the man throwing his phone to the pavement, irately stomping on it. It had been less than fifteen minutes since Emory's dad's cryptic warning. He had already seen someone losing it. With that thought, he picked up the pace.

They had made it about three quarters of the way home when the footsteps behind them picked up speed. The blow took Emory off his feet and slammed him face-first into the sidewalk. His face burned, partially from the pain but mostly from the rage building up inside of him. Scott. He knew it even before he rolled over. How long had they been following him? This was the last thing that he needed.

"Get up and take this ass whipping like a man, bitch," Scott snarled as his two cronies cracked up behind him like cackling hyenas.

“Real tough, sneaking up behind me,” Emory responded, the rage burning white-hot inside of him, choking his words.

“Better watch that mouth, faggot.” That was the trigger that released the rage. Emory swung his backpack full of chemistry and English books as hard as he could at Scott’s face.

The blow caught the boy off guard and smashed into him with enough force to take him off his feet. Instantly, the other two jackals were on top of Emory, overpowering him to the ground. Kenny smashed one of the boys in the face, knocking him off Emory, and Kenny and the goon both crashed to the ground. By this point, Scott had regained his composure and started to kick a fledgling Emory. Scott’s nose had been smashed sideways by the assault, and a cascade of scarlet soaked into his shirt. Emory lay there, taking the beating. He was losing his breath and unable to speak. The distinct sound of the car came before he saw it. It was his dad’s Charger. He looked up in time to see Emily jump out and run up to the scene.

“STOP IT! NOW!” erupted from her lips in anger.

The boys stopped the pummeling, and Scott stepped up an inch from her face. They stood there, silently staring at each other for a long moment. Emory was taken aback. This was the first time he had heard Emily show any form of anger, let alone yell. He was frozen, staring at her. Her face was flush with rage, and her eyes burned into Scott. This had to be a dream, he thought as blood ran down his face. He knew it wasn’t, though. He had never felt this much pain in any dream.

“Look at what your brother did to my face, whore,” Scott spat as blood flew from his lips.

“I’m sure he was only defending himself,” she said, regaining her sweet tone, but her eyes still shot lasers. “It’s over now, and the three of us will be on our way.”

“It’s over when I say it’s over. I have never hit a girl before, but if you try to stop this, I may pick today to start.”

Emily stepped back and let out the slightest of sighs.

Emory started to get up, ready to try to defend his sister. It was one thing to bully him and kick his ass. It was another thing entirely to assault his tiny sibling. He didn't know how, but he was going to defend Emily. He balled up his fist in anticipation of attack.

"Fine." In the blink of an eye, she open-chopped Scott's windpipe, sending his hands to his throat as he stumbled backward with a stare of disbelief.

He made a step toward her. Without hesitation, she sent a knee into his groin. As he doubled over in pain, she smashed both fists into the back of his head, causing him to finally collapse to the sidewalk. The moment seemed to last for a lifetime, and everyone else stood frozen in shock. Emory's mouth hung open. Had his sister just kicked the ass of a man three times her size?

"Get your bag and come on, Emory. It's time to go."

Emory walked over and picked up his school bag, which was now stained with Scott's blood, still confused about what just transpired.

"You two, get in the car." Emily knelt on one knee next to a pain-stricken Scott, who didn't have enough hands to cradle all the parts of him that were in pain.

He just lay there, mumbling and confused as his two brave counterparts stood back and stared at Emily, unable to hide their fear of the petite girl as they stepped back.

"What happened, Scotty? You used to be such a nice boy. Some friends you got there, just watching a hundred-and-twenty-pound girl beat the stuffing out of you. Know this: If you ever put your hands on one of us again, and I mean anybody that I care about, I'm going to take your life away from you. Now you know I can, and from what just happened, I don't think it would be very difficult. You got off lucky this time. Next time, I won't be as generous." With that, she stood, brushed her skirt straight, readjusted her blouse, and turned for the car.

CHAPTER 5

Alex tightened the black bandana under his hoodie to conceal his face as he stared into the mirror. Badass, he thought. His outfit was a black pair of jeans and an over-sized black hoodie with a hammer and sickle patch over his heart and an American flag on the back. If this didn't strike fear into the capitalist pigs, then he didn't know what would. He picked up his padlock, tied onto a length of para cord. If a Nazi got out of pocket, then he would strike him down. He put the can of pepper spray in his back pocket and his folding knife in the front.

Alex had always been the weird kid at school. He didn't have very many friends, and after he graduated, he just sat around in his mother's house. He didn't have any ambitions, and all he did was surf 4Chan and reddit all day. He barely left the house, even though his mother begged him to get a job or apply to schools. But Alex was in no big hurry. Eventually he started to follow an antifa thread on reddit. He had never been interested in politics, but something about this struck him.

He started by going to some unofficial meetings while the group was in the baby stages of forming. There he found a place where people accepted him for who he was. He made friends and going to the rallies gave his empty life a purpose. He was going to fight against tyranny and help build a stronger and more fair country. As he took one last look in the mirror, his final thought of the morning was what he could do to impress his new group of friends.

"What the hell was that?" stuttered Emory, still flabbergasted by the outpouring of violence his elder sister had just unleashed.

"There are some things that you don't know about me, Emory. Some things you don't know about this family. There is a deep crack that runs with us, and it full of darkness and mystery," she said, looking over at him briefly before diverting her eyes back to the street. His mind couldn't process the warrior that his sister had become in a split second.

"Where did you even learn how to do that?" he blurted.

"Dad taught me," she said in a cold tone.

"Why?"

Emily pulled the Charger over to the shoulder of the road and turned in her seat to stare directly into Emory's eyes.

"I'm going to tell you everything that you don't know about this family once, so sit there and pay attention. You know how Dad refuses to speak about his childhood and his family? Ever wonder why we have never met any of them? There is a good reason for that. Let's just say that Dad's upbringing in the hollers of Kentucky was colorful at best."

"Why did he tell me that we needed to go there, then?"

The color drained from Emily's face. "You spoke with Dad?" she said with a certain ring of hopefulness in her voice.

"Yeah, right before the power went out and the phone stopped working," he stated without quite understanding why she was making such a big deal out of it.

"What did he tell you?"

"Get to Grandpa. Don't trust anyone who isn't family. Beware of cops and soldiers. Why the hell does he want us to go to Grandpa's if the two of them hate each other? None of this makes any sense," answered Emory, adequately annoyed.

"Grandpa is the leader of a small militia."

"What? Our grandpa is a soldier?" Emory asked, unsure if he really wanted to go down the rabbit hole any deeper.

"Here is what I know. When Dad was a child, Grandpa had what he loosely called a militia. Back then, it was just an excuse to dress up and drink beer in the woods. They would do things like toy drives on Christmas and give out turkeys on Thanksgiving. It was just a bunch of 'good ole boys having fun shooting guns and raising hell,' as Dad put it."

"That answer isn't nearly as crazy as I thought it was going to be," he said, almost disappointed somehow at the lack of climax in the story. Some adventure might be what he needed to shake the fog of harsh memories that haunted his dreams. He looked at Kenny, who was sitting there shaking his head.

"The story gets crazier. Everything was going fine until our grandmother was killed. She was shot at a robbery at a gas station completely by chance. Bad guy got in a shootout with an attendant, and she caught a stray bullet. Dad was with her on that day. He was ten years old and covered in her blood, frozen in shock when Grandpa showed up on the scene."

"Our grandma was murdered?"

"Yes, and from there it was a slow decent into madness for Grandpa. He fell into a whisky bottle and couldn't seem to swim his way back out. He alienated his friends, only keeping the most hardcore in his militia group, which he had renamed the Redwood Militia. He started to preach about the corruption of society and the upcoming fall of the nation."

"Oh god, so the man is batshit crazy?"

"That's what Dad said. They trained constantly, and he sold off all of their possessions and moved to a cluster of cabins they had built in the hills, completely off grid. Our father was raised from the age of ten to be a soldier, waiting on the collapse of the United States." The awkwardness at divulging this had made Emily's face turn red.

"White people are crazy as shit," muttered Kenny in the backseat.

"I have so many questions that I don't even know where to start. How did we end up in Cincinnati, Ohio? Why aren't we on the side of a mountain, elbow-deep in a pot of squirrel stew?" Emory half joked.

"Grandpa and Dad had a falling out when he was seventeen. Dad had met Mother a year previous at a church function. Church was the only contact with the outside world that they were allowed. Father had never had much faith since watching his mother bleed out on a dirty gas station floor, but it was something to do that wasn't mucking out latrines or cleaning rifles. He said he knew that he loved Mother from the first time he saw her singing in the choir. He pursued her, and they quickly became close, constantly sneaking out to see each other. She showed him how the world really was. Took off his blinders, he said."

"Thank God for that," Emory stated. The way their father had always followed their mother around asking her opinions on the tiniest of decisions was starting to make sense.

"They had been planning to run away together when he turned eighteen, but events happened that made that timeline move up. One day Grandpa started growing weed. Seemed harmless at first. Then he started growing pounds of it. He took it into Louisville and traded it with gangs for ammunition and guns. Dad knew it was time to get out. He tried to convince his brother to come with him. We have an uncle, by the way. Don't know his name. Dad always called him Moose. Anyway, Moose was younger and went straight to Grandpa with his plan, and dad and our grandfather had an altercation that came to blows. Then Dad left with nothing but the clothes on his back." She exhaled.

"Okay. Yikes. Next question: why are you driving Dad's

car? He usually flips out if anyone even looks at the thing. Why in the shit would we go down to Kentucky if our grandfather is a drug-dealing, bomb-building, crazy sack of hill-jack?"

"We were hit with an EMP ."

"What's an EMP?"

"Electro-magnetic pulse. High altitude nuclear detonation," she said uneasily.

"Holy shit, someone nuked us." The panic in Kenny's voice exploded from the back seat.

"Yes. All electronics with a computer are effectively dead. Cell phones, laptops, cars. Somebody just sent us back to the 1700s, and when the grocery stores close because none of the trucks run, things are going to become ugly. People are going to kill each other for the things that we throw in the trash today. This car runs because it was built before the start of computers in vehicles. That's why Dad has it. Can take the boy out of the crazy rightwing militia, but some of that paranoia seemed too embedded for Dad to completely expel. Think that's crazy, just wait until I show you when we get home."

The shock of what she had just said made Emory numb, and he just stared out the window, lost in thought. He could deal with having some wild crazy hillbilly family members but processing the fact that they were about to deal with a whole new way of life was far from comprehension.

"Yo, pull over. I have to get off this crazy train," Kenny said. "Look, I love you guys, but this is too much for me to process. I'm going home, and I think you guys are blowing this way out of proportion. Power will be back in a couple of hours, at most a day. I will catch you later, Emory." He shook his head in disbelief as he got out of the car and jogged off, looking over his shoulder with a glance of judgement. Emory watched his friend wander off and wondered if he was right. This couldn't be real. Could it?

"You think he will be okay?" Somehow, he knew what Emily was saying was true. He could feel the truth in her words. Emily was not one to mince words. Pain twisted in his abdomen and he felt sick to his stomach. This was not the kind of adventure he was looking for.

"I really hope so, but I fear he is going to be swallowed up in the wave of violence that is about to wash over this nation," Emily said, sounding melancholy as she started the car back down the road.

CHAPTER 6

When they pulled up to the house, Eugene was sitting next to Becky on the steps to their home. Emily stopped and got out of the car. She stepped out, raising the garage door and scanning the area, hoping that nobody had seen them pull in. She slowly pulled the car into the garage and sat with her hands on the wheel after she cut the engine, lost in deep thought. Emory got out of the car and put his head in his hands, stuck in disbelief. Eugene ran into the garage with a huge grin on his face as Emily finally got out of the car.

"Emory is home early!" he said, running up to hug his brother. The boy's embrace broke Emory out of his trance and his hug made Emory feel a little better.

The boy had no idea about what was going on and his childlike innocence was something that Emory hoped he could hold on to. His brother had been down a rough road when their mother had died. Eugene didn't fully understand the situation. He didn't understand that she was never coming home again. So much grief and sadness for a six-year-old boy to deal with. It broke Emory's heart. When Emory was going through his distancing phase, Eugene was the only person that he still made an effort to reach out to. If what Emily had said was true, this was a terrible thing the boy was going to have to suffer through now.

"Becky says that we are going to go get Uncle Ronnie and then go camping." He barely got the words out, his whole body shaking in excitement.

Uncle Ronnie was their mother's brother. Ronnie was an ex-Marine and had done two tours in Afghanistan as an infantry man at first and then a third with a special forces team. Now he worked in IT at the Kroger building downtown. The death of their mother had affected him deeply. He would often talk about how God was not fair to take her when he had so narrowly escaped death in the Middle East. He used to be a regular around the house, teasing his sister while he sipped on beers with their father. Now they were lucky to see him once a month. What concerned Emory was the fact that he lived in the city, and right now that was someplace he didn't really think they should be.

"Are we going to go downtown and pick him up?" The concern showed on his face.

"Yeah," Emily said, "we are going to spend the night here and move down there in the morning. Less likely to run into looters if we go earlier."

"Are you sure that's a good idea? Is that what Dad said we should do?"

"No. He said to avoid the city at all costs, but we need Uncle Ronnie. Dad trained me and told me I was in charge of the two of you if anything ever happened to him. That being said, I would feel a lot better if a 250-pound ex-combat Marine was with us."

"I mean, it makes sense, I guess. Still feels like it's going to be an unnecessary risk."

"It's not up for discussion. We need him and that is that. Now, we need to go to Dad's bedroom to gear up. Please don't freak out at what you are about to see." She seemed hesitant to even bring up whatever she was going to show him.

This intrigued Emory, who pondered what he was about to walk into. By the time they had reached the top of the steps, he was nervous. Did he really know his father? Why didn't his father train him? Emory felt a little betrayed that he had been kept in the dark about all of this. He froze at the threshold to his parents' bedroom. He hadn't stepped foot in there in a year.

Walking in, it was like time stood still. His father had changed nothing in the room. All her makeup still sat on her vanity. Her various frilly decorations were still scattered throughout the room. Her giant girly pillows still adorned the bed. The room was spotless and pictures of the two of them were still everywhere. Emory took a minute to let it all wash over him. Maybe his father had left it this way so that he still felt close to her, he thought. Or maybe he just didn't want to admit to himself she was gone. He never really talked about it and Emory was okay with that. Whatever the reason, it made him sad.

The thoughts quickly cleared as he watched his sister walk over to the giant mirror on the wall. The mirror had been hanging in the same spot for all of Emory's life. He had never really thought anything of it. Emily pulled a small magnet from the dresser next it and ran it at the top right corner. There was a click and the mirror popped away from the wall on hidden hinges. A secret room in his house.

The room was small and at some point had been a walk-in closet, but now it looked like *Call of Duty* had puked on the walls. The far-right wall had a large work bench with a peg board above it, holding what he was guessing were gunsmithing tools. Fluorescent lights hummed a low blue glow, making everything seem more ominous.

The wall to the left was sectioned off in five rows. At the top of each row was a name written in bold block letters. It seems that each member of the family had gear and weapons that his father had been storing under them. All the gear matched. Each member had a rifle, handgun and knife hanging on the pegboard. Following that, each name had a black tactical backpack.

The rifle was an AK47 with four thirty-round magazines and one stuck in the gun. The handgun was a Glock 19 with four magazines and one in the weapon. The knife was a Gerber LMF2 sitting in a Kydex sheath. Under Emory's name there was also an intricate and beautifully engraved tomahawk. He looked to the wall on the right and there was an enormous amount of freeze-dried food, like they used when they went camping, and around fifteen cases of water.

The sight of the guns made Emory tense. He had never even touched a firearm before in real life. They made him nervous. His dad had never mentioned anything about guns to him once in his life. His mother had always told him that they were dangerous, and he should stay away from them. He had played tons of video games that had guns in them. Seeing them here in real life was something different. His hands were sweating, and he was transfixed by the wall of firepower.

He finally found the words to speak. "What is all of this?"

"Dad always called this "the social contingency plan." He said that when he left Grandpa's house, he tried his best to file all of this away but being unprepared made him restless. He put all of this up over a long span of years. Having this let him sleep at night knowing that if something catastrophic happened, his children wouldn't have to go without."

"Did Mom know?" He was saddened by seeing her place on the wall.

"Yes, and while she didn't buy into it per say, she tolerated it to make him happy. Our mom was a warrior woman. She helped with my training."

"Training?"

"When I turned sixteen, they both told me that there were some things I needed to learn. Dad was methodical in drilling into my head that I needed to know how to protect myself. Said that being a girl in this world was hard enough but being gay meant I had an extra target on my back. They both taught me self-defense, some of which you saw me show to Scott. They also made me be proficient with a firearm and some basic survival and bush craft stuff."

"How come they didn't train me?"

"Dad was going start when you turned sixteen. I was sworn to secrecy about this. He wanted to do it in his own way." She picked the Glock up off the wall and shoved the gun into the front of the black tactical pants that she had changed into. Emory decided to follow suit, went over to where the guns were and reached for one.

"No. You don't get a gun until I have time to show you how to use it," she scolded, slapping away his hand.

"You point it at the bad guy and pull the trigger. How hard can it be?" Emory said, annoyed.

"A gun in an untrained hand is a very dangerous thing. Take the knife and the tomahawk, and I will teach you how to use the gun later."

"Why didn't Dad teach me how to do any of this? Why only teach you?"

"He wanted to wait until you turned sixteen like he did with me. He said he didn't want to interfere with your childhood like his had been. Now help me get the car packed up; we're going to leave at first light."

"I guess the old saying is true. You can take the boy out of the crazy militia, but you can't take the paranoia out of the boy," Emory said as he took a minute to look uncomfortably about the room.

CHAPTER 7

John, over the fit of rage directed at his old junk truck, got out and stared at the truck in disgust. Something just didn't sit right with him. First the phone and then the truck. Was he having a string of bad luck or was it something more? He slowly made his way back into the trailer and flipped the switch for the lights. Nothing. Power out too. Had to be something he was missing, and whatever that was started to flare up his paranoia.

He went to the edge of his dirty, unkempt bed, reached underneath and retrieved an old, tattered shoebox. Slowly raising the lid revealed a black bandana wrapped around a nickel plated .38 revolver. It was the only thing of value that he had not sold off, being a family heirloom from his beloved grandfather. It had been years since he had put it away, but it was still as shiny as the day it had been placed away. Sitting next to it was a 50-round box of .38 ballpoint ammo. He picked up the revolver, popped the cylinder open and spun it. He slowly loaded six rounds in and snapped the cylinder shut with the flick of his wrist. He stood and shoved the revolver down the back of his pants, wishing it was a snub nose instead of the four-inch barrel. Time to see what the hell was going on.

Walking down the road in the hot Kentucky sun was not a pleasant experience. He lived in the middle of nowhere. Nobody lived nearby, and he liked it that way. The solitude gave him time to do whatever he wanted to do. He could be as drunk and loud as he wanted without any busybodies around to get in his business.

Because of his body lacking alcohol and nicotine, he had to make a pit stop to vomit and wretch every half mile. The walk to his friend Hank's house was five miles, but today it felt like he wouldn't make it. He had made the journey to Hank's house a million times in the old truck. Even drunk, he eventually found his way. Today, though, with the onset of the shakes setting in, he thought he might as well roll in the ditch and die. Not like anyone would miss him, he thought bitterly.

Hank and John had been friends since they were both boys. The two had raised a lot of hell together over the years. The thought sent his lips curling up in a sick smile. In high school they had run the school, bullying anybody who dared to question them. After school, they had decided to save up money and buy houses near each other. Hank was a good man, he thought. After moving in, the two of the them decided that they were sick of working day jobs just to have their checks taxed by the federal government. Just to give it away to all the damn minorities, as they put it.

So, they quit and become outlaws of sorts. They had decided that the easiest and cheapest way to get rich was to get into manufacturing crystal meth. That was not anything new to these parts, but the demand was high, and they knew it would be easy to move. It had been a learning curve, but eventually, after a few failures and explosions, they had a product that was more-or-less smokable.

Now they had a more unique problem: how the hell they were supposed to sell it. Luckily for them, Hank had a cousin in the Aryan Brotherhood. They had a meeting arranged for them, and it had gone so well that John had decided to join Hank and his cousin in getting SS bolts tattooed on their upper arms. They had made a lot of meth, but the money was just enough to get by. His train of thought was interrupted when he saw Hank's 1977 Ford F-150 pull up.

"God damn, partner. You look like warmed-over horse shit." Hank laughed.

"Piece of shit truck wouldn't start," John replied, spitting out the side of his mouth.

"No shit. We done and got ourselves nuked last night. Get your ugly ass in and I'll tell you all about it," Hank said, giddy as a schoolgirl.

As they drove down the street toward the one gas station near them, John quietly looked out the window. Hank had come to the rescue with some smokes and a small bottle of whiskey that he had stashed away in the glove box. As he puffed and blew the smoke out the window, Hank rambled on. Hank laid it out for him about what had transpired. Hank told him about the EMP and the effects that he had learned from online survivalist forums.

Hank was really into conspiracy theories. He always had been. He would spend hours of his day online, reading various stories from crackpot websites. He spent hours at a time watching things like Info Wars on YouTube. He took the crazy as fact and spewed it out every time they were around each other. This annoyed John to no end. John was a quiet man. The only thing that he ever questioned was where he was going to get his next drink, but he let Hank ramble on. Pulling into the gas station, they were the only car in the parking lot.

"So, you are saying nobody is coming to help? We're all alone?" John asked with a nervous shake in his voice.

John didn't know what to believe. It was strange that the power outage had affected his car and phone. Maybe Hank was right. There was a first time for everything, he supposed. Then again, this was the same man who told him that the chemicals in the water were turning the frogs gay. So maybe he should take it with a grain of salt.

They walked into the front of the gas station. Hank stood and looked at him with malice because he could tell what was saying wasn't sinking into John's thick skull. Hank looked around the store with his arms raised in a grand display. He walked over to the cooler, pulled out a forty-ounce of beer, cracked it open and took a long swig. John was confused about why he would do such a thing. Behind the counter sat the owner of the store, an Indian man in his mid-fifties.

"Hello, gentlemen. Can I help you with anything?" he said in a cordial and inviting voice as he raised an eyebrow at the sight of Hank drinking a beer.

"I'm trying to show this dill hole about the new way of the world there, Abu." Hank was amused with himself for causing the demure, happy man to have a frown that almost touched the floor.

"I would like for you boys to lea--" The man never got to finish the sentence.

Hank pulled a Colt 1911 from his waistband. Without another word, he had put the pistol to the man's head and pulled the trigger in one fluid motion, sending brain matter to coat the window behind him. The man sat there for a moment, and then his body slumped to the floor with a sickening thud. John watched in complete horror. They both stood frozen in place, looking at the blood that now covered the window.

"You gonna need a couple more towels on your head to clean that up, man," Hank said, turning his head and spitting on the twitching body of the man.

"God damn, man, what the hell was that?" John said, stepping back a few feet.

It wasn't the first life that the men had taken, but a little warning would be nice, he thought. They had seen their fair share of violence and death. It was never like this, though. When they had killed before, it was out of self-defense. Drug deals gone wrong. Bad guys killing bad guys was how John always self-rationalized it. They had never just outright murdered someone who was innocent for no apparent reason. He looked at Hank with a feeling he had never had toward the man before: fear.

"We got to get out of here, man. Somebody probably heard. The cops are probably on the way right now." Panic engulfed John's head.

"I told you, man, we is on our own. Ain't nobody coming. We are gonna take our time here. All the beer and all the tobacco we are gonna load up into that truck out there. I figure four trips should do it, and hell, if we got time we can take the food too. Now let's load up. We are wasting time here."

CHAPTER 8

Emory hadn't slept but maybe a half hour that night. He tried but just rolled around in his bed, looking at the ceiling. His head swam trying to figure out what was going on. As the sun slowly crept in the window, he reflected on yesterday. After they had gathered up the gear in their dad's secret bunker, they had made their way downstairs, putting as much as they could squeeze into the trunk of the car.

They took as much food and water as they could fit, and Emily had insisted on putting two of the rifles and ammunition in as well. The trunk was hard to close with the amount of supplies that they had put in. Emily insisted that they be ready to roll out as soon as they returned. She had placed one of the rifles between them in the front seat. Emory had protested, saying they would be in a world of trouble if a cop pulled them over. Emily was steadfast in her decision. Seeing how much it was bothering Emory, she laid it in the backseat and covered it with an old blanket. A thin layer of cotton over it didn't do anything to quell his anxiety.

She had given Becky a pistol and a rifle to keep at the house. Becky had protested, but Emily insisted that she keep the handgun on her at all times, at the very least. It was clear that Becky was not a fan of firearms. She had put the rifle in the closet of their room for safekeeping. She also removed the magazine and placed it high on the shelf where a curious Eugene couldn't reach. Then Becky took off the top plate and removed the bolt, placing it in her pocket. Emily protested that she wouldn't have enough reaction time to put it back together if needed, but Becky had coldly said that if Emily wanted her to keep the weapon, this was the way it was going to be. Becky was trying to be patient with Emily, but Emory could see her doubt in the situation. She was playing along to keep Emily happy. Emory hoped that she was right and that this would all blow over.

He had decided that he would keep his knife on his belt and keep the tomahawk in his pack. Emily had taken his guns and put them with the others in the trunk of the Charger. Apparently, Becky had made some trips to the range with Emily and their father. He had been impressed with her performance and ability to learn quickly. He had told her she was a natural. She didn't know about the secret room or the paranoia; apparently Emily had kept that a secret from everyone.

Emory was a little mad that their father had taken the time to teach Becky to shoot. Emory understood his father's desire to let him have a normal childhood, but he still felt excluded. These revelations about his family had added to the bitterness of his mood. He had a bad feeling about what was about to happen on the expedition into the city, knowing that they probably had one of the few running cars around, but Emily had ignored all the pleading, to his dismay.

They had sat around the kitchen table and heated up MREs for dinner as they discussed plans for the next morning. The plan was pretty straight-forward: Get in the city. Go to Ronnie's apartment. Hope he was home. Collect Ronnie and come back. Emily made it sound cut and dry, but Emory knew it wouldn't be easy.

They had run into trouble just walking home from school, and this was way more dangerous. He trusted his sister, but this was a bad plan. He would just have to cross his fingers and hope for the best. At least he had spaghetti and meatballs, something familiar, to take his mind off the lunacy going on around him, though it left something to be desired. If this is what they were going to be eating from now on, he better invest in a lot of salt and pepper.

The plan was for Emily and Emory to go into the city, leaving Eugene in the relative safety of their neighborhood. Emory didn't like the thought of them being separated. He trusted Becky one hundred percent, but he didn't share that trust in the people of his neighborhood.

If the annoying neighbor across the street had almost come to blows with his father in the past over the color of their siding, what would he be like now with no police to call? Emory thought back on the man who had destroyed his cell phone. The fabric of society was thin. Thinner than he had ever thought. He was stuck with a feeling of nervous anticipation. Little did Emory know that the events of this trip would change his life forever. A gentle knock came at his door, and he rose to answer it.

"We leave in ten. Get dressed and meet me in the garage. Don't wake up Eugene." Emily's tone was authoritative, something that took him by surprise.

After getting dressed, he slowly made his way down the stairs. He had decided against wearing the tactical clothes that his father had set back for him. He pulled on a flannel jacket and wore jeans. He did wear the boots. It was better to blend in. Kind of a silly effort when you were cruising the town in one of the few running cars.

What he saw waiting for him in the garage took him by surprise.

Emily, who he rarely saw not wearing a dress, was waiting for him, leaning against the car. She had on a pair of black tactical pants and a black tank top. Her heels had been replaced with a pair of black combat boots. Her long blond hair was pulled into a tight bun on the back of her head. She wore a gun belt with the Glock 19 holstered on her side and the combat knife adorning the adjacent side. She looked like a cross between Lora Croft and Sarah Conner.

In the front seat of the car sat the AK-47 with a magazine inserted. Apparently, she had decided against leaving it in the backseat. He stood in silence, not knowing how to process his sweet sister looking like a mercenary ready for war. She looked like something out of a *Call of Duty* cut scene. Except this was reality, and Emory didn't feel like he was prepared for it. Becky brushed past him to hand a travel mug full of instant coffee to his sister as he stood awkwardly, trying to take in the person in front of him.

"Coffee for the road," Becky said. "Be careful out there. Emily Ellison, I have loved you since the day I met you and don't think I can go on without you. Come back to me." Tears rolled down her face as her vulnerable side became visible for the first time.

Under her tough exterior, Becky was worried like everyone else. It was refreshing to know that he wasn't the only one with jitters. Emily gently put her finger under her chin, lifting her face until their eyes were level.

"I love you too. More than I ever thought I could love anyone. I will come back to you, sweetheart." She gently leaned in until their lips touched in an uncomfortable display of affection that made Emory cough uneasily.

"Yeah, yeah, I get it, pretty boy. A little too mushy," she said, regaining that tough outer layer that she usually maintained.

"Hurry back home, babe. You are looking sexy as all get-out in that getup, and I'm ready to get it on the floor." She playfully slapped Emily on the butt as a mortified Emory stood in silence.

With no other words spoken, Becky simply brushed past Emory to go back into the house. Both a bit stunned by what had just happened, Emory and Emily stood there for an awkward thirty seconds until Emily opened the garage door. Neither spoke until the house was far in the rearview mirror. It remained quiet until they left the neighborhood. This was going to be a slow process. Most people had left their cars where they had died in the street, creating a maze for them to navigate. Seeing all the empty cars was eerie. A trip that usually took thirty minutes on the freeway was about to take them hours.

"Here, eat this," Emily said, breaking the silence and handing him a breakfast bar.

He was glad to know that though the outside may have changed, at least the maternal inside was still there. He took the bar and fiddled with it in his hands as he thought.

"What if he isn't home?"

"He will be home."

Emory had no idea where her faith in that was coming from, but he shut up and bit into the breakfast bar.

Either way, he thought, this was about to be the most dangerous thing he had ever done. As he chewed, he wondered if he would ever see Eugene or his home again. He hoped that she was right, and this was going to be easy. Hope was just a feeling, and at this moment, a fleeting one. Just like the dry cereal bar that was hard to swallow.

CHAPTER 9

Alex was one of the first people to show up to the rally. Luckily for him, the walk to the battlegrounds was only fifteen minutes from his mother's apartment. There was a group of about twenty of his friends roaming around now. A sea of black-clad justice warriors ready to face the opposition. Rumors had muttered through the crowd about what was happening. Some people said it was an attack from Russia. Some said it was a GOP grab for power. Alex didn't care, whatever it was. Out of the ashes, his group could rise. They had a grandiose vision of power growing fantasies in his head.

All the people in his life who had messed with him... Now it was his turn.

Eventually, everyone there realized that nobody else was going to show up and they wandered up and down the block, chanting. He was loud and boisterous, hoping to catch the eye of the girl he marched next to.

When nobody showed up for that, they got louder, and a few of them started breaking the windows out of cars. They quickly figured out that nobody was coming to stop them and grew emboldened. Now on a path of crushing and breaking anything in sight, their bloodlust was rising. No pigs to stop them today. A car pulling up in the street caught the groups attention!

A gas-guzzling hot rod with an American flag sticker on the back window next to a grandsten flag decal. My god, he thought, finally some right-wing scum to feel the wrath of the people. The crowd, like an angry pack of wolves, made a mad dash toward the car. Screams and snarls were thrown so loudly that they were indecipherable. The small mob had grown out of control, drunk on destruction.

Alex was the first one to make it there. A girl in all black got out of the car. Only forty more feet, he thought as he pulled the knife from his pocket. He turned to see what his comrades were doing. They had all stopped in their tracks, fixated on him. If they wanted a show, he would give them one, he thought, raising the knife. Time for the revolution.

His head was still turned as three swift cracks of the gun erupted. The impact of the hollow-point bullets had all been at center mass, taking him off his feet and to the ground quickly. Blood started running out of the sides of his mouth, his breathing becoming more labored by the second. The blood pooled quickly underneath him. The last thing he heard was the heavy thudding of boots walking toward him. The last thing he saw, his head still jarred to the side, was his friends running away from him. He took his last breath alone and cold, still holding the knife in his hand. At least in dying for the cause he would be remembered.

CHAPTER 10

Ronnie sat on the couch in his two-bedroom apartment, eating a peanut butter sandwich and looking at a map of Ohio spread across his coffee table. His time in the military told him exactly what he was up against. He had trained for this very event several times. The boys were out there trying to restore order right now, that was something he was sure of. He was conflicted on what he should do next. He had two paths set in front of him. He could grab his go bag and Beretta and rendezvous with the closest Marine patrol that he could find and rejoin the fight, or he could go protect his sister's family.

He had a duty to do both and was digging deep to try to make a decision. One thing he knew for sure was that war was coming, and he better be ready for it. His best guess was that nobody could sucker punch the United States like this. During his time in the Special Forces he had seen the capabilities of this country. No, this strike was internal, he was sure of that. The federal government was making a play for power, and in no way would this make America great again. He had watched the commander in chief all over the news for months. The man was an unstable lunatic in his eyes.

Chances were that the federal agencies promising relief were already deployed to ensure a smooth takeover. Homeland security had an army all on its own complete with vehicles and heavy weapons. FEMA was being rallied to set up internment camps, he was sure of that. America was about to be taken over, and nobody was going to see it coming.

The modern-day aristocracy forgot about one thing, though. The military took an oath to protect against all enemies, domestic and foreign. He highly doubted his brothers in the armed forces would turn on their own people. A civil war was brewing, and the results were going to be bloody and the loss of life catastrophic. He had seen from his time in Afghanistan and Iraq what scared, starving people were capable of. He had to get his family someplace safe. Then he could find his way to the front lines.

Making his decision, he went to his bedroom to retrieve his weapons and gear. Ronnie was a large man, standing six-foot-two and stacked in muscles. He kept his black hair buzzed short and had a large, bushy beard. He had the same soft green eyes that his sister had. His body was covered in scars and tattoos.

His transition back to civilian life had been a rough one. The nightmares and screams of war infested his subconscious at all times. He looked scary and he knew it. He had tried going on a few dates since his retirement, but he felt so different from most people. He always had to sit with his back to the wall. When his date was talking, he was scanning the room for potential threats. He still reached for his rifle every time he stood up from a table. When he was driving them home at night, he instinctively swerved around trash accumulated on the sides of the road, fearing an IED.

The few times that he had had a woman spend the night, she had been run off by the night terrors. His dreams were haunted with the horrors of war. He had been shot, stabbed and caught shrapnel from an IED while he was fighting. All of that paled in comparison to the pain that the dreams inflicted on him. He was haunted each night by the faces of the men he had killed. Explosions and gunshots flooded his brain every time he closed his eyes. When he lost his sister, it had made everything ten times worse. She was the only person that he had felt comfortable with when speaking about his emotions.

Most people had feared him when he came back. It was a

hard obstacle to overcome. When Ronnie lost his sister, it was something that almost broke the grizzled, hard man. He had lost himself in his grief. He had seen his fair share of death over the years. He had lost people that he shared the bond of war with, but this was different. She had practically raised him. Watched out for him after they lost their parents.

He drowned himself in the bottom of a whiskey bottle for six months following. He had turned to the bottle to forget his woes, but he had become enslaved to it. Each day he swallowed his feelings from a roux glass. He would drink all day and into the night to blast the feelings away. He would drink until he blacked out, hoping that it would keep the dreams away. It didn't.

He was ashamed that he wasn't there for his niece and nephews. He knew what they were going through. Ronnie and his sister had lost their parents a few years ago. That was hard enough for two grown adults to deal with. He'd had his sister to lean on. The kids had their dad, but still, Ronnie was the only family that they had left. He knew they needed him. Especially Emory. The few times he had seen the boy recently, he could see how lost he was. He needed someone to talk to who was not his father.

Finally, Ronnie had decided that it was time for treatment and saw a therapist and went to AA. Two months sober was something he was proud of, and he was ready to go to them when this happened. He reached into the closet, pulled out his bag and dumped it on the bed. The contents were one surefire flashlight with three sets of backup batteries, four MREs, the map from the coffee table, a compass, a Nalgene water bottle, a Kayden water filter, four seventeen-round magazines for the Beretta, four thirty-three round magazines for his Beretta CX4 storm carbine, and a Ka-Bar fighting knife.

He refilled his bag with its contents and pulled the AR500 steel-plated body armor and laid it on the bed. Next, he opened the pelican rifle case, laid his carbine and handgun down and took a step back to look at the collection. It sure wasn't what he had used when deployed, but it would do, he figured. He sat at the edge of the bed and bent over to tie the laces of his boots when a loud crash echoed into the room.

At first, he thought somebody had kicked in his front door, but then the screams coming from his neighbors' apartment next door started. Since he had been home, he had seen the family next door on many occasions, but they never made an effort to befriend him. Looking at the mirror across the room, he understood that he could be pretty uninviting.

The family was from somewhere in Asia. Korea, he guessed from his time on the continent. There was a mother and a father and a teenage girl. They had a big-ass rottweiler that lived there as well, and the growling and barking was fierce enough to travel into his room. He stood and shoved the Beretta into a kydex holster in his pants and pulled his shirt over to conceal it.

On his way out of the room, he picked up the Benchmade 940 folding knife that he carried every day and put that into his front right pocket. Glancing out the front door the entry to the apartment next door was wide open. It was very dark in the hallway. He looked up and down the hall and didn't see anybody, so he slowly crept around to the door frame.

Peering inside, the girl was backed into a corner on the ground, crying and shaking in fear. The rottweiler, 140 pounds of fury, stood in front of her, snarling at the two assailants, who were screaming at the dog. The men looked like typical crack heads. Dirty clothes, unkempt hair and matted facial hair. The smell of the men was noticeable from the doorway, and they didn't smell good. One of the men held a three-foot length of rebar, and the other man had a large, goofy-looking bowie knife, the type that you could pick up from the flea market.

"Tell the damn dog to back off. Look, we just want some

money and food, then we will go away," Dirtbag Number One said.

"Speak for yourself. One way or the other I'm gonna usher this bitch into womanhood." The second man laughed as he licked his lips.

Ronnie hated rapists. Especially when they were involving kids. In his eyes they were as bad as murderers. They all deserved the same fate. In war-torn countries, he had seen many men prey on people who were weaker than them. Now they wanted to hurt this child, and he was going to make sure that these vultures never hurt anybody ever again.

"Hey, shit stain, how about you pick on somebody your own size?"

The men about jumped out of their skin. The man with the knife turned toward him with rage in his eyes.

"You ain't a part of this, tough guy. So hows about you turn around and get your faggot ass out of here," he said, taking a step toward him.

"Now, that ain't no way to talk in front of a lady. Plus, I don't appreciate that slur. It's just ugly. This is only going to play out one way. I'm going to kill the two of you. I know you are thinking that there are two of you and one of me. But trust me, fellas, I have been against some bad dudes in my lifetime, and you two little rascals are not even going to make me break a sweat. So go on, make your move so I can go about the rest of my day," Ronnie said calmly, staring directly at both men.

The men had become so confused that they didn't know what to do. The brave demeanor they had started with faltered. They just stood there like white trash statues, looking at him. Their confidence was shaken by his calm.

"Look, man, we will just go, no harm no foul," pleaded the man with the rebar. He was trying to sound tough, but his voice was shaky and uneven.

"Too late for that, boys. I let you go, then you are just going to do this to someone else. Now, I'm a fair man. I could have walked in here and just shot you two turds, but I'm going to give you a chance now." He lifted his shirt to reveal the handle of his handgun. The two men's eyes became large as saucers, but they still lingered, staring at him.

Time to kick it off, he thought, and slowly reached for his weapon. This snapped the men out of their stupor, and the man with the knife put it straight ahead of him and charged at Ronnie at full speed. Ronnie simply stepped to the side and brought one fist down hard on the inside of his elbow. His other hand grabbed the man's fist with the knife in it. The inertia of the slam on the elbow coupled with Ronnie's control of the knife easily pushed it into the man's eye, sending blood spraying out of the wound. The man took two steps back and collapsed in a heap to the floor, blood still hemorrhaging out of him.

Rebar man didn't get off so easily. He had turned his back on the rottweiler when his friend had attacked. This proved to be a fatal mistake. The big dog had sunk its teeth into his Achilles tendon and, with one hard shake, snapped it, sending the man to the floor. In a flash the dog had attached its teeth to the man's throat and lacerated it. It was brutal and ugly and took Ronnie by surprise. Momentarily stunned, Ronnie stood there looking at the beast. The dog stood there with its prey subdued and lifted its head to Ronnie.

"Easy, girl. You sure killed the hell out of that prick. Good girl," he said as he made his way over to the girl on the floor.

"You okay?" he said calmly, careful not to get too close to her as she tried to regain her wits.

"They wanted to rape me," she said with tears in her eyes.

"They are not going to hurt anybody ever again," he said gently as he stood. "Where are your parents? Are you here alone?"

"They flew to California for my sister's wedding. They are supposed to be back again on Sunday." The statement made Ronnie's heart sink. He couldn't leave her here alone and defenseless. He knew it was going to slow him down, but the girl and the small bear were coming with him.

"Pack a bag. You and the killing machine are coming with me. I got a niece and a nephew about your age you can stay with them. What's the beast's name?" he said, staring at the dog that still had blood matted in its fur.

"That's Lola, and I'm Margot. Thanks for what you did there. No disrespect, but what do you want out of this? You going to try to get some too? I'm not going to have sex with you for saving me." She averted her eyes.

"Miss, I'm old enough to be your daddy. Trust me, no funny business. I just don't feel right about you being stuck here all alone. You can trust me. I'm one of the good guys." He flashed a cheesy smile from ear to ear.

"I don't know,"

"Here," he said, handing her the pistol. "You know how to use this thing?"

"Dad took me to the range a few times," she said with growing confidence.

"If I do anything wild, just put me down. Now, we ain't got time for this. Go in there and get a bag of clothes and meet me in my apartment. Come on, Lola." The dog refused to budge.

"Fine, be that way," he said as he walked next door.

It took her about twenty minutes to poke her head in the door. Lola barreled in at full speed, making sure the path was safe. Ronnie sat in his Laz-E-Boy with his glasses on, reading a book. He slowly sipped on a water bottle, staring at the pair as they stood there. He assumed she was trying to figure out if this was a trick in some way. After a long awkward moment, she walked over and handed him his pistol.

"You sure? I got the long gun if you having this makes you feel safer," he said in a confused tone, pointing at the gun next to the chair. She lifted her shirt to show the Smith and Wesson now on her hip.

"I got Daddy's out of the safe. I should have had it when those two kicked in the door. I won't make that mistake again. My parents travel a lot, and I barely see them. My father was worried about me being alone so much, so he gave me the combination to the safe." She patted it softly. My god, he was really starting to like this girl.

"What now?"

"Now we go pick up the rest of my family and we--" The shouts of numerous people from outside gave him pause, and he stood and walked over to the window.

What he saw made him grumpy. His brother-in-law's Charger sat running out front and Emory and Emily were standing outside of it. Some douchebag in all black was hooting and hollering and running straight at Emily. She was frozen, just watching the man descend on her. They were going to have to learn a lot and fast if they were going to make it through this, he thought as he opened the window and raised the Beretta.

About forty yards. He had made longer. He pulled the trigger three times, dropping the threat instantly to the ground. Emory and Emily just stood there, looking at the fallen man. He assumed this was the first person they had watched die. The loss of their innocence made him sad, and he reflected on the first time he had been forced to take a life. It was a hard thing to come back from. Lola barked and ran all over the apartment. Oh, those two were gonna get an ear full, he thought as he beelined out of the apartment.

CHAPTER 11

It took Hank and John ten trips to clean out the gas station. The two men had started off strong, but they decided that it would be better to drink some of the beer while it was cold. Some beer turned into gallons of beer, and toward the end, they could barely keep the rusty old truck on the road. They took all the alcohol and tobacco that they could find. Then they cleaned out the register and pulled the safe out of the wall with a chain and their truck.

Next, they moved on to all the food and random stuff that crowded the middle shelves of the store. They brought a generator and a submersible pump and stole as much gas as they could, filling the few cans for sale in the store and the ones kept at the property. About fifty gallons in total. Could always come back, they figured. In the end they had even taken all the lottery tickets.

Their last act was to pick up the gas station attendant they had murdered and throw him in the dumpster behind the store. The dumpster was full to the top; must have been trash day. Hank then doused the dumpster in gas, took two steps and lit a cheap cigar and flicked it into the dumpster, starting an enormous, engulfing flame. Hank had always been the more violent one on their two-man team. John still had a sense of guilt about the things that they had done. He was quick to wash it away with three quarters of a bottle of whisky. Hank made some kind of joke about burnt Indian food, and John tried to wash it away in the bottom of a forty-ounce.

After the plundering, they were on their way home when a motorcycle came toward Hank's house. The man on the bike looked the part. Short and stubby with a bald head and a big mustache. He had on a leather vest with no shirt underneath, ragged old jeans and cowboy boots. This was Hank's "brother" Cecil, who he had met on his last stint in prison. Cecil was not in a gang, but he did hang around them. He was their connect for the meth and came and went when batches were ready for pickup. Both vehicles slowed to a stop in Hank's driveway.

"What you two peckerwoods up to? Nothing good I can figure," he said, looking in the back of the truck at their bounty.

"Just some Indian takeout from down the road. We done claimed it as ours," Hank said with a grin.

"What the owner have to say about that?" Cecil said with a laugh.

"Kinda hard to talk when a forty-five splits your skull in half," Hank proclaimed, pointing finger guns at the other man.

"You killed him. Ain't you worried about the heat that will bring us?" All sense of amusement was gone from Cecil's face, now replaced with panic.

"Nobody is coming to get us now. I got some things I need to tell you about how the world is. So, let's get wasted, and I'm gonna tell you how we are about to live like kings."

CHAPTER 12

It was slow going moving into the city. Emory didn't feel much like talking, but luckily for him, neither did his sister. He just looked out the window, watching the streets devoid of people pass. The lack of life surprised him a little. It was pretty early in the morning, but he had seen maybe ten individuals. Must be trying to figure out what to do, waiting in their houses for the power to come back, he thought. The few people they did see were just out talking to other lost souls, and it appeared that everybody was just trying to figure out what was going on.

Eventually they pulled up in front of their uncle's house. The group of chanting people in black grew louder as they rounded the corner as they parked. This made him very uncomfortable, and he wished he had a gun stuffed in his pants. He and Emily both got out of the car, and before Emily could say one word to him, one of the crowd broke from the pack and raced toward them with a knife in hand. Emily froze. She didn't even make a play for her gun as she stood there in shock. Even with all her training, she wasn't ready for this.

When the man was closing in about thirty feet away from them, three loud reports from a firearm behind echoed dropping the man. They both just stood there, unsure what to do as the rest of the black-clad people ran off as fast as their legs could carry them. Their uncle walked past them without a word and walked up to the man bleeding out on the pavement. He stood there for a moment with his gun on the man, trying to make sure he was not a threat. Then he squatted next to him, muttered something they couldn't hear, and briskly walked back to them.

"What the hell are you two doing here? You know how stupid and dangerous it was to come into the city! In a car, no less, that somebody could have easily taken from you." His face was red and his words were forceful. Apparently, Uncle Ronnie was as unhappy about the plan as Emory was.

"It's nice to see you, Uncle Ronnie. We are here to save you. I wouldn't have let somebody take the car," Emily said in a whisper, her face growing red with embarrassment.

"You, you just killed that guy," Emory said, not knowing what to feel.

"Third one today. Actually, second, I guess. Dog did the work on the other one. Look, missy, next time somebody is coming at you or a member of this family with a knife, you shoot them right in their face. Hesitation will get you killed. Uhhh, enough out of me. You're here now. Let me get my bag and we can go. Also, we are bringing someone else with us. Two, actually, but one is a dog. Hold on." He stomped back the stairs and out of sight, leaving the pair looking at each other.

"What just happened?" Emory said, even more confused than before.

"Not sure. I'm sorry that I froze up like that. I really thought I would be ready for something like this happening," she said, kicking at the ground.

Ronnie was only in the apartment for about four minutes before he came stomping back out, his face still annoyed. Behind him was a giant bear of a dog, and behind the dog was a girl around Emory's age. Emory's heart skipped a beat when he saw the girl. He had never seen anything so beautiful before, he thought as his throat tightened.

She was about five foot eight and very slender. Her jet-black hair flowed behind her in the wind. His dad had said he knew he loved his mother from the first time he saw her. Now Emory knew what he was talking about. With a dead man thirty feet away from him, it was crazy as hell feeling this way, but for some reason he couldn't control it. As they approached the car, the rottweiler stopped and growled low, staring at Emory, who was snapped back into reality.

"Easy, Lola," Margot cooed to the dog.

"Uh, hi, I'm Margot," she said shyly. She held out her hand.

"I'm Emory. This is my sister Emily," he said, abruptly feeling his face turn red.

What a first impression, he thought. Why would a beautiful girl like that want to be with a dweeb like him? He had never been very successful with girls. His sister told him that he was too shy and needed to gain confidence. He had many friends who were girls, and some of them were probably interested in him, but he had never worked up the courage to ask one of them out. The few times he did go out with someone, they had asked him. Something about this felt right, though. He just wished it didn't take the United States falling apart to find love at first sight.

"Pop the trunk," Ronnie said, walking behind the car to put in his bag.

"It's full," Emily said, walking around to oblige him.

"Of what?"

"Stuff Dad had put away for a rainy day," she said, taking a step back from the trunk as Ronnie peered in.

"Oh my god. I have just so many things to say I don't know where to start. What if somebody had car jacked you? Bad enough to lose the car, but all this stuff could be the difference between life and death. You shouldn't have come to the city, Em, but I sure as shit am glad to see you two. Now, I'm assuming that Eugene is at home with Bec. So, let's get this freakshow on the road. I'm driving. The dog sits in the backseat. Lastly, I knew how your daddy grew up, so none of this is a real shock to me. I just don't understand why in the hell he put back a damn commie gun," he mused as he pulled one of the AKs out, checked the mag and cycled the bolt.

"I'm gonna go ahead and keep this up here with me," he said with a look on his face like a toddler getting a new toy.

The ride home was just as slow as the ride there. People were milling about as they left the city limits. Just wandering around with no particular direction. They passed a Kroger, and the line outside was around the block. The first police officers that they had seen since this all had started were there, patrolling what looked like a pretty unruly crowd. The officers were dressed in full riot gear and were controlling the flow in and out of the store. Emory wondered how long the items would last, but more importantly, what would happen when they ran out. He hoped that they were far away from the city when that happened.

The car was silent except for the steady panting of Lola, who was staring at Emory. He felt like the dog was trying to size him up. To see if he was a good person or not. Emory sideways glanced at Margot without turning his head. She quietly sat there, lost in a book she had brought with her. One hand held the book and the other slowly stroked the back of the dog's head.

He had to talk to her, he thought quietly to himself. Problem was every time that he tried, the words got caught in his throat before he could get them out. He sat there trying for a half hour with the dog silently judging him. Just thinking about something to say that wouldn't make him look like a dingus. *Just ask her what she's reading,* he thought. That couldn't be contrived as awkward. He finally turned his head to speak and staring right back into his eyes was Lola, looking straight into his soul. He was going to get blocked out by a dog. The dog, looked at him slightly, turned its head forty-five degrees. Suddenly, like a bolt of lightning, she licked his face. She decided to like him after all, he thought.

"Ugh, gross." He wiped his face with the back of his sleeve. The slobber was all over him. This must have been amusing to Margot, who giggled and pulled the beast off him.

"Thanks, I needed something to take my mind off this. She must like you. Take that as a compliment; that is a pretty small group of people," she said with a smile.

"I'm honored, then. How are you doing? Did Ronnie say where we were heading to?" Her smile had him feeling extra nervous.

"I'm okay, I guess. He just said that he knew of someplace safe. Your uncle saved my life today, did you know that?" The smile faded when she spoke about Ronnie.

"No, he didn't mention anything. Uncle Ron has always been the badass in the family. If anybody can keep you safe, it's him."

"After what happened this morning, having two men break into our home, from now on I'm going to protect myself," she said as she lifted her shirt, revealing the grip of the Smith and Wesson.

"I think everyone has a gun except for me. Makes me feel a little unprepared." Emory said.

"Why don't you have one? From seeing the trunk of this car, seems a bit odd."

"My sister told me I can't have one until she can train me," he said, feeling like a scolded child.

Margot pulled the gun out of the holster, removed the magazine and racked back the slide, ejecting the round in the chamber. Even with a gun in her hands, she seemed so elegant and mysterious, Emory thought as he tried to play it cool.

"I can show you something if you want. My dad was a shooting instructor, when he wasn't off doing lawyer stuff." The sound of the racking of the slide made Ronnie look back from the front seat but really didn't seem to hold his interest. She handed the gun to Emory.

"First rule is always point it in a safe direction. Second rule is never point it at something you don't want to destroy. And finally, don't put your finger on the trigger until you are ready to fire. Now, this here is the safety." She pointed and accidently brushed Emory's hand. His heart skipped a beat, and he felt his face get hot and was blushing now.

Before anything else could happen, the car slowed. They both looked to the front, and Lola started a low rumbling growl. In front of the car stood two policeman who had set a roadblock. The roadblock had been concealed around a corner, making Ronnie stop with no chance at simply driving away and avoiding it. The two cops slowly walked toward the car with their hands on their pistols, one on each side of the car. Margot snatched the gun out of Emory's hand, re-racked the magazine in and shoved it in her holster, quickly covering it with her shirt.

"Everyone be cool," Ronnie whispered, holding his hands up as they approached the window.

"Hello, folks, how you all doing?" Cop Number One said, peering into the window and scanning the car.

"We are okay, officer. We are just trying to get home. My little brother and friend are there waiting for us," said Emily, batting her eyes at him.

"We have been having some trouble with some folk here in the city. You all need to be careful," he said, eyeballing his partner.

"The governor has declared a state of emergency, and we are to confiscate all working automobiles and firearms for emergency service use." His tone was authoritative. "I'm gonna need you all to step out of the car."

"You can't just take our car, sir. I'm gonna reach for my ID now. Here, I'm a Marine, and I need to get back to my unit. We are all on the same side here," Ronnie said as he handed over the ID, maintaining eye contact.

"I don't give a damn about who you are. We are taking the car! Now get out!" Officer 1 shouted.

"Okay, you got it." Ronnie reached over and turned off the car, put the keys into his pocket and stepped out. Everyone else followed suit, and Cop Number Two stepped back toward his partner. Lola growled loudly, pulling at Margot's hand as she kept a firm grip on the dog's collar.

"Give me the keys now. I don't want this to get ugly," muttered Cop Number Two as he stepped toward Ronnie.

This was a mistake, and Ronnie knew it. As the cop reached for Ronnie's pocket, Ronnie grabbed his arm, spun him around like a top and put him in a choke hold. He used the cop as a human shield. Cop One took two steps forward and raised his gun. What he hadn't seen or paid attention to was Emily, stepping behind him and pulling her gun.

"Put it down, sir. I really don't want to have to do this," Emily asked politely while she pointed the gun at the man's head.

"Fine," responded the police office as he lowered his gun to the ground.

"Get their cuffs and take their weapons," Ronnie commanded as he removed the officer's gun belt.

Ronnie cuffed the two men together with their hands behind their backs. He took their guns to the old truck that they were using as a roadblock. He removed the magazines from the guns and took the chambered rounds out. He popped every bullet out of the magazines, put them inside the truck and locked the doors. Then he removed the slides off the guns and took out the barrels and springs. He locked the barrels and springs in the other car at the block. He took the handle and slides and tossed them in opposite directions off the road. He took the handcuff keys and placed them on top of the cars. He did this without saying one word, glaring at the two men cuffed together. Finally, he walked over and squatted next to them.

"Names," he grunted.

"You don't know who you are messing with, man. You are gonna have the whole department up your ass now," spat Cop Number Two.

"Shut your mouth, Rob. I'm Billy. That is Rob," said Cop Billy, not maintaining eye contact.

"I'm going to say some things now. You are going to answer. Truthfully," Ronnie said, looking directly at them.

"Take these cuffs off and we can go at it like men. Fist to fist," Rob said angrily.

"Boy, I was killing terrorists in the sandbox when you were still taking algebra class. Trust me when I tell you to be glad those cuffs are on. If I wanted to hurt you boys, I would put that big nasty dog behind me on you. I don't want that."

"I noticed you didn't take our guns. Thank you," said Billy.

"I'm not going to leave you out here defenseless. Even if old Robby over here is a dick head."

"I'm thankful for that, sir. Ask me whatever you want, and I will give you a straight answer."

"How do you know about the governor's decree? I highly doubt that any of your long wave communication is working."

"We had training on this very event last week."

"You don't think that is suspicious?"

"Didn't until today."

"What's next?"

"House to house in the suburbs taking survivors to a mandatory FEMA camp."

"Jesus, how would you have enough manpower for that?"

"National Guard. They were here training this week when it happened."

"Look, man, I'm going to level with you. You are clearly putting the pieces together in your head. There are gonna be two sides coming. Choose the right one. Now, we are going to get in that car and leave. I hope you make the right decision." With that, Ronnie got back to the car with everyone frozen, staring at him.

"Get in, you knuckleheads." Everyone piled into the car, and they took off, leaving the two men bound in the middle of the road.

It was silent for a while. Emory had never had an interaction with the police before. Being a white kid in the suburbs, they had never bothered him. It felt strange having them come on them like that. Maybe it was his turn to feel some of the systematic oppression that other people faced on a daily basis.

His best friend Kenny had told him about a few times that his dad had been harassed by the cops. This made Emory's thoughts drift to Kenny. He hoped that he was okay. Maybe their paths would cross again at some point. He hoped so as he brooded, looking out the window.

"What did you mean, two sides coming?" asked Margot, breaking the silence.

"Civil war is coming. It's going to be us vs. the federal government. I'm pretty sure that they had something to do with this mess. That's not really the pressing issue at the moment. I'm more worried that when we get home, Becks and Eugene are gonna be stuck in that FEMA camp." Worry showed in Ronnie's voice.

"War," Emory stated as the fear grew inside him.

CHAPTER 13

Becky had gone back inside after seeing Emily and Emory off. She was worried about them going leaving alone but understood why Emily asked her to stay back and watch after Eugene. She went to the fridge and pulled some bacon and eggs out. Better to use it up before it went bad. She pulled the small Coleman camp stove they had found in Emily's dad's storage and fired it up. She put the pan on and added the bacon. A very tired Eugene stumbled into the room, wiping the sleep from his eyes.

"Good morning, slugger. You hungry?" Becky asked, trying her best to sound maternal.

"Yes, ma'am," Eugene replied, half awake.

Before another word could be spoken, the front door exploded, sending splinters flying everywhere. Becky ran to Eugene and pushed him behind her instinctively. The boy didn't even have time to blink. Five soldiers burst into the room with weapons drawn, surrounding them. Becky held her hands down beside her best she could to shield Eugene.

"Hands up," shouted the man in the lead.

Both of them complied and jumped at the harsh tone the man had taken with them. The team surrounded them, still with their weapons raised. One man lowered his rifle and frisked Eugene. Becky was taken aback by the thought that they would frisk a little boy. It upset her. Seeing him stand there scared with a grown man running his hands over his little body. She wanted to tell him it would be okay. But at this point she didn't know if it would be.

A woman walked up and frisked Becky. She wasn't gentle about it, either. The woman ran her hands up her inner thighs and cupped under Becky's breast. Becky felt more violated that she ever had in her life. That was upsetting, but what she was worried about was what would happen when they found the Glock concealed in her waistband. Slowly making her way to Becky's midsection, the woman found the Glock and handed it to the soldier behind her.

"Any more weapons?" she asked loudly, giving Becky a cold stare.

"No," Becky responded, still in a daze about what was going on around her.

"You are going to be moved to a FEMA camp near here. They will provide you with the necessary items." commanded the soldier.

"Can we just stay here?"

"No. Mandatory evacuation for your safety."

"Why didn't you just knock on the door?" Becky asked.

"We don't know what you have behind that door. Safer for us this way. Now, no more questions. Move," the soldier said as she pulled Becky out the door.

Becky looked down to see Eugene being pulled behind her. The boy was scared, and tears streaked down his young face. That was when the fear in Becky turned to anger. She would go with them, but by god, she would figure out a way to get out of this. How big of pieces of shit did those guys have to be to treat a little boy like a criminal? What did they expect him to be packing? No child should have to go through something like this. Her fingers were in tight fists at her sides, and she couldn't calm herself down.

As they exited the house, soldiers were coming and going from all the houses on the block. A parade of people were being led out of their homes. None of the crowd looked scared. Some of them were even laughing and making jokes as they made their way to the trucks. For some reason, this made Becky even madder. As they threw her in the back of the deuce and a half, her last thought was of Emily and how the Emily and Becky would make them pay for this.

CHAPTER 14

After Kenny had gotten out of the car yesterday, he had started slowly walking in the direction of his house. He watched as the brother and sister drove toward their house. The nonsense Emily had been spouting had annoyed him enough to make the walk in the rain. He loved the Ellison family, but that was too much to take in one sitting.

He lived in the same subdivision as Emory, on the other side of the massive development. Where they had dropped him was a path that he had taken hundreds of times before. There was a large field he would have to cross that led straight to his back door. Normally he traversed this hike alone, but now something was strange. Other people were crossing toward the subdivision too. He found something about it unnerving.

He picked up the pace, his shoes making sucking noises as they sank in the wet ground. He tried his best to keep his distance from the other people. It wasn't hard, for the most part. Most of them paid no attention to him as he mucked his way past. He moved swiftly and with determination, finally making it to the tree line that divided his home from the field.

He had a new problem to address now. The small creek that ran through the narrow strip of woods had swelled into a small river. The water was moving quickly and was so dirty that there was zero visibility. He stood there, confused about what to do next. It was a long hike to get to the road. He was already soaked and shivering. He didn't really want to make the trip around, so he decided that his best bet was to try to swim across.

He bent over, pulled off his shoes and put them in his backpack. Most of the schoolwork was soaked anyways. Next, he slowly stepped into the fast-moving water. The current was swift. Kenny was a stout and strong young man. Foolishly he assumed that he would be able to make it across.

He inched in deeper and deeper until the water smashed into his knees. It hit so hard that he had trouble keeping his footing. Taking a few more steps, his feet slipped out from under him, and he fell face-first into the water. Panicking, he splashed around as the water pushed him farther down the creek.

Luckily for Kenny, the creek made a ninety-degree turn just a little downstream. He looked up in time to see a downed tree across the water. He was going to have one shot at hitting the tree and stopping himself from a watery grave. He focused on the downed timber that was moving closer and closer. He lifted his body with as much force as he could muster, made contact and held on with everything he had.

Grabbing the tree was a miracle in itself. Now he had no idea what to do next. He was pinned against the oak, the water smashing into his body with enough force that he was starting to have trouble breathing. Gasping for air, he looked up to see a boy about his age holding his hand out. With no hesitation, Kenny grabbed his hand, and the boy got on his knees and crawled, dragging Kenny to the bank.

Kenny collapsed, sucking in as much air as his lungs could hold. He turned and looked at the boy standing over him. He was probably about sixteen, but Kenny had never seen him around before. He was average height and a little chubby. His light brown skin glistened with sweat. He had light brown hair and eyes. The boy stood over him, looking down with bewilderment on his face. His eyes were wide as he regained his composer after the episode. Finally, after they shared an awkward silence, he looked down at Kenny and spoke.

"Well, that was stupid."

After the incident with the two police officers, the rest of the drive home was pretty uneventful. Ronnie kept a decent pace, much faster that Emily had taken it on the way to his apartment. It was clear that he was in hurry to get back to the house. He didn't speak another word the entire ride home. He just drove with steel-faced determination, gripping the wheel so hard that his knuckles turned white.

Emily stared out the window, apparently in a mood not fit for discussion. It was a strange thing for Emory to see, since Emily was usually the chatty one in the family. Her bubbly and pleasant demeanor was long gone. Everyone had their breaking point, he figured, and she had found hers. He couldn't imagine the stress and pressure she was feeling, trying to keep everyone alive and safe.

Emory couldn't stop looking out the corner of his eye at Margot. She sat with her legs crossed, gently stroking her dog's head.

People milled about on their paths to nowhere. They all looked like zombies, trying to recreate the routines of the past. The strange thing was that everyone looked like they were ready to go about their daily lives. Businessmen in suits, construction workers with their gear, and so on. Emory just figured it was easy to stick with what was familiar rather than think about reality.

The car got people's attention. Everyone they passed looked at them like they were a spaceship out of an old science-fiction movie. Groups of people yelled at them as they passed. Most asked for a ride, but some actually tried to step in the path of the car and stop it. Their eyes would grow wide as the car kept racing toward them. Ronnie was not going to stop for anyone or anything, and at the last minute they would move, screaming curses at the car.

When they got close to their neighborhood, He didn't see anybody. Not a soul. The streets were abandoned with no signs of life. The smell of the smoke filled his nostrils. Somehow, deep inside of himself, it was their house, but he held out hope. The fear choked up in his throat. If he lost Becky and Eugene, he didn't think that what was left of his heart could take it.

When they were two blocks away from home, the billowing smoke was cascading into the sky. His heart sank. By the time they pulled onto their street, that old familiar feeling of sorrow invading him, overtaking his mind. The house was engulfed in flames. The fire covered every square inch of the home. There was no saving it. Ronnie hit the brakes, and the car crept into a slow stop.

"No, no, no," Emily pleaded as she jumped out of the car and ran to the house.

She was hysterical as they tried to run to what used to be their front door. Ronnie was quick behind her and had to grab her by the arm to keep her from running in what was left of the house. She thrashed around in his arms, sobbing and trying to break free from his embrace.

"I have to get in there. I have to help them," Emily pleaded as she tried to pull away from her uncle's grasp. Twisting and pulling, she made her best attempt at getting lose.

"Look at the door, Emily. Those markings mean FEMA has been here. They are at a camp," Ronnie said, pointing to the neighbor's house.

"Why would they go with them? They knew we were on our way back," Emily said, still hyperventilating.

"My guess is that they didn't have much of a choice. We need to find that camp. We will get them back, Em," Ronnie said matter-of-factly.

Emory couldn't find the words to speak; he just stood there catatonic, staring into the blazing flames. Seeing his sister's outburst sent his heart fluttering. In the last two days, he had seen every range of emotion from her. Something he hadn't seen in his entire life, and the whole situation made him very uneasy. The sadness that poured out of his sister seemed to be infectious. Not a single person had a dry eye.

Looking at the raging inferno of his home was surreal. He had been so ready to turn eighteen and leave this home. Watching it burn, he wondered how stupid he could be. His whole life and his childhood had been spent in that house. All of his memories of his mother were in that house. Then it hit him like a Mack truck. Every family picture had been in there. He had no way to remember his mother's face. All the mementos that he had tied to memories of his mom were going up in smoke.

He tried to hold back the tears, but they invaded his face, slowly trickling down to the ground. A nuzzle pushed against his leg and looked down to see Lola, rubbing against him with a low whine. Margot put her hand in his, and he turned to look at her.

She didn't say a word, just stared into his eyes, gave him a small nod, and looked back at the inferno. His mind fired in ten different directions at once. Half of his brain thinking about his broken family and the other half wondering if Margot's actions were out of pity, or maybe something else. It was a crazy thought, having only known her for less than a day, but something in her eyes made him calm down a little.

One thing he knew to be true was that he was going to get Becky and his brother back or lose his life in the process. God had already taken one person he loved, and come hell or blazing flames, he would not lose anyone else.

CHAPTER 15

Kenny stood on wobbly feet and tried to brush some of the muck and debris off of himself. It was futile effort. He looked up at the boy, who was now sitting against a tree. The boy had pulled a can of Copenhagen out of his pocket and was packing it into his lip. Kenny could have died, and he knew that. The boy had saved his life. Walking over, he was filled with gratitude to the point of becoming overly emotional.

"Thanks, man. I'm Kenny." He held his hand out.

"I'm Marco. That was some crazy shit, brother," he said, standing and shaking Kenny's hand.

"Yeah, I don't know what I was thinking," Kenny said, embarrassed and running his hand over his head.

"One of these houses yours?" Marco asked.

"Yeah, that one." He pointed at his house.

"Cool. How about we go in there and get some dry clothes?" The boy spat a long strand of tobacco juice.

"Sounds like a plan to me..." Kenny said.

The two boys walked through his backyard, making their way to the back door. Kenny retrieved his keys and opened it. They walked into the kitchen, and Kenny took his soaked bag off and chucked it into the yard in frustration. He would have to get some new books when he was back at school, but that was something he could worry about later. He walked to the fridge, pulled out two still-cold Gatorades and handed one to Marco, who accepted it and took a long drink.

"Nice house, man. Your parents rich or something?"

Marco asked as he walked around the kitchen.

"My dad's a doctor." Kenny took off his shirt and put it in the sink.

"Wow. That's cool. My dad is a farmer. Our house doesn't look anything like this."

"Guess I never really thought about it. Just been this way my whole life."

"You're lucky."

"How did you get here? I've never seen you around before."

"I was driving into town when my truck died. Tried to use my phone. Messed up thing is that it was dead too. Walked in here hoping I could find someone kind enough to let me use theirs. Then I saw your attempt to swim." He chuckled.

"I don't know how long the power is going to be off, but you are more than welcome to stay here. I mean, you saved my life. I owe you big time."

"Thanks, I appreciate that. How about we go find some clothes? I'm soaked to the bone."

"Sure thing."

"Hope you got something that will fit a big boy like me."

"I'm sure Dad does."

"Will he be mad if I wear his stuff?"

"After what you did today, you can wear his two-thousand-dollar suit. Hell, I will throw in one of his watches too."

CHAPTER 16

The truck was crowded and smelled slightly of sweat and urine. Eugene cried and clung to Becky. *How could they do this?* she thought. Something about this was wrong, and she couldn't put her finger on it. She looked at all the other distraught faces that surrounded her.

Everyday people just like her, nothing special about them. Most had been upbeat when they got on the truck, sporting smiles. Those smiles had faded in the overcrowded conditions. Nobody spoke. They just clung to their loved ones and jostled around with the bumpy ride. All the passengers looked like cattle going to auction, and it dug into her struggling mind.

Where were they taking them? What were they going to do with them? The questions were setting her mind on fire. Through all the burning, she had to protect Eugene. She had come to think of him as her little brother, and his panicked sorrow destroyed her. It also made her angry. Very angry. These people came and took her away from Emily.

Becky and Emily had met their senior year of high school. They had English class together and had been assigned to work on a project as a team. Becky had been out as a lesbian for a long time, ever since middle school, but that was a hurdle that Emily had yet to jump. They had gone to school together all of high school but didn't really know each other.

In the time they spent together, they had quickly become close. One day they had decided to go to the park to look at the Christmas light display. There, under the lights, they had shared their first kiss. From then on they were together. Emily had feared telling her mom and dad that she was gay and dating a black woman, not knowing how they would react, but to her surprise, her mother and father were very accepting and took Becky in as one of their own. Becky had always appreciated that unconditional love, and now she feared she would never see them again.

The truck came to an abrupt stop, and the engine turned off. Wherever they were, they had apparently arrived. The soldier came to the back, dropped the gate, and started ushering people off. Becky looked up, and what she saw put her into shock. They were at a Walmart.

Behind the Walmart were hundreds of big canvas tents. In the distance, soldiers were putting up fencing around the tents. The part that confused her was that the top of the fencing had razor wire. Only problem was, it faced inside the camp. Even from this distance, it was being put there to keep them in, not to keep them safe. There were too many people to count and more trucks coming.

They pushed and pulled the captives from her truck in a line toward some folding tables that were covered in logbooks with people sitting behind them. These people were not soldiers. They looked like everyday citizens, the kind of neighbors you would run into at the supermarket. The only similarity that she could see was that each of them wore a small American flag pin with a cross in the middle of it.

They stood for what seemed like forever. The crowd behind them were talking about how lucky they were to be able to stay in a government camp. Eventually Becky was at the front of the line, and a large angry woman sat behind the table staring at them.

"Name, address," she said unpleasantly.

"I'm Becky Standard, and this is Eugene Ellison. Address is 101 Maple Street. What's all this about? What going on?" Becky said unintentionally giving them the Ellison's address.

"No questions. We are saving you. What was your occupation? Are you the child's legal guardian?" the woman said, abruptly looking over the top of the thick black glasses that had slid down her nose. This set off Becky's rage, but she swallowed it down, fearing being separated from Eugene.

"I am his stepmother, and I was a student before all of this," Becky said as pleasantly as she could.

"Job detail will be manual labor. I will allow the child to stay with you. You can report to tent 114. You will be sharing the tent with another family. If there are problems, you will be punished. Severely. Report to your tent, and the resident advisor will get with you," the woman said with a tone of visceral and bile.

Becky made her way past the store, which was full of soldiers. They didn't look like normal soldiers. Their uniforms were all black and had DHS on the back. The national guard units didn't come past the gates. It was like the camp was segregated, DHS soldiers on one side and guardsmen on the other.

Once they had made their way past the gates, they were stopped at a checkpoint and re-frisked for weapons. At least they had the courtesy to have a woman pat Becky down. They even searched Eugene again. The man who stood before Eugene took his time doing it, and Becky was repulsed at the thought of a forty-year-old man with his hands all over the boy.

Once they were thoroughly violated, she took Eugene's hand and started down the rows of tents. The faces of the people they passed were happy, even jubilant. Eugene had not said a word this whole time, just followed Becky with his eyes wide in bewilderment. The boy had been through so much that she was worried about his mental health. This didn't seem like a very hospitable place for a child. They walked for what seemed like forever, but eventually they found their temporary home.

From the outside, it looked okay, she guessed. She was glad it wasn't winter, because she couldn't imagine the canvas walls being very warm on the inside. She pulled back the flaps, revealing a bleak and poorly-lit interior. Inside the canvas walls sat three people. It seemed like they would be sharing their tent with a small family.

The father was a small man, thin but muscular and sporting a thick, fluffy mustache. Next to him sat a short, thin woman. She was very pretty, with long black hair that was braided down her back. Between them sat a young boy around the age of seven. For the longest moment they all stared at each other, nobody speaking.

"Hi, I'm Juan," said the little boy to Eugene, breaking the awkward silence as he walked over to the pair.

"I'm Eugene," he said, finally finding the courage to speak.

"Want to see the toys I brought with me?" Juan said as he made his way to the back of the tent.

Eugene looked to Becky for permission, and she gave him a small nod. The boys ran to the back of the tent, leaving the adults alone. It was nice to see how happy Eugene could be, and for at least the moment, her worries about the boy lifted the slightest bit.

"Hi, I'm Becky," she said, extending her hand to the couple and taking a few steps toward them.

"I'm Ricky, and this is Maria. Nice to meet you," he said, shaking her hand.

"Any idea what this place is? Why did they bring us here?" Becky said.

Before they could answer, two people walked into the tent. The one in the back was a soldier of some sort, Becky thought, wearing tactical gear with the DHS stamp on his vest and carrying a large black rifle. The woman who stood in front of him wore a plain white blouse and a long khaki skirt.

Her glare was sullen, and her air of superiority hung in

the air like a thick fog. Everything about the unhappy-looking woman made Becky's skin crawl. Her brown hair was pulled up into a bun, and she wore thick black glasses with a crucifix hanging around her neck.

"Welcome to Camp Hope. I am your resident advisor and will be helping to assist in your rescue. My name is Haley Nicklewell, and before all of this I was a simple bartender and was just like you people. Before you ask any questions, I want to give you my little speech. The United States was attacked. We have no idea what kind of cowards would inflict this amount of pain and suffering. That doesn't matter at this point, though. What matters is that you stay safe while you are here. Everyone is given a work assignment. Nobody stays here for free, except the children. You have been assigned to work as a maid in the soldiers' barracks. You will report for work from eight am to eight pm. While at work, you will do whatever the soldiers and camp staff ask of you. Now, there are five main rules. Listen closely; any deviation from the rules will result in great punishment. Rule one is no stealing. Stealing anything will result in ten lashes with a cane, and for each subsequent offense, five lashes will be accrued. Rule two is no violence. Violence of any kind will result in isolated imprisonment for you and your son for five days. Rule three is insubordination. Any back talk to the staff will result in loss of meal privileges for you and you son for the day. Rule four is no weapons. Any person found with a weapon will be summarily executed on the spot, and any dependents of that person will be put in the care of the state in the orphans' tent. Rule five carries the same punishment, and the rule is no escape attempts. You are not free to leave this place, and if you do you will be put down. Now that you understand the rules, I must be leaving. I have many more families to meet with. If you follow these rules, your stay here will mean the difference between life and expiring out there on your own. Goodbye and god bless." The woman had spat all of this as fast as her lungs would allow her to speak, and upon finishing her statement, abruptly spun on her heels and stomped out of the tent.

Becky stood with her mouth open in shock. She had no words to describe how she felt. What had just happened? Had that lady who looked like she had a stick up her butt just told her that she was now a maid who had no rights and had to follow the instructions of every person who had abducted her and forced her into this place? The anger welled inside her heart and started to bottle up. She tried to hold it back, but the tears streaked down her face. A gentle hand touched her shoulder, and she jumped as she turned around to look at Maria.

"It's okay. I'm a maid as well. We will get through this together, watching each other's backs," she whispered as she rubbed Becky's shoulder.

If this was the way things had to be, Becky would go with the flow now and swallow her pride for Eugene's sake. Emily better get her out of this somehow before somebody got hurt.

CHAPTER 17

When the beer cans had piled up on the floor of ratty old house, Hank demanded that John clean them up. Hank was quickly declaring himself the king of their little rat pack. John pushed the mountain of cans out of the house with a push broom into a mountain of cans off the back deck. They had been so wasted last night that he couldn't really remember much of what had happened. Cecil was passed out in the old, stained Laz-E-Boy in the living room, and the whole house stank of stale beer. Hank walked out of his room and kicked Cecil's leg.

"Get up, you lazy slob, and come in the kitchen. We need to have a talk." The three men followed Hank to the kitchen table and watched as he popped open a warm beer and ripped into a bag of corn nuts.

"I had a revelation last night, gentlemen. We can do whatever we want now, right? So why the hell are we staying in this shithole?" he said, raising an eyebrow.

"Where else would we go?" asked John as he lit a cigarette.

"Wherever we want, dummy. I say we take that big house up the hill down Route 49." He viciously chewed on the corn nuts.

"Ain't that house got a bunch of towel heads in it?" asked Cecil as he spat a long dark brown streak of spit into an empty Pepsi bottle.

"Yeah, so what?" Hank said incredulously.

"So, what we do with them?"

"Well, I figure the old man catches a bullet. Hell, his terrorist ass probably deserves it anyhow. Maybe the president will give us a medal or something. As for the mom and daughter, I don't know about you, but the lack of female companionship round here is something that needs remedying." He chuckled.

"I don't think them ladies is gonna be too keen on keeping us warm at night if we kill the old man," John replied.

"Oh hell, booger brains, we ain't gonna give them a choice. They is in our country, they gonna pay for it one ways or another," Hank said with no expression.

John opened the bottle of whiskey that was sitting on the table and took a long draw of it. If he was gonna do this, he would have to sedate that conscience that pecked in the back of his brain. He sat and half-listened to the plan that Cecil and Hank were rambling on about. After he had heard as much as he could stomach, he walked out on the back porch and sat and watched the sun come up. If God were watching him now, he knew that he was gonna burn in hell. Hopefully hell had booze.

Emory woke with a start. The sun was coming up, and he was twisted in a very uncomfortable position in the backseat of the car. Margot was cuddling up against the giant dog, her pistol sitting in her lap. She looked beautiful in the slow-filtering morning sunlight.

After the shock had worn off yesterday, Emily and Ronnie had decided to canvas the neighborhood, looking for signs of anyone who had escaped being detained. They hadn't. What they found were flyers. Hundreds of them. They told of the location of the camp and explained to survivors that they were to report there and would be welcomed with open arms. The camp was called Camp Hope. How bad could a place called Hope be? Ronnie had decided that they would go to the camp today, and two of them would sneak in. Emily and Emory would be the ones to do it. Ronnie said that he would stick out like a sore thumb, and there was no way that dog would leave Margot's side.

After the plans had been discussed, they sat around in the evening and shared a meal of MREs from the trunk of the car. It was eerily silent among the group, and nobody had much of anything to say. Emory figured it was everybody's nerves getting to them, so he let it be. After they ate, Ronnie said that he and Emily would be sleeping in two separate locations away from the car so that they could avoid being ambushed.

This made sense to Emory, but the thought of being alone in the backseat of a car with Margot made his stomach turn. He had imagined that the first time he was in the backseat of a car with a girl would be on a date, not during the collapse of a nation. She read her book before falling asleep, and Emory stared out the window, lost in thought of the fragments of his family. Before he fell asleep, he wondered if he would ever see his dad again. Getting out of the city seemed daunting and hopeless. His emotions getting out of sorts again, he gently wept until he passed out from exhaustion.

Margot started to stir, and he abruptly looked out the window, hoping she didn't catch him staring at her.

"Good morning," she said, her words sweet and soft.

"Good morning," Emory replied nervously.

"Congratulations," she said with a straight face.

"Uh, for what?" said Emory, thoroughly confused.

"You are the first boy I have ever spent the night with," she said with a devilish grin.

"I, uhh..." Emory blurted.

"Relax, I'm just messing with you," she said, laughing.

"Oh, well, you got me." He blushed.

"Ugh, I barely slept in the back of this thing." She contorted her neck until it popped.

"Yeah, it really wasn't pleasant. Hey, about yesterday, I'm really sorry that you had to see me get upset. I don't usually lose composure like that. I don't cry that often," he said, trying to save his manly integrity.

"It's okay. I think it's really sweet that you care that much about your family. You don't have to hide your emotions from me," she said, holding his hands and staring into his eyes.

"Thanks," was all he could say with her touching his hands.

"Well, I have to take this beast out so she can pee. By the way, you messed up, mister." She got out of the car, looking back through the door frame.

"What? How?" he said with a tone of panic.

"You were supposed to say I was the first girl you ever spent the night with," she said, giving him a wink.

Cecil and John lurked around the corner of the garage. The three men had parked about a half a mile down the road and crept under the cover of the woods toward the home. John had hoped that nobody would be home, but they had seen the mother come out and hang up some laundry to dry. John pulled the flask out of his pocket and took a long draw of whiskey. He couldn't get over how content and peaceful the woman was as she went about her daily task. What was about to happen was wrong but he couldn't find it in himself to walk away. Cecil lit up some meth next to him. *That's not good,* John thought as the bloodlust in Cecil's eyes fired up. The man looked crazy, and it added to John's anxiety about this plan. Hank walked up and knocked on the door.

"Hello," the girl said, barely opening the door a crack.

Through the crack in the door, the girl was visible. She was young. If he had to guess, she was fifteen or sixteen. That was okay with Hank. She was slim and still wearing her pajamas from the night before. He had an urge to kick in the door and take her right now. The smell of her perfume was driving him crazy. No, he thought to himself. Better to stick to the plan. The look on her face was not inviting. She looked confused with her brows furrowed and arms crossed at the arrival of visitors, but after seeing Hank's appearance and smelling the whiskey on his breath, the look turned to concern with her casting her face down.

"Is your daddy home, sweet thing? I need to speak with him; it's important," he said with a toothy half-smile. She stared at him for a moment, trying to run though her head what this man would want with her father.

"Uh, sure, let me go get him," she said, closing the door and locking the deadbolt.

Soon enough the door opened, and the old man walked out on the porch, closed the door, and locked it behind him. The man was small, barely coming up to Hank's shoulder. His skin was weathered and wrinkled from age. He was bald and sported a thick, full beard. The man looked at Hank, sharing the same confusion as his daughter.

"Can I help you with something, sir?" the pleasant father asked as he forced a smile. There was anger in the man's eyes. For a split second he wondered if this was a good idea.

"Sure can. I'm here to take this house and them women folk off your hands." The words flowed smoothly out of Hank's mouth without a second thought.

The old man didn't react. He just stared at Hank. The man didn't have any idea how to react to this proclamation. He had never had someone so boldly threaten him.

"How about I take my wife and daughter and leave? You

can have this house. Please don't hurt my girls," the man said, staring Hank in the eye.

The man hoped that Hank had some form of compassion someplace on the inside. He had seen evil men before, when he was growing up in the mountains of Afghanistan. He thought he had left all of that behind him. On this day, here and now, no sliver of mercy was coming. The hate in Hank's eyes burned with the intensity of a thousand stars.

"Nope. Look, you jihadi son of a bitch, I'm gonna kill your ass. Now, I ain't no animal; I know them bitches can see you from the front window. I will walk you around the corner where they won't see it go down." Hank laughed, drunk with the power of the situation.

The man looked at Hank, and Hank pulled back his jacket to show the handle of his pistol. The old man took a moment, then nodded and made his way toward the side of the garage, where Cecil and John waited. The man desperately searched his mind, trying to find a way out of the situation. Hank was bigger than him and twenty years younger. He couldn't try to fight his way out of this. Hank also looked like he had the intellect of a stump, so he figured that he may have a small chance at talking his way out.

"You don't have to do this," the man stated. He spoke in a soft, unthreatening tone and looked Hank squarely in the eyes.

"Sure I do," Hank taunted. He was loving every moment of this. The power he felt was making him bolder and bolder.

"I forgive you for this. I hope that Allah has peace on your soul" the man said without his voice wavering.

"Shit, stop. You know what, that touched me. I ain't gonna kill you. He is."

A tweaking, methed-out Cecil came around the corner. He carried a three-foot section of pipe. The man's reflexes kicked in and he tried to run, but Cecil was too fast and smashed his kneecap with the pipe, sending him crashing to the ground, screaming in pain. The screams didn't last long, though. The fury and ferocity that poured out of Cecil lasted for five minutes, and the carnage was indescribable. Cecil, covered in blood, finally stopped and leaned back against the wall, panting for breath.

"God damn, man. You are one sick son of a bitch. The president would be proud," Hank said, laughing.

"How about we go collect the prizes now?" Cecil said, giving Hank a wink and tugging at his crotch.

"John, clean this shit up. Me and Cecil did all the work, so we get first crack at the pussy. I call dibs on the young one."

John stood and listened to the words. He didn't have any interest in raping anybody.

"Sure thing, Hank," he said, not looking him in the eye.

Hank and Cecil made their way to the door, and Hank stepped up and slammed the door hard. While hearing all of this, John took a moment to look at the man, or what was left of him. Something about how the man had told them that he forgave them dug into John's brain. He couldn't get the image of the man's shock and horror out of his head. While he listened to Hank and Cecil slamming on the door, he sat down and wept. He didn't want to do this anymore, but he was sure Hank would kill him if he tried to leave. Standing and wiping his tears away, he went to look for a shovel and a bottle of booze. He was going to burn in hell for the things he had done. Figured he better show up drunk.

"Open up. Your new daddy is home," he snarled.

Nobody came to open the door. Getting annoyed, he took two steps back and kicked the dead bolt with every ounce of energy he had, sending the frame splintering and the door flying into the room. The mother and daughter both ran, screaming, and Hank sprinted over to the girl, grabbed her by the hair, and dragged her up the stairs into the bedroom, slamming the door behind him and ignoring the crying and pleading of her mother.

CHAPTER 18

Kenny and Marco had rummaged through Kenny's father's closet. They had many choices of things to give to Marco. Kenny's father had a wide arrangement of clothing. Eventually Marco settled on an old pair of jeans and a black tee shirt. Kenny had offered him a shot at his dad's watch collection, but Marco had declined. The boys had changed, throwing their wet clothes half-dazedly into the bathtub.

"Feels good to be dry again," Kenny muttered as he dried his hair with a towel.

"That it does, my friend." Marco said, sitting on the edge of the bed and lacing up a pair of boots he had found in the closet.

"You hungry?" Kenny asked.

"Always."

"Let's go find something to munch on."

The boys walked back downstairs into the kitchen. Kenny opened the dead fridge and scanned the shelves. There weren't many choices. His family ate out for most meals and didn't keep a well-stocked kitchen. With the power out, they couldn't cook anything. Kenny reached in and pulled out a gallon of milk, setting it on the counter.

"Cereal okay?" Kenny asked, opening up the pantry.

"Fine with me."

"We only have Trix and Honey Bunches of Oats."

"Well, considering I'm not ninety, I'll go for the first one."

“Yeah, me too.”

He pulled out two bowls and poured them both full of cereal. The milk was still cold and smelled okay. Taking the chance, Kenny topped off both bowls with the jug. They sat there munching away. They had both spent an enormous amount of energy in their little adventure and needed to recoup some of the calories they had spent. Nearly dying had filled Kenny with hunger. They sat and ate until the box was empty.

Kenny was putting the bowls in the sink when they heard it: a loud crash and screaming coming from next door. They ran to the window. Barely separating the curtains, they peered out. Neither of them were ready for what they saw.

There were military vehicles lining the cul-de-sac. Soldier were moving all over the place. They were dispatching in small teams, going house to house. They were kicking in the doors to the house on the left of his. They sat and watched as the soldiers dragged people out and ushered them into the backs of large trucks.

“Holy shit,” Marco said, exhaling.

“Yeah. What do you think we should do?” Kenny stepped back as a team was forming at the edge of his drive.

“Well, I’m pretty sure we should try to get away,” Marco said, stepping back from the window.

“Yeah, I feel that. Follow me.”

Kenny stepped back and turned, running up the stairs in full stride. Marco was right behind him and moved fast for a big dude. They ran into Kenny’s room. Kenny closed the door and locked it. It was a feeble attempt to keep them from entering, but he locked it out of instinct.

The front door smashed open and footsteps parading into the house. Kenny tapped Marco on the should and silently pointed to the closet. Marco followed him into the walk-in, not confident in the hiding spot. Kenny got on his knees and pushed a pile of clothes to the side, revealing a small access panel. He opened it and crawled inside. Marco followed and shut the panel behind him.

Looking around, Marco could barely make out anything. The room was bare and full of insulation. His best guess was that in a house of this size, there were multiple panels like this to work on things like pipes and the ducts.

Footsteps were coming up the stairs, and Kenny leaned over and tapped Marco on the shoulder. Kenny pushed himself as far back as he could and lay down. He quickly and franticly covered himself with the insulation that was blown everywhere. Marco decided to do the same.

They had barely covered themselves all the way when the soldiers kicked in the door. What seemed to be two sets of footsteps were walking around the room. Things being thrown around filled the silence and the dresser being knocked over thundered outside of their hiding spot. Kenny's heart nearly jumped out of his chest when the closet door opened. Voices started to filter through the thin walls of the room.

"Don't make any kind of sense."

"I know someone is here someplace, or why would the door be locked?"

"Maybe they went out the window."

"Nah, it was locked."

"Yo, look at this."

The access panel being opened squeaked and they both held their breath. The men shined flashlights in, illuminating the dark space. The lights shining through the insulation were moving all around the space, looking for signs of life.

"Ain't nobody in there. You would have to be crazy to hide in that shit."

"Should we look anyways?"

"You want to be itching the rest of the day? I sure as hell don't. Let's just call it clear and move on. We have a lot of houses to hit today."

"Yo, if you are in there. We are just here to help."

The soldier stood there for a split second, waiting to hear any kind of response. None came. They left the room with the panel wide open. The boots clopped away from them and faded as they were leaving and walking down the stairs. They lay hidden for what seemed like forever. Eventually Kenny sat up, brushing the insulation off himself.

"I think they are gone," he said, his whole body on fire with itching.

"Yeah, probably," Marco said, sitting up.

"I don't think this is a regular power outage," Kenny said as he crawled out of the closet.

"Yeah, I assume not."

"I used to hide my weed and booze in there. Never in a million years would I think I would be hiding in there," Kenny said, trying to get the insulation out of his hair.

"Any idea what's going on?" Marco said, walking around and sitting on the edge of the overturned dresser.

"Yeah, maybe. My friend's sister had an explanation, but at the time I thought it sounded crazy."

"What is it?"

"Good thing you are sitting down."

CHAPTER 19

They squatted in a marathon station just out of sight of the camp. Emily was looking at maps in the corner, pretty much staying to herself. This introverted version of his sister was starting to make Emory worry about her well-being. She had barely spoken to him since they had found the house on fire. She was blaming herself for what had happened. If they had been there, then they would be in that camp too, and who knew if Ronnie would have ever found them. She was being too hard on herself.

Margot and Lola were taking a nap in the corner, leaving Emory to himself. Emory sat there and was inspecting the tomahawk that his father had bestowed to him for the first time. The handle was made of wood. Hickory, he thought. It was grooved and fit his hand surprisingly well. The head was steel and had tarnished over time. It was hand engraved. One side of the head had a roughly etched American flag. The other side had a one-word etching: freedom.

Emory had a hard time thinking about his father using any weapon, but for him to have a tomahawk like this made sense. It was no-nonsense and ready for work. The weapon reminded him of his father. His father was a loving man who was always quick to help when asked, but he was always so serious. Knowing his past now gave Emory a sense of why he was so serious. He couldn't imagine what it was like to grow up like that. It was amazing that his father turned out the way that he did. A lesser man would have been consumed by his roots. Emory wondered if, had he grown up under the same circumstances, he would have been strong enough to free his mind the way his father had. He missed him. Wherever he was, Emory prayed to God that he was okay.

Ronnie returned from his reconnaissance around the camp. He came back in and sat down beside them, placing his rifle against the counter behind him. He carried a notepad full of handmade drawings and numbers. He had been gone for a long while. His face was glum and full of worry. He didn't look very optimistic about what they were doing. This was something that Emory hadn't seen before, and it shook him a little. Ronnie was usually a very confident man. Emily rushed over to sit next to him. Reading his face seemed to make the nervousness contagious, as Emily's face soured.

"I have good news and bad news. The good news is that I saw them reporting to the breakfast line," Ronnie started.

"Oh my god. Were they okay? Did they look hurt?" Emily interrupted.

"They looked fine. They were wearing gray jumpsuits. Do you have clothes for them?" he asked as he looked to Emily.

"I think their bags were in the house," she said, letting out a sigh.

"That's going to be a problem. While you two are in there, Margot and I will find them something to wear. Maybe Becky can wear some of Margot's things. We will find something for Eugene."

"What's the bad news?" Margot asked, waking up from her slumber.

"The place is heavily fortified. There is a decent number of soldiers and cops defending the place. We are only going to have one shot at this. If we fail, somebody is going to die," Ronnie said harshly as he made eye contact with the small group.

"Tell me that you have a plan," Emily pleaded.

"I do. You and Emory are gonna stroll up there and say

that you found the flyer and are looking for help. After you are in, I'm pretty sure that they will put you in Beck's tent. From what I could tell, it looks like families are staying together. At least for now. I'm assuming that there is a curfew, and the cover of darkness is our best chance at getting away with this. So, at midnight tonight, you will need to sneak out to the gap in the back gate and fade into the darkness."

"How are we going to do that with all of the soldiers?" Emory asked.

"I'm going to cause a distraction to get their attention. Margot will be waiting for you and know the escape route."

"Where are you going to be?" Emily asked.

"On the other side of the camp causing the previously-mentioned distraction. There is a good chance that I could be captured or killed. I need to know that you will leave no matter what you see or hear." Ronnie's eyes burned with determination.

"No, no way are we going to do that. I can't do this on my own," Emily said, a tear streaking down her face.

"You have to. You are strong, Em. I can see your mother's strength burning deep inside of you. You will lead this family to safety without me. If I didn't believe that there is a way, I wouldn't even propose this plan. Now buckle up, buckaroo. We are going to go over the details until you know them by heart."

Emory's heart was racing as he made his way toward the line that had formed outside of the camp. The bile was rising up his throat and he hoped that his breakfast didn't make a reappearance. Emily walked with determination and fire in her eyes. Great, he thought to himself. *One of us is going to puke and the other is going to start a fistfight.* They stood in line for what seemed like forever. The people in the line were chatting away without a care in the world. It seemed that most of them were going to be content with joining the ranks of the camp. He heard many people saying things like, "Thank god for the president. At least we will be safe. Things will turn around eventually. Heard the power will be back on soon." Nobody seemed to be questioning anything. It startled Emory that so many were so confident in the intentions of this place. Nobody cared that they were sheep led toward the slaughter. Scarily enough, they embraced it.

Finally, it was their turn, and they stepped up to the folding table across from a morose looking man in his mid-thirties. The man looked like he didn't care about anything. With a frown he muttered, "Name, address." He didn't even have the courtesy to look up from his papers.

"Emily and Emory Phillips. 101 Maple Avenue," she muttered with a stare that could melt ice cubes. The man thumbed through the large stack of papers until he finally found what he was looking for. He looked up at them, then back to the paper.

"We have a Becky Standard and Eugene Phillips listed at that address already liberated to Camp Hope. What is your relation?" he said with a devious glare.

"Becky is...." Emily tried to say.

"Our step-mom. Eugene is our brother. After Mom died, Dad went a little wild and married a nineteen-year-old. Kind of weird, you know, but oh well, shit happens," Emory blurted, not quite sure if the man bought it or not.

"Well, that matches what it says in here. Good thing, too. We don't let sodomites in this camp. You can move on to the next station." He was clearly annoyed that they dared interrupt his brooding.

Without a word to each other, they walked past the table and down an aisle that was sectioned off with rope, leading them to the next phase of entering the camp. A pair of armed

Department of Homeland Security guards stood in front of the entrance. They were dressed in full combat gear complete with black uniforms and body armor. Just above the left shoulder was a patch of an American flag. This wasn't the normal American flag. In the middle of the patch was a large black cross. Neither one of the men looked friendly.

"Step forward. There are two booths up ahead. There will be agents entering with you. Remove all your clothes, and you will be inspected for contraband. A female agent will be assisting with the lady," one of the men said in a flat monotone. Both Emory and Emily stood stunned at what they had just heard.

"NOW," the soldier said with force.

Emory stepped up hesitantly and gave Emily one last worried look as she vanished into the booth with a woman in a Homeland Security uniform following her. Emory stepped into the booth and removed his clothes, an older agent behind him. He was glad Margot hadn't come with him. At least she would be spared this indignity. This was the first time he had been naked in front of anyone since he was a child, and the whole process made him feel cheap and belittled.

"Turn around. Now squat and give me three hard coughs," the man told him with a smile on his face that made Emory want to rip his heart out. The man touched him in ways that made his stomach curl, and after what seemed like forever, the man tossed him a jumpsuit and watched him put it on.

"Good job, buttercup. Now you can head on to the next station," he said as he gave him a pat on the butt on the way out.

Emory exited the tent and was filled with a silent rage. Had they done this to Becky? Even worse, Eugene. Something stirred inside of him. Something dark. He wanted to hurt these people, and that scared him. He had never felt this level of shame and rage at the same time before.

He watched as his and Emily's clothes were carried off

and thrown into a burning trash barrel. It made sense to him. They build you up with the hope of peace, and as soon as they get you through the gates, you are property of Homeland Security. Then they can treat you however they want; the gloves are off. They were burning the clothes and giving them the hideous jump suits so if they escaped, they would be easier to find. Also, when everyone looked the same, it was easier for people to assimilate to the way things were now.

They stepped up to the next station. There was a row of chairs. On the ground was tons of human hair. They made their way up and sat down in the chairs. Emory looked over to Emily, who had a worried look on her face. A woman walked over to Emily, pulled out some combs and started brushing through her hair. After she had found no detections of lice, she cleared Emily and sent her on her way.

A large, greasy-looking man walked up behind Emory. Apparently, he was not going to be as lucky. With no words, the man pulled out a pair of cordless clippers and started cutting off Emory's hair. He sat there watching his hair rain to the ground. Emily watched, holding her hand over her mouth. He had always had long hair, and watching it fall to the ground made him think. New world. New hair. Maybe it was time for a new him. The man reeked of stale tobacco and took his time, not in a rush. After he was done, he simply walked away, and Emory got up and joined his sister.

"How's it look?" Emory said, trying to make the best of the situation.

"Makes you look ten years older. Why cut yours and not mine?"

"Less attachment for guys, I guess. Probably don't want to upset the ladies," Emory thought as he ran his hand over his freshly shaved head.

His mind was on fire as they reached their third and final destination. It was a mini amphitheater of sorts. About twenty or so chairs lined up around a podium. They took a seat as the place started to fill with a sea of gray jumpsuits. The smell was foul. People without running water were losing hygiene fast. He wondered if he smelled like that too.

"Why did you say Becky was our step-mom? I'm not ashamed of who I am, Emory," Emily said in a low whisper.

"I could see the book from where I was standing. That's what Becky told them. Plus, I didn't like the way that human trash bag was looking at you. I assume it was Beck's way of not getting split up from Eugene," he said in a low whisper back.

Before they could converse more, a large man came off the side stage and stood in front of the crowd. The man was every bit of six-foot-six and three hundred pounds. He was bald and sweating profusely. He wore a black suit with a large patch of the cross and the American flag above his heart. The man looked like he was about to pass out at any minute, and his wheezing was audible from where he sat.

"Hello everyone, and God bless. I hope that you all made it here to Camp Hope without much trouble. My name is Max Pruner. I am civilian deputy chief of this camp, and I am here to give you an introduction of sorts and tell you what is going on, as far as we know. We will start with the events that led us to these dire circumstances that we find ourselves in. A nuclear bomb was detonated in the atmosphere above New York City." The man had to stop for the gasp and mutterings of a shocked crowd. He looked very annoyed that he had been interrupted.

"Do we have to worry about fallout? Is it safe here?" one man shouted from the back of the crowd.

"There will be no fallout, since it was detonated so high. Now, no more interruptions from the crowd. It will not be tolerated. We know that this act was commissioned by the Democratic Party and carried out by terrorists from Iran. It seems that the left hates our heroic president so much it was willing to put all your lives in danger. But fear not, good people. Out of the ashes of the old comes a new birth for our country. Most of the satanic left has fled for the west coast and won't be much of a threat to us now. We have a chance to start a new country. One where God is at the center. We will rebuild a better world. Our fearless commander had the foresight to put systems in place for camps like this one all across this nation. As I speak, we are making sure that all of you good people are safe. Now, on to the rules of this camp. The days of the free ride are over. Everyone here works. You will all be given work assignments when you get to your new temporary housing. The camp staff is here to ensure your safety, so you will be cordial and inviting to all their requests. Any disobedience or back talk will result in your loss of meal privileges for the day. Any violence or weapons will be dealt with by a quick and efficient firing squad for you and the adult members of your family. Any children will be put under the care of the state."

"You can't do that. This is bullshit," a man in the front row screamed, standing and glaring at Max. Max stood there for a moment, wheezing and catching his breath from his long speech. His face had turned red from the audacity of someone else daring to interrupt him.

"Yes, I can. People need rules or they are just unruly animals. Now you, sir, have lost your family's meal privileges for the day. Sit down and be glad it wasn't your life." The man sat down, face beet-red, and Max's face twisted back into the fake smile he had tried to portray since waddling onto the stage.

"You will all be fine if you follow the rules that have been given to you. Welcome to Camp Hope and God bless." After he finished his statement, he walked off the stage, and guards at the gate to the camp opened the door.

People stood and looked dazed and confused. They shuffled out, looking like a large group of zombies. It was eerily quiet, and nobody even looked at each other. There were no more smiles or jokes. Emory wondered how many of them were second-guessing their decision to come to this place. After they were about twenty yards away, Emory looked over to Emily.

"You believe any of that garbage?"

"I'm sure there are chunks of truth in there. It kind of makes sense that this happened from the inside. I just can't imagine that somebody would do this to their own people. All I know for sure is that he doesn't deserve to wear the cross of our God," Emily said, looking to the sky.

"Your God. I haven't felt him since Mom died," Emory said flatly, staring straight ahead.

They had grown up in a religious house. The only time one of them missed a Sunday at church was when they were sick. Emory had struggled with his relationship with God when his mother passed away. How could God let that happen? He had stopped going shortly after. He could tell his father was upset by this, but he let him slide, not wanting to force him to go. The preacher had sat down with him and explained that his mother was in a better place now. How could it be a better place, devoid of the people who loved her? He had sat and listened to that man all afternoon one day. It was still a bitter pill for him to swallow.

They walked in silence to where they were told their tent was located. They went up and down the rows. People were out and about around them. Most of the people just walked around, their faces hidden from any emotion. There were DHS soldiers everywhere. Their eyes were burning into them as they walked. Ronnie had better cause quite the diversion to pull them away, or they were going to be stuck in this place for who knew how long.

Emory held his breath as he walked through the door. The tent was dark and smelled musty. A man with a thick mustache sat on one of the three cots in the room. When Emory saw Eugene playing in the corner, a tear rolled down his face. Eugene hadn't noticed them and continued to play with his new friend in the corner of the canvas house. Emory found it insane that in all this madness, his younger brother could carry on with a child-like innocence. It somehow inspired him with hope. Eugene seemed happy and content, and for a split-second Emory wondered if they were doing the right thing by taking him away from a place that was technically a "Safe Zone." Little did he know that he was about to learn a lesson about giving up his freedom for false safety.

Kenny and Marco both had to change their clothes once again. Their skin was burning from hiding in the insulation, and the water wasn't running. Fearing going outside, they had settled on wiping off with a couple of baby wipes they had found in the bathroom. It didn't help much, but it was enough to slow it down. They sat quietly in Kenny's room for hours in case they had to make a dive back into the wall.

Kenny had explained everything that he had learned from Emily to Marco. The boy had taken it surprisingly well. He didn't seem shocked and had no panicked reaction. He just sat there like a sponge, taking it all in.

"What the hell do we do now?" Kenny asked, keeping his voice low.

"We wait until night, and then we high-tail it back to my family's farm."

"Why?"

"Well, we got food, water and even an outhouse. We can weather out any storm there."

"I don't want to be a burden on your family."

"No burden. It's the Christian thing to do. My parents are good people; they will take you in."

"How long will it take to walk there?"

"Better part of three days, I reckon. What if your parents show up and you ain't here?"

"They are at a medical conference. They won't be back for a long while. What if your parents were taken by the soldiers?"

"My dad wouldn't let that happen. He would be hiding in the hills at the first wind of those booger eaters."

"Okay, then what's the plan?"

"Wait until night and then start humping it. We will have less chance of being seen at night."

"Makes sense."

"Now we can spend the rest of the day gathering supplies. Please tell me you all have some guns."

"No guns. Dad doesn't believe in them. We have some old camping supplies in the basement, though. Been years since they have been touched."

"Well, let's go take a look."

The boys crept into the basement, trying their best to stay away from the windows. Kenny couldn't resist and peeked out the window into the living room. All signs of the military were gone. So were all signs of people in the neighborhood. Nothing moved outside except for a random cat walking down the street.

Once they had located the storage totes labeled "camping," they pulled them out and dragged them back up into Kenny's room. They had found four large totes in total. Marco opened the first one to reveal three large backpacks shoved in. They were external frame and heavy-duty. He laid them out on the bed.

"You do a lot of backpacking?" Marco asked.

"We did for a summer. Dad is like that; hobbies change with the season."

"Shame. These are some nice packs."

Opening the second box revealed three sleeping bags. They were light-duty bags, and Marco laid them out on top of the packs. Marco's spirits were rising. They may not have a gun, but at least they would have reasonable comfort on the trip.

Opening the third box revealed cooking supplies. Kenny found a couple little rocket stoves, the kind designed to put out a large amount of heat from being fed small sticks and leaves. There were some cook sets that Kenny pulled out and laid on the bed. The bottom of the tote was a hodgepodge of miscellaneous freeze-dried food bags. Luckily, they lasted a long time. He laid them on the bed.

Marco pulled out a few wide-mouthed water bottles. His heart nearly stopped when he found a brand new, never-used-before water filter at the bottom. Rich people never ceased to amaze him. The filter had probably been at least a couple hundred dollars, and it had never even left the package. It was a huge score and would keep them from getting sick. Last thing he wanted was to try to hike with the mud butt.

The last tote was filled with all sorts of treasures. A couple of expensive multitools. Lots of flashlights and batteries. Wool socks and rain gear. Marco couldn't believe the amount of stuff they had bought to use only for a summer. Reaching in, he pulled out two machetes. They were top of the line and in good shape. Setting them on the bed, he stood and looked at Kenny.

"There is enough stuff here to live like kings," he said with a chuckle.

"Thinking about camping right now doesn't remind me of kings," Kenny said, looking at the bed.

"That's cause you ain't never went without before, city boy," Marco said, annoyed.

"I won't apologize for the way I was raised."

"Well, you better toughen up quick. We ain't going to have it easy again for a long while."

CHAPTER 20

Becky had woken up and for a moment forgotten where she was. The sky was crimson as the sun started to break its way into day, and a dull light shone in the front of the tent. Then the realization of what was going on hit her, and she frantically felt beside her for Eugene. Her hand found his chest, and she let it stay there to feel the rhythmic in and out of his breaths. She lay there and stared up at the top of the tent. Hopefully Emily and Emory would show up today, but inside she truly doubted it. She felt alone. On top of that, she felt the pressure of taking care of the boy on her own. It was going to take everything she had to get through. She looked over to see Maria getting out of bed and slipping into a gray jumpsuit.

"They came this morning. We all have to wear them. How good do I look in this thing?" she said, striking a little pose with a smirk on her face.

"You look better than I will," Becky said, smiling back.

At least she had found a friend in here. They had stayed up yesterday talking and quickly took a liking to each other. Maria had told her about their little home and that she was a paralegal before all of this. Her husband had been a freelance writer and traveled a lot. She was grateful that he was home when all of this rained down upon them. Their son had been at school when the power blew, and they had to go get him.

Luckily, they had an old truck that had been her father's, and after some minor tweaking, they had gotten it to fire up. After picking up their son, they had been on their way home, and they had come up to a newly-constructed road block. Soldiers in black uniforms had come upon them with weapons drawn and forced them out of the car and on their knees at gunpoint. One of the soldiers kept asking them if they were illegals and demanded their IDs. Maria was not sure, but from their tone and mannerisms, she didn't think that illegals were going to be treated very well. Finally, after seeing their credentials, the soldiers put them on a truck and shipped them here.

"Come on. I don't think that we should be late on our very first day. Who knows, maybe it won't be so bad," Maria said.

Becky looked over at Eugene, asleep on his cot. He looked so peaceful that she didn't want to wake him to say goodbye. Ricky was going to stay with the children. The schedule for families was staggered daily so that one of the guardians would be with the children at all times. Part of her wondered if this was done to be kind. The other part of her knew that this was being done so that the camp didn't have to tend to the children.

As they left the tent, the early morning sunlight hurt Becky's eyes, and she lifted a hand to shade her face. It was early, but the camp was bustling with activity as people started their daily jobs. They walked to the mess tent that was located in the middle of the camp and stood in line. Luckily, they had gotten there early, as the line behind them swelled into a giant gray mile.

They were served one scoop of oatmeal that had been cooked to mush with a cup of water and a biscuit that was as hard as a rock. They sat and ate their breakfast in silence. Maria prayed before eating her food, which was something that caught Becky a little off-guard. Religion had always been the Ellison family thing. Becky didn't know what she believed, but she had a hard time being thankful for such a meager breakfast. At least they were being fed, she rationalized. They turned their metal trays in and started toward the barracks that they were responsible for cleaning.

"A bunch of men living together in here; I'm guessing this

is about to be a pretty dirty job," Maria said, bunching up her nose.

"I shudder at what the bathroom is going to look like," Becky stated.

"It's only been one day. How bad can it be?"

They walked into the barracks, and the odor assaulted their noses right off the bat. It smelled like a dirty locker room. There were twenty bunks, lined up ten on one side and ten on the other. There were clothes and gear thrown everywhere, with disheveled, unmade beds as far as the eye could see. Each bunk had a footlocker at the front of the bed with a name in bold letters assigned to it. At the far end of the room were ten men sitting around a table enjoying their breakfast. The men wore smiles and appeared to not have a care in the world. It was a stark contrast to what they had just witnessed at the workers' mess tent. They approached the table.

"We are here for maid duty," Becky said, staring at what the men were eating.

While there were children outside eating slop, these guys had a full spread. There was a large plate of scrambled eggs in the middle of the table and a platter of donuts and Danishes. Each man had a cup of coffee with a pot in the middle of the table. The men were wasting more food than the people outside were eating.

"You can clean me up anytime, sexy," said a man who looked like he was about twenty and had his finger between two donuts he was eating.

"Shut up, Roberts. There are cleaning supplies in the closet. I'm afraid you are going to have your work cut out for you; these boys are messy as hell. Now if you will excuse us, miss, we have to report for duty. Roberts here will be your chaperone for the day," the leader of the group said without the courtesy of even giving them his name.

He stood, grabbed his rifle and headed for the door. The rest of the men minus the man named Roberts followed suit. The men had simply left the dishes and food on the table, figuring that they would clean it up. Their lack of courtesy made Becky feel cheap and used. Like she wasn't even human enough to show an ounce of kindness or respect to. They walked into the bathroom, opened the closet and pulled out the cleaning supplies.

"I guess we should start on one end each and meet in the middle. We can change who does the end with the bathroom each day. What side would you like to start on?" Maria calmly said.

"Did you see what those pricks were eating?" Becky said as calmly as she could, trying to keep her temper in check.

"Warriors need fuel," Roberts said, sneaking up on them with his best attempt to play it cool. "Don't worry your pretty little head about it. Now, that could be a loss in your food privileges for the day. Or you could turn that frown upside down and take a couple of these fine pastries with you."

"I'm sorry," Becky said half-heartedly as she thought of Eugene, ignoring the urge to break the asshole's face.

"It's okay, sweetie. Now, you clean up this mess, and I'm going to go lie in my bunk. Try not to disturb me again," he said, giving her a wink and slinking off while blowing her a kiss over his shoulder.

"Yikes." Becky whispered as she pulled the items out of the closet.

"Yeah, for sure. Guy is a grade A creep-burger. Anyway, I'm going to start here in the bathroom today; you go on and start on the other side. It's going to be okay, Becks," Maria said gently, patting Becky's hand reassuringly.

Becky walked to the other side of the building and stared at the mess. She didn't even know where to start. She started to mindlessly pick up clothes off of bunks, folding them and laying them on the bed. She made some pretty good progress, and about an hour and a half into it had most of the clothing folded and on the bed. She started on the trash. She was finding chip and candy bar wrappers all over the place.

This camp was starting to make a little more sense to her now. It was not about safety at all. It was about making slaves and living like kings. Her blood boiled as she found more and more. Empty dip cans. Spit bottles. For the people living in here, it seemed nothing had changed. Even their vices had carried into this new world. She started putting clothes away in the footlockers while her blood was boiling.

She was just about to Roberts and he got up and gave her another wink and walked to the bathroom where Maria still was. She opened his locker to put his clothes away, and something glimmered, catching her eye. She pushed away the penthouse magazines to reveal a boot knife underneath.

Without thinking, she opened her jumpsuit and slid the knife's belt clip into her underwear. She had a feeling that she may need it in the future. She had never so much as hit anyone before, and now she was shoving knives into her underwear. Would she even know how to use it? Could she even use it? The doubts bounced around in her head. What was she thinking? This could mean death for her and Eugene. This was a stupid thing to do, she thought. Before she could put it back, screaming interrupted her from the bathroom.

"I said no! I'm married, you pig," Maria shouted in a tone that was full of fear and panic.

Becky ran to the bathroom as fast as her feet would carry her. The knife bounced around under her jumpsuit, and she hoped that Roberts didn't spot it. She closed the distance fast and slid to a stop upon entering the bathroom. The scene she walked in on took her breath away. Maria was in the corner, and Roberts stood over her, exposing himself. He stood there with his bits out, laughing and waving it around, having the time of his life. Maria's face was tear-streaked and flushed from fear. She cowered in the corner behind a toilet, trying to fend off his advances. It took him a minute to figure out Becky was behind him, but after noticing her, he carried on. Roberts looked over his shoulder at Becky.

"Oh, hell, it's gonna happen sooner or later. Be your turn next shift, unless you all want to give me a two-for-one discount. I'm trying to explain to your friend here you take care of my needs, and I will keep you up on treats like donuts and--" He never got to finish that statement.

While his head was turned, Maria had gotten up and taken the top of the toilet tank off. Her hands gripped the porcelain so tight that her fingers were turning white. With all the force that she could muster in her small body, she hit him across the back of the head with it, causing a sickening thud as the porcelain shattered in her hands. He crumpled to the floor, still exposed, and blood began to pool from his head on the tile. His eyes were open and staring at Becky, and he still had a shit-eating grin across his face. Eventually his breaths stopped coming, and his eyes rolled into the back of his head. Just as that happened, another one of the men from the breakfast table walked into the bathroom and raised his weapon on the two of them. He stood there trying to assess the situation, looking wildly all around the room.

"He tried to rape me," Maria managed to get out between sobs as she stood there, still holding a piece of the shattered top.

The man looked to the floor, then back up at Maria. Becky stood frozen at the sight of all the man's blood on the floor and the cascade of violence that she had just witnessed. The man raised his rifle and fired a single shot into Maria's head without warning, sending a sea of crimson against the back wall. Her body fell to the floor, and Becky just stood there looking at the soldier. The man was stone-faced and unfaltering, meeting her glare. There was no remorse in his eyes for what he had just done. Her fear had paralyzed her, unable to process the events that had just unfolded.

"Violence will not be tolerated. Just be glad I walked in here to take a crap and caught her red-handed or you would be going with her. Now go back to your tent. I will call the hazmat crew to clean up this mess. One other thing: You are here to take care of us. That means anything that we say. Anything," the man said with no emotion, pointing at her.

Becky exited the tent in a state of shock. Did he really just say that they were to take care of the men here by all and any service they requested? She had never been with a man and was not about to start. Her senses started to come back to her after her adrenaline had dumped, and the realization of what just happened hit her like a ton of bricks. The woman that had showed her so much kindness lay dead in a shitty bathroom in a shitty camp. They were going to come for Ricky now, she thought, and she ran to the tent. Maybe if she got there in time, she could warn him and he could try to make a break for it. Their son was going to be put in group care. She couldn't imagine what kind of hell that would be.

"No running!" a guard screamed at her, not even bothering to get up from the chair he sat in.

She slowed her pace as the tent came into view. She was too late. The guards were leading Ricky out at gunpoint and had the boy trailing behind him. The man looked thoroughly confused about what was going on. The boy wore a face of fear that would be burnt into Becky's brain until the day she died. There was nothing she could do, and she knew it. What kind of world was this? Sick and defeated she moved forwards. If this place was trying to defeat her spirit, it was winning. She was feeling hopeless for the first time in her life.

She squatted down and began to weep. She let it all out. All the sadness for her new friends. The sorrow for missing the

Ellison family. How on earth was she going to explain this to Eugene? Could a child even process what she was about to tell him? All hope was starting to leave her at a rapid pace now. She thought that she was strong. She thought that she could handle anything that life threw at her. Apparently, she was wrong. She didn't even notice the footsteps walking up to her. She just sat there, falling to pieces and didn't care who saw her. She looked up to see Emily standing there in a gray suit.

"You didn't think I was going to leave you here, did you, beautiful?"

CHAPTER 21

Kenny and Marco slipped into the darkness after sunset. Their packs were full, and Marco wore his machete at his side. They felt good about their chances. They stood in the thin strip of woods, letting their eyes adjust to the night. After they felt like they had good enough visual competency to navigate the woods, they started walking. They were silent as they walked. Marco had suggested that they keep a six-foot interval in between them in case one of them came under attack.

They moved quickly and with purpose. They cleared a lot of ground on that first night. Their stomachs were full and their spirits high. Marco had suggested that if they could clear the city limits by daybreak, they would be in a much safer spot. Less people around meant less of a chance of running into government people.

They did pass by numerous groups of people on this first night. They slipped by undetected. It was easy to spot the people. Most of the small groups they passed had been huddled around small campfires, lighting up the night. Kenny thought it seemed like a pretty bad idea to advertise their location like that, but at least it made it easier for them to avoid.

The only problem they had encounter on that first night was a run-in with a group of people at a house on the outskirts of town. They had come upon the house, but they could hear it from a half-mile down the road. People were laughing and loud as they drew upon it. They could see about fifteen people in the front yard. The house was surrounded with lit tiki torches.

They were having a party. In all of this mess, these people

had decided that the best course of action for them was to knock back a few. The boys huddled up and devised a plan to make a large arc around the house and through the woods that sat behind it.

As they crept their way through the woods, they kept their eyes fixated on the people at the house. Kenny had been so concentrated on the house that he didn't see the two people who had snuck into the woods for some private time. He walked upon them and didn't turn his head until he heard the muffled sounds of copulating.

They had been so wasted that they had not noticed his approach either. They both realized each other's presence when Kenny was only feet away from them. The man stumbled to his feet, butt naked, and zig-zagged to a tree where a shotgun was sitting. Kenny moved faster than he ever had before in his life, with the naked man trying to chase him. Kenny kept running for a few hundred yards and sat down in a clearing.

Eventually Marco came huffing and puffing into the spot. He sat down, laughing while trying to suck in air. The two sat and made jokes about what had just happened. It felt good to laugh. With all the crazy stuff going on around them, at least they hadn't lost their sense of humor.

They hiked for another few hours, eventually making it into a field. Kenny was glad they were stopping. His feet were on fire in the still-pretty new boots. He knew they would take time to break in. Sitting on a stump, he pulled them off and set them to the side. Marco whistled at the huge number of blisters that were forming on Kenny's feet.

Marco pulled out a roll of duct tape that he had found in one of the bins. He went to work on Kenny's feet, covering up the hot spots. He showed Kenny how to properly lace the boots tightly so that his feet wouldn't move around so much in them. Marco kicked himself for not showing him earlier and maybe saving Kenny some pain.

The night was nice enough that Marco had suggested they sleep without the tents. He still set a tent up about thirty yards away from Kenny and Marco's camp. He told Kenny that if they had unwelcome guests that they may spot the tent first to investigate and they could slip out the back. Kenny was thankful that Marco knew his stuff. He would be helpless on his own.

They were to sleep in shifts, with one of them watching for people. They had boiled up two of the pouches of the freeze-dried food. Kenny had beef stroganoff. It was okay but left something to be desired. Marco was up for first watch. Kenny slid into his sleeping bag. He watched the sun breaking into the sky. He hoped that his parents were watching the same thing. As his eyes felt heavy and he felt sleep taking him, he thought of the Ellison family. He hoped wherever they were, they were okay.

Ronnie watched his niece and nephew walk into the front gate of the camp. He was worried, though he wouldn't admit it to himself. He didn't know if this plan was going to work, and he knew if he lost them, he would lose himself.

He had seen insufferable human cruelty from his tours of combat and facing it now in this country was a horror he had always prayed would be spared from his family. The amount of evil that people were capable of still haunted his dreams. But for now, he had to push it out of his head.

There were too many things to do and not a lot of time to do them. He walked back over to Margot, who was leaning up against the bumper of the car, watching Lola run around chasing butterflies. She was a remarkable young lady, he thought. The way she had bounced back from their traumatic first encounter. He could see the way Emory looked at her, all nervous and goofy. The boy was in love.

"We need to find them clothes first thing," Ronnie stated as he put the binoculars back into his bag.

"We passed a thrift store on the outskirts of town. I could go there while you do what you need to do," Margot offered, snapping her fingers and signaling the dog back to her side.

"No thanks. We are going to stay together. We are stronger together. Especially with the man detector over there." He pointed at the dog, who was jumping at the butterfly again.

"She sure looks vicious like that, doesn't she? What a dork," she said, laughing.

"Come on, let's go," Ronnie said, picking up his pack and his rifle from the hood of the car. He walked past the car in the direction of the store.

"Are we not driving?" asked Margot.

"No. Less chance of being spotted on foot. We will move it after dark. Less chance of being seen with no headlights."

They walked down the back ally that adjoined the road. They didn't see a soul on their way there. In a place that used to be a fluster of activity now sat a bleak nothingness. The door to the shop was unlocked. Whoever owned the place must not have cared if someone came in and took this stuff.

The store was still relatively untouched. Ronnie pulled the list from his pocket and made a beeline for the men's clothing. He looked over at Margot, who was wandering up and down the aisle. She seemed like nice girl. He was glad that their paths had met. She would be a good addition to the group. He was still torn about what path he would follow after getting them to their grandfather. But hell, he could die today, so he would worry about that later.

They piled their bounty into two shopping baskets and made their way back to the car. The smirk on her face twisted into a smile.

"What's with the silly grin?"

"Oh, I found the perfect shirt for Emory. It's a surprise; can't wait for you to see him in it," she said, trying to hold back the giggles.

"Look. I need to ask you something," he said.

"Uhh, okay. Go for it." Her grin was replaced with nervous anticipation.

"If something happens to me tonight... If I don't make it to that car on time... You get my family in there by any means necessary. Don't let them try to come and save me. You know they will. Just get them the ham sandwich out of this mess," he pleaded while trying to hide the worry in his voice.

"What makes you think they are going to listen to me? They barely know me. I'm just some girl along for the ride," she said.

"Emory will. The boy is sweet on you," he stated flatly.

"What? How do you know that?" she said, her face flushing and her eyes diverting to the floor.

"I've seen the way he looks at you. Be careful with that boy. Behind that sorrow in his eyes, I'm pretty sure a warrior is brewing, waiting to explode out of him. At least if he is anything like his daddy."

"I, umm..."

"It's okay. I have probably said too much already. Just please get them out of here." With that, they didn't say another word for a long time.

Ronnie wondered if it was the right thing to do, to out poor Emory's feelings like that as they walked back toward the car. Emory sure was going to be pissed if he found out about Ronnie's statement. As they grew closer and closer to the car, Ronnie started to hope that maybe the two would have a relationship.

The way Margot looked at Emory when she thought nobody was looking. It was like the two had an unspoken bond. The kind that ran deep and couldn't be explained. He knew that they hardly knew one another. An outside observer would have no idea of that, though. They were natural together. They both deserved to be happy and cling to whatever they could in their bleak new lives. For a moment sadness at the fact that he didn't have anyone took him, but he found solace in the fact that he was going to take care of these kids, come hell or high water.

He wondered if their dad was still around. Frank Ellison was a good man. Ronnie hoped to see him again someday. While Ronnie was off trying to get drunk enough to block out the fact that his sister was dying, Frank never left her side. Ronnie respected him, and respect was not something he gave out easily. The kids needed Frank more than they needed Ronnie.

When they finally arrived at the car, Ronnie opened the trunk. With his mood souring on the shortcomings and failures of the past, Ronnie started messing around with weapons and gear in the trunk. Ronnie's mood was turning. Margot began to worry that the man she had seen kill somebody with no effort was starting to show his nerves. She distracted herself by placing the clothes and shoes in their respective bags.

As she put the clothes away, she reflected on Ronnie's statement about Emory being sweet on her. She did feel something too. She hardly knew him, but for some reason she liked him. Ronnie finally came around the edge of the car and looked at Margot with a big smile from ear to ear, apparently recovering at least momentarily from what was bothering him.

"Come on, I'm gonna teach you how to blow up a car."

CHAPTER 22

Hank rolled over and looked at the girl who lay in bed with him. She had a black eye that was puffy from crying. Her hands were bound to the headboard. She was not more than sixteen, he thought as he sat up and reached to the nightstand, lighting a cigarette. Sitting on the edge of the bed, he took a deep breath. His plans were coming together perfectly, and his confidence in himself was growing exponentially. In a bathrobe that he had found in what he assumed was the dead father's closet, he wandered down the stairs and into the kitchen. He had put John on moving the contents of his house over here. John was carrying in two cases of beer, and he put them down and stared at Hank.

"She is up there if you want sloppy seconds," Hank said with a wink.

"No thanks," John said, not meeting his eyes.

"Your loss," replied Hank.

Cecil pounded into the room and pushed the woman out in front of him. She seemed catatonic, like a zombie. She was covered in bruises and was in her underwear still. Her face had been beaten pretty badly, and she could barely see from her swollen left eye. She walked over to the counter and started looking at the food John had brought and putting it away without making a sound. Cecil sat down and pulled a can of grizzly winter green out and put in a huge pinch. He didn't have a shirt on and was only wearing black sports shorts. He was riddled with tattoos, and the giant swastika tattooed on his chest had faded over time, but it still made its point.

"That was sweet, man. Like real sweet. It's done been a minute since I had a woman. She was fighting it real hard at first, but I made her see it my way. I told her to come put the kitchen up and make us some food or we would take turns on the girl and make her watch. Straightened her out real quick like," he said, pushing a big spit into his empty coffee cup.

"I think we could make this a real good home for a while. We need to set up an ambush site back in them woods past that old-ass log cabin. That trail will be hot, and we should be able to pull a lot out of there," Hank said as he turned his head and cracked his neck.

"Ain't them crazy-ass militia boys back in that direction? I think we should avoid running into them," John said, taking a drag off a Busch Light.

"Nah, man, I'm pretty sure they ain't been that way for a while. Besides, them boys pretty much keeps to themselves. I don't even think they would give two shits if we was back there anyhow," Cecil said, stepping up from the table and walking over to open a pack of Ho Ho's. He smacked the woman on her behind, and her whole body flinched. Laughing, he walked back over and sat down.

"We will go check it out later. For now, I'm gonna get upstairs. I got some business to be tending to. Been a hell of a long time since I have been with a sixteen-year-old, and boys, I gotta tell you, ain't nothing like it," Hank said as he walked past the mom and slapped her behind as Cecil had, sending a quiver up her body. He went up the stairs, and John opened another beer. This shit was too far. He was going to have to be extra sedated today.

Becky stood and fell into Emily's embrace and continued to weep for a good five minutes. This was the only time that

Emory had seen Becs so upset. When their mom had died, she was sad and shed a few tears, but watching her fall apart like this hurt Emory, and the rage inside of him was hard to contain. He was used to her being so strong and brave that whatever had happened inside of these walls must have been truly horrible.

"Go cry in the tent, ma'am. None of us want to see that," said the same man who had told her to stop running.

As they made their way to the tent, something made him stop dead in his tracks. Scott was making his way there. The same Scott who had beat him just two days earlier. He was wearing a Department of Homeland Security uniform. How in the hell did he get that? Emory was flabbergasted. It was like this day couldn't stop messing with him. He wondered if they would ever catch a break. They rushed into the tent, and Eugene finally noticed them and came over with his eyes full of tears, and all of them embraced.

"They took my friend," Eugene said between sobs.

"I know, buddy. Becs, what was that about?" Emily asked sweetly, trying to calm her down.

She told them the whole story. While they spoke, Eugene attached himself to Emily's side, hanging on for dear life. Becky told them of the kindness that she had been shown by the family. How Maria had helped her to stay calm and collected. How Eugene had made friends with the couple's child.

Then she told them about what happened leading up to Maria's murder. Emory watched as she regained her composure, speaking slowly and more clearly. The fear left her eyes and was replaced by hate. He could tell that she wanted to hurt these people. Emily told her of the plan in place to get them out under the cover of night. Told her about how they had met Ronnie and Margot, who were waiting for them on the other side. Tried to reassure her that in only a few more hours they would leave this place forever.

"We have to get them out of here with us. We have to--" She was interrupted by Scott walking into the tent.

He was wearing the black uniform and carried an AR15. He had an unsettling smile. His face was still black and blue from their last meeting. He had a wild look in his eyes that made Emory's senses go on alert. He stood there like he was waiting for something to happen, lightly tapping his boot on the ground. Just then, a solitary gunshot was fired.

"That was your partner-in-crime's husband facing the rapture," he said with a chuckle.

Emory stood, walked over and got in Scott's face until their noses were just inches apart. He didn't say a word, just stared into his eyes. For a split second, fear flashed in his former friend's eyes. It was quickly replaced with disdain. Scott pulled out his handgun and put it up to Emily's head, never taking his eyes off Emory.

"Go ahead. Give me a reason. We all know she deserves it from what she did to me. You all do," he said, flicking the safety off the Beretta.

Emory backed off and sat back down. Threatening to hit his sister was one thing, but this was a step over the line. Scott would pay for this, he thought while staring at Emily. Eugene whimpered and clung even tighter to his sister. Becky took Emily's hand. There was no fear in this meeting like last time, just rage.

"What are you doing in that uniform, Scotty?" Emily asked, somehow keeping her head while a gun was pointing at it.

"Dad had some connections, I guess. Came here and we both got uniforms. They looked past the age thing," he said, running his hands through his hair. "Looks pretty good, don't it? I saw your names on the list and decided to pay you all a visit. See, I know something that you don't. They don't like your kind here," he said, pointing to Becky and Emily. "I could tell them now about what abominations you are, but that seems too easy." He re-holstered the pistol.

"I'm gonna make you all suffer. I'm gonna make your life hell while you are here, and when I'm done playing with you, I'm damn sure gonna get you all a date with the firing squad. Then you all can have a family reunion in hell," he said with every ounce of hate that his miserable soul could muster.

"I think you are a scared little boy trying to play tough in his new soldier uniform. Once a bully always a bully, huh, Scotty?" Emily said, not showing an ounce of fear to the man.

He was taken aback by that statement. He had walked into the tent with the intention of striking fear. All he got in return were three faces looking at him with nothing but contempt. Frustrated, he turned and walked out of the tent with two middle fingers up over his shoulders. They all looked at each other in disbelief.

"I don't know how, but I'm going to kill him before we leave this place," Emory said, breaking the silence. His hands balled into fists, and his body shook trying to hold all his anger inside.

CHAPTER 23

Ronnie carefully lined up the sights on the AK. He had the guard by the front gate at center mass. The military had shown back up halfway through the day, setting a camp outside the main gates. He had decided to move the show to the front corner of the camp. Ronnie didn't have that much of a problem with shooting these Department of Homeland Security scum bags after he had watched them execute a man in front of his child earlier, but he wasn't going to shoot at a fellow soldier. He looked at his watch. It was a G-Shock and somehow had survived the event.

Ronnie had made a pit stop at the hardware store, and they had gotten a few rolls of duct tape. Together Margot and Ronnie had covered the lights and reflectors so that they were completely blacked out. Carefully they had moved the car to the rendezvous point, an access road in the woods that lined the back of the old Walmart.

They had left the car at the back of the road to try to keep from it being uncovered. The clock struck midnight. Now or never. Ronnie let out a breath as his finger squeezed the trigger and the report of the rifle broke the stark silence of night.

All was quiet for a moment, but in what seemed like an instant, all hell broke loose. Lights scanned the area and rifles fired in unison. The noise was all too familiar to Ronnie and took him back to his day of fighting insurgents. Except this time, he was the insurgent. He watched as the man fell to the ground, clutching his chest, and Ronnie bolted to his next position.

Earlier in the day, Margot and Ronnie had cut T-shirts from the store and soaked them in kerosene. Then they had shoved them into the gas tanks of abandoned cars using a wire hanger. Ronnie had said at least the giant paperweights of useless cars wore worth something. The T-shirt extended about nine feet out of the car. He figured that would give him at least a little time to flee the area.

He pulled a Bic lighter out of his pocket and set the shirt ablaze. It moved a little quicker than he had hoped, and the massive explosion lit up the night sky. He put himself behind the engine block of an old F150 and waited.

His position was revealed just as he planned. A team of six men sprinted towards the car. They were moving slowly but methodically. Their guns were raised, and they cleared everything they went by. Thank God Ronnie was not up against real soldiers, he thought, or he would have been in trouble by now. When they were about fifteen feet away from the burning car, Ronnie raised his carbine and fired three quick shots. All of them rang true and hit the men in their vests, making them fall to the ground.

Ronnie turned and looked at the gas tank of the F150. The T-shirt fuse was even shorter than the first. It gave him pause for a moment, but he figured it was too late in the game to do anything about it. He lit the shirt and ran, but the concussion of the blast took him off his feet.

The DHS boys saw his position and opened fire. He took a bullet through the front of his shoulder and fired a few bursts back at them. This was not the first time he had been shot, and he was thankful that it was only a shoulder wound. He could work with that. He had to find a way out of this, but his options were quickly running out as a second team came in his direction.

He turned to peek over the hood of the car, and when he looked back, there was a rifle in his face. The man was a Marine in uniform with a neck twice as thick as any normal man's. His stature was short, but his muscles bulged under the digital camo fatigues. He stood there looking at Ronnie, not saying even one command.

"Holy shit. Ronnie, is that you?" the booming voice commanded, the man's face going from all-business to a smile.

"Luke?" He stood up, and the two men lingered there awkwardly for a minute, sizing each other up.

Then Luke stepped up and embraced Ronnie in a giant bear hug. Ronnie grunted in pain. He was so pumped up on adrenaline he had forgotten that his shoulder was on fire. The man let him go and took a step back.

"What in the hell are the chances....?" Luke didn't get to finish that statement. The two men were confronted by four Homeland Security forces. All of them had their rifles up.

"Sir, step away from the prisoner," one of the men demanded.

"He is my prisoner. I will take him to my camp," Luke replied.

"That man is ours. Now step away or we will call your commanding officer over."

"Listen here, fellas. I know that you are real excited to have all these toys and play dress-up and pretend to be soldiers. Normally I would be willing to let that slide. That man in front of you is a Marine, and a damn good one. While you were over here jerking each other around, he was in the sandbox killing terrorists all over Afghanistan. The man is a warrior. He chews glass and eats cigarette butts, and he is coming with me." The look in Luke's eyes dared the man to do something.

"I'm calling your commanding officer over here." The DHS guy obviously was over it and was starting to look a little concerned about the way Luke was talking to him.

"I am the commanding officer, dingus. Also, there are more of us than you." He pointed past the man's shoulder.

Behind them stood six Marines. Ronnie had never been so happy to see his brothers. They stood there with expressionless faces that let the DHS guys know playtime was over. All of them had their rifles slung, but their hands were on the grips, ready to end this. The DHS ringleader threw up his hands in frustration and stormed off like a child throwing a tantrum. The men watched as they retreated back to their camp. When they were out of earshot, most of them laughed. Luke walked toward their camp with the others in tow.

"Hey, Luke, thanks, man. Can't believe I ran into you out here. Guess somebody is looking out for me," Ronnie said, thinking of his sister. "Why are you home? What's going on?" Ronnie placed his hand over the bullet hole in his shoulder, which was bleeding at a pretty rapid pace.

"We have a long time to talk about it. Most of us from overseas were recalled back home. Also, congratulations, you just re-enlisted. Welcome back, Devil Dog. I hope you are ready," Luke said, not looking back.

"For what?"

"War."

At 11:45, Emory peered out of the tent. Nobody was moving. It appeared that everyone was sticking very closely with the curfew, not even daring to leave their tents to use the latrine. Two guards sat next to each other near their tent. One was asleep, and the other looked bored out of his mind, flipping through an old magazine. Emory closed the flap and looked at everyone.

"We only have one shot at this. If we get caught, we are dead," he stated.

"I don't want to die," Eugene said, tears welling in the corners of his eyes.

"We are not going to die, little man. We are going to just slip out the back," Becky reassured him.

"You have to stay close to us and do everything we tell you. We are going to be okay," Emily chimed in.

They sat for what felt like an eternity, time barely moving. The shot broke the night and sent them into action. Emory ran to the flap as the two guards sprung to their feet and ran toward the gate. They waited for the explosion and slipped out the door of their tents and ran as fast as they could toward the back section of fence that wasn't completed yet. Emory kept his hand grasped tightly in Eugene's.

They didn't see a single soul. Not one person had come to see what the fuss was about. Then three quick shots exploded and a volley of gunfire answering back. Then everything went silent. No more explosions. No more gunshots. Emory's heart sank. Something had happened to Ronnie.

No time for him to think about that now. His mission was to get the people he loved out of there. They made it past the missing link of fence and slowed at the tree line. They had made it. Part of Emory couldn't believe it was so easy. They slowed their pace and made their way to the car. Margot stood there with Lola faithfully by her side. They stopped and caught their breath. Seeing her again was the best feeling Emory had had since this whole mess had started.

"Stop right there," a voice yelled from behind them.

Had they been trailed this entire time? Nothing was ever easy. He turned to see Scott and two other men come out of the trees with their weapons raised.

"Somehow I knew that that explosion had to do with you assholes," Scott said as he made his way toward them. That wild look in his eyes was amplified by ten now. The three men slowly closed on them. Scott and his men came within three feet of them and stopped.

"You don't have to do this, Scotty," Emily pleaded, her face red with frustration.

"I know I don't have to. I want to. I will be the hero that caught the first escaped prisoners." His eyes gleamed with pride.

He stood there like a proud little kid who was showing his report card to his mother. It made Emory sick with anger. Lola foamed at the mouth, and Margot was having trouble holding the beast back as she almost pulled Margot's arm out of its socket.

"Put that dog in the car, bitch," Scott snarled as he pointed his gun at the dog.

"Watch your mouth," Emory replied. The response was involuntary. He didn't know why it came out, but he could not stop himself.

"Don't tell me what to do, trash. I'm trying to figure out who we should shoot first. I don't need to bring all of you back, just a couple. Hey, Pete, go put your gun in Dreadlock Girl's mouth." The man to his left walked up and pulled his pistol out.

When he was almost there, Becky put her hand in her jumpsuit. The man, unsure what she was doing, hesitated. That hesitation was enough for Becky to retrieve the boot knife. In one swift motion, she pulled it out and plunged it into the man's neck. The man grasped at the wound as blood sprayed out, staining the grass in front of him. He swaggered from side to side, trying to say something, and fell to the ground in bloody heap. Becky stood there covered in his blood, still holding the knife. She figured she could use it after all.

Everyone was frozen for a second, but Emily was next to react. She grabbed the barrel of the rifle held by the guy on Scott's right and slammed the butt into his face, making him lose his grip and release the weapon. She stepped forward and kicked him in the testicles with everything that she could muster. The man grunted in pain and fell to his knees. Standing, he pulled the knife from his belt and made an effort to come at her.

She punched the inside of his elbow with one hand, and he dropped the knife. Her final blow was a kick to the man's larynx, sending him to the ground aspirating. He rolled around, choking trying to get air until he went still under the light of the moon.

While she was doing this, Scott turned and raised his rifle. Emory tackled him and took him to the ground, the force from the blow knocking the weapon from his hands. Scott had been caught off guard and didn't react fast enough. He didn't even get a chance to raise his hands before Emory straddled him and pummeled Scott's face and head with his fist.

It all came out. The rage of losing his mother. The rage of losing his father. The fact that this former friend of his was willing to kill his family for a promotion. He beat on him until he started to run out of breath and lost feeling in his fist. A gentle hand laid on his shoulder and turned to see Margot with tears in her eyes. He stood, Scott's blood dripping off him, his knuckles bleeding from the ferocity of the impacts.

"He was going to hurt you. He was going to hurt all of us," Emory rationalized looking around at everybody for validation.

"It's okay. He did want to hurt us," Margot whispered.

"I'm sorry," he said.

"Nothing to be sorry about. You were brave." She placed a hand on his shoulder.

He didn't feel brave. He felt sick. Memories of the good times at Scott's house flooded his brain, and he walked away from her and vomited. Scott was a dickhead, but had he deserved what Emory just dished out to him? His thoughts tore at him as he was confused from the entire situation. Looking around at the carnage they had just unleashed made him wonder how much more that they could take. He stood back up and looked at his shirt, covered with blood and vomit.

"I hope you brought me a change of clothes."

Ronnie flinched as the medic dug at his wound, trying his best to clean it. He had been stuck in the medical tent for an hour now. One thing he knew about the medics in the Marine Corps was that they were not gentle, and this one didn't disappoint. Whenever Ronnie grimaced in pain, the man would stop and look at him, annoyed. He needed to work on his bedside manner, Ronnie thought as he bit the inside of his lip, trying his best not to look like a child getting a shot.

At first, he wondered if the kids had gotten away, but after not hearing any more gunshots for a while, he assumed they had. The luck that he knew a Marine here was not lost on him. There was a total of fifteen marines stationed here. From his recon on the base, he assumed there was at least three times that amount of Homeland Security staff. There had been a large National Guard presence, but they had been sent to a new location, luckily, or he knew he would have been toast. He figured that they had moved on to evacuate another town.

They were outnumbered for sure. He had done a rotation in Afghanistan with Luke. He was good man and a damn good Marine. He had saved Ronnie's ass more times than he could count. He was glad that Luke was the one who had his back. Finding someone you could trust was hard. Finding someone you could trust while taking enemy fire was something else entirely. Luke had earned both of those.

For his short stature, he made it up in toughness. They had some good times in those mountains, and some really bad times. When you faced death together, there was a bond that couldn't be explained. Seeing Luke made him think of some of the brothers he had lost, and he hoped that he wouldn't lose any more. He knew he would, though. He was just glad someone was there to go through it with him.

"That's about as good as I'm going to get it here. Didn't help much with you flinching like a damn baby. The bullet is going to have to stay in for now. I can't get it out; I'm no surgeon. You should be fine until we can get back to someplace more suitable," the medic said, standing and stretching his back.

"Thanks, Doc. I'm a big boy. I will deal with it," Ronnie said, imitating a baby by sticking his thumb in his mouth and giving him his best "goo goo gah gah." Having been through worse, he would make it through it.

"Wrap it up tight. We got some shit to talk about," Luke said, entering the tent and taking a seat next to Ronnie.

"Yes, sir," the medic replied, applying a generous amount of tape and slapping the thumb out of Ronnie's mouth.

"I checked on your family, Ronnie. They are gone. Found three DHS up there where you told us to look. Two were dead. One boy beaten to a pulp, but they think that he will make it. No sign of any car or the kids. They must have made it out." Luke set his rifle next to him against the exam table.

"Thank God for that," Ronnie said, letting out an exhausted breath.

"I gotta say, they left quite the mess up there. Did you think they would be capable of that level of violence? It was an ugly scene," Luke said, raising an eyebrow.

"I was not sure, but we both know what people can do when they are backed into a corner and forced to fight. They are in for a tough road. We've both seen the devastation of human bleakness. In this new world, they are going to have to become hardened. My only hope is that they don't become jaded." Ronnie's eyes cast down to the floor, knowing that was a tough obstacle to overcome.

"Like us," Luke replied, knowing exactly what Ronnie was implying.

"Yeah. What the hell is going on, Luke? Who did this to us? What are we going to do back?" Ronnie had so many questions, and he was not entirely sure he wanted the answers.

"Well, I don't even know where to start. The new Republicans have set these fine camps up in the Midwest and parts of the south and the whole eastern seaboard. The party was overcome with extremists, and most of the moderates were either executed or fled. Their story is that this was an inside job perpetrated by the senior leadership of the Democratic Party and was carried out by Iran. The president has the Department of Homeland Security and the big-city police departments that he is using as his own personal army," Luke explained.

"What about the west coast?" Ronnie asked, wondering how the hell this could happen.

"Right before the event, most of the House and Senate Democrats fled across the country to the west coast. Same story. The far left forced their way to the top. We both know that the loudest and most violent people can seize power in times like these. They expelled the Congressmen that didn't agree with them. The latest reports even from an hour ago state that they have rallied the people of the biggest blue states on the western seaboard. They have declared that this was an inside job by the president and the Russians. They also have control of the police departments, and as of an hour ago, they have overtaken most of the military bases in their area. They are arming the public, and now they have an army too," Luke said in an overwhelmed tone.

"Well, what the hell are we doing? There is no way we are picking a side in this battle of corruption, is there?" Ronnie prayed the answer was no.

"No. As of now we are attached to DHS. The joint chiefs are meeting on our next plan of action. The Department of Defense has been moved to Texas, and all branches of the military are based out of there now. A large group of senators have fled to Texas, under the protection of the four branches. We also recovered President Bush's family and the Obama family. The collective group of politicians are helping to formulate a plan to retake the country, working closely with the joint chiefs. Did you ever think a day would come where Presidents Bush and Obama would work together? This shit's crazy as hell. If I had to guess, we are just playing nice right now so we can keep tabs on these assholes while they formulate a plan of action," Luke said.

"I guess we did take the oath to protect against all enemies foreign and domestic," Ronnie said as he laughed at the thought of the former presidents working in unison.

"That is exactly right. The scary thing is that the Navy has to turn away un-peacekeeping troops that were trying to enter the country, mostly made up of Chinese and Russian troops." Luke chuckled.

"That does not look good for the president. Do we know anything about who actually did it?" Ronnie inquired as he tried to rotate his shoulder.

"Military has their best investigators on it now. The bomb was smuggled in on some sort of unmarked freighter. We know the location from tracking it. Whoever fired it was smart enough to scuttle the boat and let it sink to the bottom of the Atlantic," John replied, giving Ronnie a hand up.

"Ron, I have one question for you."

"Shoot."

"How in the hell did I sneak up on you?"

"Civilian life must have made me soft."

"Well, you better toughen up, buttercup. We are about to be in a two-front war."

CHAPTER 24

Kenny woke up to change shifts with Marco after his four-hour post was over. He was groggy and walked around half-asleep, trying to will himself back to being fully awake. He felt like he had only slept for a few minutes. It had been a deep, dark slumber that was devoid of any kind of dream.

He watched as Marco crawled into his bag. The boy passed out as soon as his head hit the ground. Apparently, he could sleep anywhere. Kenny walked over, sat on the ground and retrieved his pack. Opening the front pouch, he pulled out one of the five-hour energy bottles that he had found in the kitchen. He downed it in one go and pulled out some strawberry Pop-tarts to munch on.

The first two hours of his shift went by pretty uneventfully. He lay on his back watching the clouds pass. It was boring. More boring than anything he had ever experienced. The loss of his phone had been more devastating than he had ever thought it could be.

He didn't realize how heavily he had relied on the pocket-sized entertainment source. Every minute of every day he'd had something to do just with the click of his finger. From music to YouTube, he seldom had time to sit in the absence of noise.

The silence was deafening. His mind and ears were not ready to adapt to taking in so much ambient noise. As he lay there, mourning the loss of his phone, movement in the bushes behind them set off alarms in his head.

He sat up, listening as the noise grew louder. He gripped

the machete and inched his way to a sleeping Marco. He crept on all fours, trying to stay as low as he could. When he was within ten feet of Marco, a large German Shepard came out of the bushes.

The dog sized up Kenny. Kenny had always hated dogs. He had been bit by a dog as a child, and now he didn't trust them. The dog looked well taken care of. Its coat was full and shiny. It had a collar hanging around its neck. The dog took two steps toward him, lowered its ears and let out a low growl.

Kenny didn't know what to do. He was woefully underprepared, gripping the machete in his hands. They sat there in a stalemate, both looking at each other. Kenny wondered if the dog's owner was nearby. This filled him with concern. He looked down in his hands and was holding a bag of beef jerky that he had pulled out of his pack.

Curious, he took a piece out and threw it at the dog. The dog bent over, smelled the jerky and swallowed it down with two chews. It was hungry. The dog's owners must have been taken away, he figured. They sat there for a long while, with Kenny throwing jerky at the dog. Eventually he ran out, and the dog cocked its head to the side, wondering where the rest of its food had gone.

"All out, boy," Kenny said, tossing the bag to the dog.

The dog smelled the bag and looked back at Kenny. Satisfied that there was nothing left for him, the dog wandered off, leaving Kenny shaken. He looked at the still-snoozing Marco in disbelief. He couldn't believe that he had slept through the whole encounter. Kenny wondered if Marco would even believe him when Kenny told him the story.

Kenny walked back over to his pack and lay down, using it as a pillow. As he gazed into the sky, he wondered what would become of all the household pets that were roaming around with nobody to look after them. He figured that the cats could probably survive on their own.

He wondered how many hungry families would enjoy a meal of cat when everything else was gone. The thought made him feel ill. Then he had an even worse thought. All the loose dogs would be roaming the cities and countryside. A shiver went up his spine as he thought of packs of Chihuahuas and pit bulls roaming the streets.

Emily drove for three hours before she would even consider stopping. Her face was determined as she white-knuckled the wheel, trying to drive as quickly as she could. Everyone was tired, and eventually they crossed the border into Kentucky, going over the Ohio river.

Emory wondered if they would fare any better here than Ohio. Probably not, he thought, struggling to stay optimistic. Everyone looked glum in that way. Nobody talked, and Eugene was fast asleep in Becky's lap in the front seat. Margot had fallen asleep with her head on Emory's shoulder.

After turning down some back country roads, Emily eventually found what seemed to be an abandoned farm house that was secluded and pretty far off the road. After a close inspection, they couldn't find any signs of habitation. Emily volunteered for the first shift of guard duty, telling the others to go get some sleep.

"I will be in that tree line about fifty yards away," she told Becky.

"What? Why so far away?" Becky said shakily, still nervous from her time in the camp.

"If somebody gets that close to me at the house, it's too late. Out here, I can draw fire away from the house and keep them busy so you guys can ambush them," she said as she pulled the fresh clothes from her bag. They had all been too paranoid to stop to change out of their jumpsuits.

"Whatever, babe. Me and Eugene are going to get some sleep," Becky said, grabbing the boy by the hand and leading him into the house.

"Goodnight, Emily," Eugene said.

"Goodnight, buddy. Sleep tight," she said as she picked her bag up and trudged off to the woods.

This left Margot and Emory standing alone by the car. Emory, still covered in Scott's blood, looked at Margot, who was pulling her bag out of the car. When he had lost his composure and was beating Scott, she had been the one to stop him. In one of the darkest moments of his life, she was the light. When he had first met her, he had had a bit of a crush, but now it felt like more. It was hard for him to explain but it just was better when she was around. She stood and walked over to him.

"I saw a creek over there; you should probably go wash up. You look like hell. Your new clothes are in your bag. I'm going to go inside." She pointed over his shoulder with a smile.

"Thanks." He grabbed his bag and walked toward the creek.

It was small creek, but the water rose to his waist. He pulled the small bar of soap out of his toiletry bag and started to undress. At first, he looked around to make sure nobody was going to see him nude, but after a while he didn't care. He was too tired to care. The water was cold and made him shiver, but it felt good against his body. He scrubbed and scrubbed until most of the gore washed down stream. He lay down, dunked his head under the water and floated around for a minute, looking at the clouds in the sky peeking at him through the trees that surrounded him. If Heaven was real, he hoped that his mom was looking after his dad, making sure that he was safe.

He stood and walked over to his bag, realizing that he didn't have a towel. He folded over the jumpsuit until he found a section that was clean and dried his body with it. He reached in and pulled out his clothes. He put on the pants and belt and sat down to put on his socks and boots. Standing, he pulled out the tee-shirt. He stood there confused, taking the shirt in. It was brown and covered in kittens. Not just one kitten, but like, the faces of thirty kittens. He shook his head. At least she has a sense of humor.

Walking back to the house, he looked around at the landscape. It was beautiful and full of rolling hills. He assumed that it was about four in the afternoon, and he really couldn't remember the last time he had been this tired. He was thankful that they had gotten Becky and Eugene back from that awful place.

He was worried about what had happened to Ronnie. He had wanted to go back and look for him. He had insisted on it. Margot had told him about what Ronnie had said to her. After a few moments of pleading, he gave in, and they took off.

He walked onto the porch and sat in a rocking chair, propping his feet up on the small table in front of him.

"Long bath," Margot said, stepping out of the house carrying a candle and sitting in the chair next to him. He figured it was to keep the mosquitos away.

"Had a lot of grime to wash away." She had brought a first-aid kit.

"Let me see those hands."

"They will be okay," he said hesitantly.

"Let me see them," she insisted, pulling his hands over to her. They were raw and bleeding from the fight. She pulled out some antiseptic wipes and started to clean them.

"We don't want this to become infected," she said as she worked. She cleaned them and wrapped them in gauze and sports tape.

"How did you know that boy?"

"We were friends once, in a different life."

"He didn't seem too friendly."

"He changed. Still, I hope I didn't kill him. I mean, I just lost it. What am I becoming?" he said, sadness overcoming him as he hung his head.

"You did what you had to for your family. For me."

"You don't know the darkness that is inside of me. Sometimes I lose myself in it."

"From this short time we have been together, for some reason I feel like I have known you forever. If you ever lose yourself in it, I will be here to pull you back."

"Yeah, I know what you mean. And thanks, that means a lot to me. Just hope I don't fall in too deep," he said, meeting her gaze.

"You are a good man, Emory," she said, leaning in close to him.

Emory's first kiss was under the covered porch of that farmhouse on that fateful afternoon. The coldness inside of him was chased off by her embrace. He knew now what his dad had spoken of, about love at first sight. He didn't know why, but it felt right. She gently pulled away and stood, taking his hand in hers.

"You know, the one good thing to come out of this mess was that we found each other," she said.

"Yeah," was all he could say with her leading him toward the bedroom.

"Come on, let's go to bed. We will feel better after some sleep," she said, taking him to the bed.

They lay down, and she rolled over to stare into his eyes. They just lay like that. Neither spoke. Lola lay on the floor next to the bed and passed out the minute her head hit the pillow. Wrapped in each other's arms, they found the safety that they craved in each other. Both felt like a missing piece of themselves had been found. Fate worked in a funny way, Emory thought as he brushed Margot's hair from her face. He had finally found love. The irony was they could be dead tomorrow. Trying to shake that last thought from his head, he tried to think of something he could say to lighten the mood.

"It was the kitten shirt that made you fall for me, right?" he said, joking.

"No. It was that big heart of yours. You may not know it there, but I can see it. The way to care for your little brother and your sister," she said, snuggling close to him, their lips touching again. "The shirt helps though."

Ronnie adjusted the plate carrier as he walked out of the supply tent. No comfortable way to align it with his wounded shoulder. He had worn body armor and fatigues most of his adult life, but it felt strange being back in the Marine uniform. It had only been a few years, but it felt almost foreign to him now. Ronnie had forgotten how heavy it all was as it strained on his back.

He had traded in his AK for an M4. Having the rifle back in his hand again felt right. It had been a part of him for the better part of his life, following through all his deployments around the globe. For lack of sounding cliché, it made him feel whole. As he pondered how ridiculous that made him sound in his head, Luke came into the room. The look on his face told of how bad the coming conversation was about to be.

"First off, it's good to see you back in that uniform. Second, we got orders, Ronnie. It's not good. I hope you are ready to get back in the field," Luke said, flipping through a stack of papers on a clipboard and tossing it to the table beside them.

"How bad can it be? Last time I saw that look on your face,

it was 120 degrees and there was sand everywhere. I shook sand out of everything I owned for two months after I got stateside," Ronnie stated, trying to lighten the mood.

"It's bad, man. California is now calling itself the Socialist States of America. They are pushing east hard, swallowing up everything in their path. It appears they had an insurgent group lying dormant in Chicago for who knows how long. A day ago, a man only known as Mateo attacked a church that was housing refugees in Bucktown. They moved through it, killing everyone they could find. I mean, nobody was spared, not women or children. When they were done, they soaked everything in kerosene and lit the place on fire. They did all of this in Department of Homeland Security uniforms. We are guessing that they are here to destabilize the Midwest." Luke's eyes stared off in the distance as he spoke with that hollow look Ronnie knew all too well.

"Jesus," was all Ronnie could get out.

"I know. I haven't seen this level of depraved, morose evil since Afghanistan, and it here in our backyard. They are calling him the Butcher of Bucktown. Intelligence says that he is moving in this direction. Our orders are to find him and terminate him and his group. They think that he is somewhere in Kentucky at this point. Personally, I hope I am the man who puts the bullet in that sick son of a bitch's skull." Luke's face snarled as he spoke.

"When do we move out?"

"In an hour. Put on your game face. This shit is about to get ugly." Luke walked out of the tent.

Ronnie had seen some bad shit in his military career. Evil stuff. It took a lot to get Luke worked up like that. Whoever this Mateo was, he sent a shiver up Ronnie's spine. He also knew one other thing about men like Mateo: They needed killing.

CHAPTER 25

Mateo rode in the back seat of the Humvee they had pillaged from a DHS unit in Chicago. He had the backseat to himself and took the opportunity to stretch out and try to get some rest. The two men in the front seat made their way down the road quietly. He didn't allow his men to speak to him. He found that their drivel made him annoyed quickly.

He had met most of the men while being an underground agent in Chicago. He selected the most ruthless and depraved people he could find to keep by his side. He had wondered when the time for violence had come if they would be able to complete the task that they had been assigned to perform.

After the church in Chicago, he was riding in the presence of killers. The men had set out with the simple wave of his hand. These were hard. None of them even flinched at taking the lives of the women and children. Most of their faces bore depraved pleasure while carrying out the task. He had chosen wisely.

Mateo had never been one to stray away from violence or death. He didn't really ponder on the things that he had done. He did enjoy the power of holding someone's life in his hand. He would be lying to himself if he didn't say that he got a sense of sick satisfaction from watching people suffer and die. He liked to watch their final seconds. The look in their eyes was fascinating to him.

The men all shared a common tattoo that he had insisted on. An AK47 held by a clenched fist. He didn't have the same marking. He wanted them to feel like he had ownership over them. He wanted them to know he was the boss. They were to heel to him like a pack of obedient dogs.

He pulled a pack of Marlboros out and slid one into his fingers. Lighting it, he leaned his head back against the seat. His orders were simple. Drive through the small towns without DHS presence. Kill and rape his way through them. The plan was that the people left in these areas would spread the word that the DHS were murderous thugs that couldn't be trusted. It was a job that Mateo had been perfect for.

Margot woke before Emory and watched as his chest rose and fell as he slept. They had been so tired that they had passed out in each other's arms and lay that way for hours. She barely knew him, yet somehow, she felt like she had known him for years. She had watched him beat a man nearly to death, but she didn't fear him. She saw the darkness that brewed behind his troubled blue eyes, but she trusted him. He had been so gentle as they lay there in bed together. She had never met another boy like this. He was complex, but sweet and gentle. She gently leaned in and kissed him on the forehead.

"Time to get up, handsome," she whispered in his ear.

"Ugh, how long did we sleep?" Emory asked, wiping the sleep out of his eyes.

"Best guess is it's noon. Come on, let's go find something to eat." She took his hand, and they walked to the kitchen.

Emily and Eugene sat at the table with re-heated dehydrated meals. Neither looked too thrilled about it. Emory went to his bag and thumbed around. He found two power bars and pulled them out. He handed one to Margot, and they sat down at the table.

"Where is Becky?" Margot asked.

"On sentry duty. I'm going to go get some sleep before we

leave again," she said as she scooped a spoonful of eggs in her mouth.

"This is not very good," whined Eugene as he pushed chili mac around in his pouch with his fork.

"It's okay if you don't want it right now, buddy. Why don't you go lay down? I will be in there in a few minutes. I want to talk to these two for a minute first," Emily replied.

"Okay, Em, I will go lay down," Eugene said, handing his bag to Emory, who picked up the fork and started eating what Eugene had refused.

"Night, bud. Thanks for the food," Emory said, chewing up the noodles, and Eugene left the room.

"He didn't sleep well last night. He kept waking up crying. I'm afraid about how this is going to affect him," Emily said as she took a drink out of her mug. "Also, I'm not trying to pry, but I saw you two making out yesterday on the porch by candlelight while I was on sentry duty."

Margot looked down, and Emory's face went flush. How could they not have realized that Emily was out in the woods watching the house? Emory thought to himself. It was foolish. At least Emily got to see his first kiss. Which was a weird thing for her to see.

"I'm not saying it's a bad thing. I also just noticed that both of you came out of the same room. I'm assuming you slept together," Emily said, raising an eyebrow accusingly.

"We didn't have sex," Margot replied defensively.

"It's not any of my business what you do behind closed doors. You just need to be careful if Margot gets pregnant. We don't know how long this lawless land is going to last. Do you want to raise a baby in this? That is one challenge I wouldn't want to face. It's hard enough looking after Eugene in this nightmare world," Emily said as the two gave her blank looks. "Nice shirt, by the way. Maybe that is your form of birth control.

I can't imagine that something like that can be found sexy." Emily cracked a smile.

"No," they both said in unison.

"Well, think about it. I'm going to get some sleep for a few, and then we can get a move on it. Should be able to make it there tomorrow." She stood and walked to the bedroom.

"Well, that was awkward," Emory stated, letting out a breath and looking down, hoping that Margot had gotten him another shirt.

CHAPTER 26

Kenny told Marco about the dog when he woke up. Marco's reaction was not what he had expected. The boy laughed for a good long while until he was holding his side. Marco, having been raised on a farm, thought the fact that Kenny had been so afraid of a dog was a pretty funny thing.

They sat around, talking and shooting the shit, waiting for the darkness of night to come over them. Eventually, when night had overtaken the day, they set out. They moved swiftly. Slower than the previous night, with Kenny's banged-up foot, but still at a pretty good pace.

The countryside seemed empty. Mostly all they saw were cows and corn fields. The lack of people this far out was comforting. Surrounded by the sounds of nature, it was peaceful and tranquil. They stuck to the side of the road. Lucky for them, most of the cornfields hadn't been processed yet. The corn was tall, giving them a quick escape route.

They only had to flee into the field once that night. Seeing the headlights of a vehicle in the distance, they took refuge in the corn. Squatting next to each other, they watched as the truck pulled up onto the road and stopped close to where they had hidden.

Two men stepped out and shined flashlights into the corn, looking for them. Both men looked the part of typical country folks. Big boots, jeans and tee shirts. One of the men sported a cowboy hat and a thick curly mustache. They stood there for about ten minutes, until the man with the hat spoke.

"We saw you boys hightail it into the corn. You can come

out; we are not going to hurt you," the man said as he stood with his hand on a big revolver he wore on his belt.

The boys looked at each other without exchanging any words. They didn't need to. Both of the men were armed. Both sported pistols on their belts, and the one without the cowboy hat carried an old lever-action cowboy gun. The boys sat in silence as the man waited for a response.

"It's okay that you fellas don't feel safe coming out. I get it, I really do. We are here to help. Me and my son here are gonna leave. We are heading the opposite direction of the way you were walking. You have my word I'm not gonna try to follow you. I hope you boys get where you are going safely," he said as he walked to the back of the truck, pulling out two old Kroger bags and setting them on the side of the road.

"These bags have some supplies in them. It ain't much, but we are trying to help the people we can. Some cans of food and bottles of water and such. We don't want nothing in return. It's just the right thing to do. We are going to be leaving now. I hope that you boys get where you are going."

With that, the two men got back in the beat-up old pickup truck and sped off down the road. Kenny and Marco waited for about twenty minutes before getting up and walking out of the field. They walked over to the bags and opened them up.

It was just like the man had said. Some cans of beans and bottles of water. The boys were a bit taken aback by the act of kindness. Kenny had known that there were still good people out there after Marco saved his life. It was still refreshing to see this.

"Awful nice of them," Marco said, opening his pack and putting one of the bags inside.

"People are good, for the most part," Kenny said, doing the same.

"I guess," Marco said doubtfully.

"My dad used to say that. He would say that it was hard to see in a world focused on the bad. With the news blasting us with everything wrong all the time, it is easy to lose faith."

"Your dad seems like a pretty good guy."

"Yeah, the best. He dedicated his life to helping people. I mean, he really cared. He was a good doctor and an even better man. He used to tell me that good was all around us, all the time. You just had to look for it."

"You worried about what's going to happen to him?"

"I mean, I would be crazy not to worry right? Luckily, he has a skill set that is going to be very in-demand now. If things don't get better, having a doctor around is going to be as important as food and water."

"Never thought of that."

"I'm sure he will find his way into something. Even in all this mess, I know that he is going to be out there helping as many people as he can find."

Becky sat with her back against a giant oak tree. The sun had finally come out and it felt good shining down upon her. She twirled the gold ring in her fingers. She had found it in the house while Emily had sat watch. She had been thinking about it for some time. She was going to ask Emily to marry her. She knew they were young, but the last 48 hours had proved her level of love for Emily. It was time, she thought. She slid the ring on her finger as a glare caught her eye.

Looking up, two black Humvees were racing down the rural stretch of road. They were heading straight toward the farm. The Hummers had no markings on them, and she couldn't pinpoint a source of origin. In a panic, she sat up and grabbed her rifle. Flipping off the safety, she held it up in the air and fired one shot, sending the Humvees skidding to a stop.

In horror, she watched as Department of Homeland Security soldiers piled out and set up a defensive perimeter. She counted eight men in total as she ran down the incline to the house. They were so close to her family that she was in a panic, wondering if they could get away.

As she ran, a man wearing a black beret stepped out of the Hummer in the back. He was tall and wearing a pair of black aviator glasses. He had a muscular build and was quite intimidating to look at. He walked around while his men were moving in chaos and appeared to just be enjoying his little stroll. While his men scanned for the threat, he casually pulled out a cigarette and lit it without a care in the world. That's when they spotted her and the volley of bullets started flying.

Emily sat straight up in the bed. Stunned in half-sleep, wondering if the shot had been a dream or real. Foggy from the lack of sleep, she had forgotten where they were. Emory burst in through the door with Margot in tow. Reality was sobering.

"It's DHS, and there looks like ten of them," Emory reported, breathing heavily from his pumping adrenaline.

"Okay, grab the bags and the guns. We are going to have to make a break for it," Emily said, sitting on the edge of the bed and putting on her vest.

"We can't leave the car," Emory pleaded.

"We have to, now let's--" Emily's words interrupted by the hellfire outside.

Without another word, they ran to the back door, Emory with Eugene in his arms. The tree line to the woods was about a seventy-five-yard dash, with a barn three quarters of the way there. There was not anywhere to take cover between them and that barn. They were just going to hope that the element of surprise from bursting out the back door would catch them off guard.

Emily turned and handed Emory a Glock 19, which he shoved into the holster on the vest. Apparently, he had just graduated to being allowed to have a gun. They ran for the barn, gunfire bursting and impacts to the ground all around them. Their lack of surprise was not that surprising, Emory thought as bullets whistled past him. Having reached the barn in a cascade of dirt from the near misses, Emory couldn't believe that nobody had been hit. Then turning his head there was Becky. Becky had made it to their rendezvous point at the barn, and she sat on the ground with her back against the wall. Her shirt was soaked in blood.

"Oh my God," Emily said, running over and leaning next to her with tears in her eyes.

"It's okay, just took one in the shoulder," Becky said shakily.

"I, uhh, um," was all that Emily managed to get out, her emotions overflowing and choking her words.

"Babe, I said I'm okay, dammit. We have to get out of here. We can fix it when we put in some distance." Becky grabbed Emily's head and looked her in the eyes, both hands leaving blood smeared across Emily's face.

Two men came around the side of the barn with rifles raised. Emory put Eugene down and stepped in front of him. The men slowly advanced on them with their rifles pointed at the group.

Something didn't look right about these two. There was something off about them. They were not clean-shaven like the men at the camp; their uniforms were a mess and their shirts were untucked.

Most telling were the tattoos. Each of them had one on the side of their neck. It was a fist holding a machine gun, and it looked like it was homemade. The men inched closer without muttering a single word. The looks on their faces sent a chill up Emory's spine. They both had giant grins, but their eyes seemed hollow and dim, like there was nothing on the inside. He knew that they were going to do terrible things by the way they were looking at the girls. He was tired of guns being pointed at him, and he wondered how many times this could happen. Maybe they needed to be more careful.

When they were about three feet away, it happened. It was a blur. Violence was usually fast and ugly like that, Emory was learning. Lola bolted from behind Margot and sank her teeth into the man on the left's leg.

The smiles turned to pure unadulterated hate, and the other man turned and fired a shot. While his attention was off them, Emory pulled his father's tomahawk from his belt and sank it into the man's head as hard as he could. The man stood there for a second, locking eyes with Emory until he crumpled to the ground. Emory turned to the other man and pulled his knife from its sheath, but he was too late. The massive dog had him on his back and was at his throat, ripping flesh as the man thrashed.

"Lola, come," Margot demanded.

The dog released the man and started to come back, but she was whining and only made it halfway before collapsing. That's when the bullet hole in her side came into view. Emily had Becky on her feet, and they motioned for the trees. Emory pulled the hawk out of the man's head and put it back in its belt sheath. Margot was sobbing by this point at her fallen protector. The dog lifted its head and gave her a look that said to run away. Scooping Eugene up and throwing him over his shoulder, Emory grabbed Margot's hand, shaking her from her trance as they disappeared into the woods.

CHAPTER 27

Mateo casually strolled to the back of the barn while the rest of his escort followed on his heels. As much time as he had spent in prison, he had learned to be patient. What a journey he had been on. He had gone from being a crystal meth addict to a home invader to a prisoner and then tapped to be a government operative. Unofficially, of course. He didn't really give a crap about the propaganda that had been spewed at him from his handlers, but freedom and the chance to engage in uninterrupted violence had piqued his interest.

At first it had been attacking people at right wing rallies and hurting people who they deemed needed a hurting. Things had changed since the event. He was a rabid pit-bull, and they had taken his collar off and told him to maul the world. Something that he was obliged to do. Walking around the corner of the barn, he smiled as he saw the gore and carnage that had been left to him like a gory Christmas present. He leaned down and inspected the bodies of the two men. He didn't really care about losing them. Hell, he barely remembered their names, but unfortunately, he would have to put on a show for the other men's sake.

"You try to liberate people from an oppressive totalitarian state, and this is the thanks you get. Fret not, brothers. These people will be found and punished for their crimes against us. Power comes out the barrel of a gun, and eventually these dissidents will all come to know our wrath. We will find them and make an example of what happens to radicals in this new world order." Content with his speech, he walked over to the snarling dog.

Every ounce of the dying dog's energy was put into its glare at Mateo. He felt that he could relate to the beast. Even while its strength wavered, it wouldn't give up the fight until the bitter end. He would show the beast mercy, he thought, and Mateo pulled his pistol from the holster on his belt and pointed it at the dog's head.

A single shot made him stop as the man next him was lifted off his feet with a massive impact. The sound was deafening, and he knew that the weapon was a high-powered sniper rifle of some sort.

The men looked around for the source but couldn't find it, and he knew they wouldn't. Mateo put his gun on the ground and lifted his arms in the air. He knew when was a time to fight and when wasn't.

A squad of Marines came around the barn with their rifles up, screaming demands. The last thing that Mateo remembered seeing was a man walk around the corner, pick up the dog and carry it off before a bag was shoved over his face and zip-tie cuffs were strapped around his wrist. A voice was muffled through the bag.

"Next time you steal a government vehicle, you should pull out the GPS transmitter, genius."

They ran as fast as they could with Becky's injury. They were moving slowly, and Emory kept looking over his shoulder, expecting to see the soldiers. He couldn't believe that they had made it away.

After an hour of off-and-on sprints, Emily decided that they could squat down for a rest. She picked a clearing in the trees that was surrounded by thick brush and was well-concealed.

Emily pulled out the small tarp from her bag, and Becky

lay down. Emily pulled out the medical kit that her father had made her. She gently laid the contents on the tarp near Becky. She packed the wound with gauze and taped up the shoulder the best that she could. Becky tried to stay quiet but couldn't muffle the screams of pain.

"Here, drink this," Emily said, holding a water bottle to Becky's lips.

Becky took a long sip and lay her head back to rest. Margot held Emory's hand. The tears had stopped falling, but the sorrow on her face spoke volumes. She buried her head in Emory's chest. Poor Eugene sat half in shock on Emory's other side. Would this be the world that his baby brother grew up in? Would he have to see things like his brother cracking open a man's skull on a regular basis?

The look in the man's eyes would be something that haunted Emory until the day he died. The shock the man showed. The fear. It ate away at Emory's conscience. Emory rationalized that the men had it coming, but it didn't make him feel any better. He figured that it was probably a good thing he cared. If not, he was crossing a line he knew that he couldn't come back from. He was thankful that at least he had what was left of his family, more or less in one piece.

Hearing the hammer of a gun pull back, he hung his head. How much more shit could they be subjected to in one day?

"Freeze right there," an older woman said, stepping into their little clearing with a side-by-side shotgun raised.

The woman was tiny and looked like she could blow away in the wind. It was almost comical, in some messed-up way. She was wearing a sundress with a kitchen apron over it. She looked like a long-lost sister to Granny in the Beverly Hillbillies. As out of place as she looked, Emory could tell from her facial expression that she was all business. Another woman, maybe in her early thirties, stepped out from the other side of the clearing, holding a lever-action rifle of some kind. She looked like a younger version of what Emory assumed was her mother. She wore a faded flannel shirt and jeans and was a taller woman. She shared the same exact sentiment on her face as the other woman.

"Y'all put them guns on the ground and stand up real slow like. I may be old, but my trigger finger is real fast ." None of them doubted her as she swayed, holding the scatter gun at them.

"My girlfriend is hurt real bad. Please help us. We are good people," Emily said, tears streaming down her face. The old woman had a flicker of tenderness in her eyes, but her ferocity fired right back up.

"What are you doing in my woods on my farm?" she said.

"Some men tried to hurt us. They killed my dog," Margot said.

"Homeland Security people?" the other woman said.

"Yes," Emory replied.

"Had some trouble with them ourselves. They are fertilizing the garden right now. Come on now, get your gear and follow us. I'm a veterinarian, but I will try my best to patch up your friend," the younger of the two said with compassion as she lowered the rifle.

They picked up their gear and followed the women back to the break in the woods, revealing the women's house. The brush was so thick that they were nearly on top of it and couldn't see it. Emory figured that Becky's screams of pain had alerted the pair.

It was a big old farmhouse with two smoking chimneys adorning the top. The house was two stories and sported a wrap-around porch that were popular in the south. Behind the house sat Tanner Veterinary. It was a steel building that looked like it had been converted from an old barn of some type. The yard was well cared for, and there were flowers growing everywhere. Assorted livestock were making noises, but they could see the animals.

They followed the women to the building, and the women unlocked the door and motioned for them to enter. Emory, Margot and Eugene sat down in the waiting room as Emily and the women carried Becky into the back.

She didn't look good. And blood was everywhere by this point. As they disappeared into the back, Emory looked around at the room around him. There were all sorts of posters with ads for cats and dogs. Eugene got up and went over and started playing with a plastic skeleton of a cat that was on display at the counter. Margot leaned back in her chair, looking at all the dog toys that were on display by the front window. The fact that her best friend just got shot and now she was forced to be reminded of it... Emory knew it had to be painful for her. Sitting back and closing his eyes, he hoped that soon they could put all of this behind them.

Emily and the younger woman carried Becky to the table with both of their arms around her. Becky was sweating profusely and starting to tremble. They carefully laid her on the steel exam table. The doctor went over to a large supply closet in the corner of the room and retrieved a tray that was full of exam tools. Next, she grabbed some rubbing alcohol and many rolls of gauze. Coming back to the table, she set them all out in order and opened the gauze. From the routine, Emily could tell that the woman was meticulous and thorough in how she did things.

"I'm Jennifer, and that's my momma Debbie. We are going to try our best to patch you up; seems like you went and sprung a leak," she said as she gently cut Becky's shirt away and looked at the wound.

It was bleeding, but it wasn't spraying as she gently pulled out the gauze that Emily had packed in. The hole on the front of her arm where the bullet had impacted was tiny. Gently she rolled Becky over, revealing a slightly bigger wound where the round had exited. She poured water over the wound to get a better look. She blotted away at the blood with a sponge and put on glasses, taking a closer look.

"Good news is it didn't hit an artery, and I don't think it struck any bone. You are very lucky, though I know it doesn't feel like it. Bad news is it tore you up pretty good. Good news is that it went straight through, so we don't have to yank any bullet out. I'm going to get you on an IV to replace some fluids and pump you full of antibiotics. Luckily, animals and people can take some of the same things, so we are pretty well stocked up," Jennifer explained as she carefully worked around the wound.

"Thank you so much. I don't know how we can ever repay you. If you hadn't found us, I don't know how much longer we could have carried on like that," Emily said, tears welling in her eyes.

"There are still some good people in this world, sweetheart, and y'all seem like some fine young people. It looks like you have been through a lot, but you have to remember to have faith. Not everyone is out to get you," Debby replied, placing a hand on Emily's shoulder.

"Still, I don't know what I would do if I lost her," Emily said, taking Becky's hand.

"Hold on to that love there, sweetie. I lost my husband in a car wreck two years ago. He was a good man, and I miss him every day. When I lost Paul, it about destroyed me, but the good times and love we shared helped me to get through it. Love is the most powerful force on this planet, and with it you can get through just about anything," Jennifer said, looking at Emily and forcing a smile.

"How about I take the rest of the bunch inside and get

them fed? Dinner was a-stewing when we found you, and we cooked up a whole bunch 'cause the freezer was thawing out," Debbie stated as she gave Emily a wink and a smile.

"That's very nice of you. Thank you," Emily replied, growing to love the old woman's spunkiness in the short time that they had known each other.

"We all gotta look out for each other now, child. I fear evil is coming in a capacity that we have never seen before. It's love that will be the beacon of light that gets us through the coming darkness. May God have mercy on our souls," she said as she slowly left the room.

CHAPTER 28

Ronnie picked Lola up from the backseat of the Hummer. The dog was limp, a hundred and twenty pounds of dead weight, but she was still breathing regularly. She half opened her eyes and looked at him for a few seconds before closing them again. It had taken way too long to pack the beast's gunshot wound. To Ronnie's surprise, the dog didn't put up a fight when he was tending to her. He felt crazy for thinking it, but Lola had given him a look like she knew he was trying to help her. Dogs must be more tuned in to the people around them than Ronnie had previously thought.

Everyone else on the scene had thought he was crazy, but he would be dammed if he let this brave animal, who had taken a bullet for his family, die. A bond with the beast was forming. They were both warriors ready to tear the throats out of anybody who wanted to do evil to someone they loved. He respected her.

He thought of the bloodstains on the back of the barn and prayed that his family was okay. He couldn't help the sinking feeling in his gut, and part of him knew that there was a pretty slim chance that they would all survive this. He didn't know whose blood was stained on the back of that barn, and it was tormenting his mind. He had to find them and made a vow that he would or die trying.

He entered the medical tent and set the dog down on the exam table gently. Lola hadn't growled or snarled at Ronnie once since he had set out to rescue her, even as he packed her wounds and tried to control the bleeding. The dog he had seen rip out a man's throat laid its head upon the table and gave him a look that made him think she was thanking him for his efforts in her own animal way. The medic walked into the tent and made an abrupt stop.

"They said you were looking for...You have to be shitting me, right?" His eyes cast down to the dog panting in front of him.

"She needs help. You are going to help her."

"It's a damn dog."

"Yeah."

"I ain't no vet."

"You are today."

"I ain't wasting supplies on a dog."

"Let me tell you something. That dog right there is a warrior. Hell, I like her more than ninety percent of the people I have met in my life, including you. You are going to fix her. If you don't, I'm gonna be real sad. I'm gonna take that sad out on you. Understand?" he said firmly while staring into the man's eyes. The man stood there and looked at the dog, then back at Ronnie. Ronnie's scowl helped to emphasize the point.

"I will try my best. I'm not making any promises, though."

"Good. Now, I have some business I need to attend to," Ronnie said as he exited the tent, his patience being pushed to the limits.

Ronnie made a beeline for the old post office down the road where they were keeping the prisoners. They had apprehended six men. They left the bodies of the dead scumbags where they sat, figuring nature would take its course. He would be damned if he dug a grave for men who had done so much wickedness. One of these men had hurt somebody he loved, but they were all going to pay dearly.

It was going to take every part of him to keep from killing

all of them. Some people were trash, and they just needed to be taken out. He had no problems when it came to being the garbage man with men like this. He walked up and nodded to the two Marines guarding the door as he entered. Making his way to the back, most of the men were zip-tied to folding chairs in the middle of the mail sorting room, with four Marines standing guard over them. The men still had bags on their heads, and they fidgeted at the sound of his boots passing them. He spotted Luke in the distance and made his way past them toward his old friend.

"Is he in there?" Ronnie inquired.

"Yep. Got two guards on either side of him. He ain't going nowhere," Luke explained.

"Look, after we get what we need from him, one of us needs to put a bullet in his skull."

"No can do, old buddy. Texas wants him alive."

"That's bullshit."

"That's the orders."

"Fine, but I bet you a million dollars he ain't going to forget me," Ronnie snarled with a look that Luke knew all too well.

"You ain't got a million dollars.,." Luke said as they walked in.

The man sat zip-tied to a steel chair, and he didn't seem to have a care in the world. He whistled and tapped his foot on the ground. He had no fear about what was about to happen to him. In fact, he wore a big shit-eating grin across his face.

"One of you boys got a smoke I can bum? I'm real stressed out here," Mateo said coyly as he looked from man to man.

"We have some questions.,." said Luke.

"Well, I bet I got some answers."

"What's your real name?" Luke said calmly.

"My name is Death, and I am coming for you all," Mateo said with a wink and smile.

"Who do you work for?" Luke replied.

"I am a slave of no man," Mateo replied, full of pride that repulsed Ronnie.

"Look, man. I really don't care about you answering these questions. They can beat them out of you in Texas, but my buddy here is going to ask you some things. He isn't as nice as me, and you will tell him what he wants to know. They said I have to take you to headquarters. They didn't say in one piece," Luke said, not losing his composure.

"Oh my goodness, that sounds scary. Let's get into it, tough guy. I'm shook." Mateo laughed, turning his attention to Ronnie.

Ronnie took his rifle off and handed it to Luke, who slung it over his shoulder. They had done this song and dance a thousand times before. He had rarely seen the man so emotional and on edge. Ronnie took off his vest, set it in the corner and put his pistol next to it. Standing, he stretched his back out and cracked his knuckles as he walked over and glared at Mateo.

"You know, I have been doing this for a real long time. I have had my fair share of terrorists in front of me. That's what you are, you know? Different flavor, but made from the same batch of shit," Ronnie said coldly, not lifting his glare.

"One man's terrorist is another man's freedom fighter," Mateo said, losing the smile and replacing it with disdain.

"What you did in Chicago qualifies you as a terrorist. I'm not gonna lie, letting you live to get information out of you is more than you deserve. I am one thousand percent sure, though, one day you will pay for your sins."

"Allegedly did."

"We both know what you did. You will pay for it eventually, and I hope that I am there to see it."

"We all pay."

"True. Who was hit and how bad?"

"You have an attachment to those kids? You do, don't you? Wish we would have killed some of them now. There is still time, I guess."

"I do. I'm guessing you don't have an attachment to anybody. I've seen your kind before. You act hard, but inside you are a little boy, scared in this big bad world. Now, who was hurt?"

"I don't recall."

"Unless you want to start losing fingers, I would suggest you answer my question." Ronnie pulled his knife from its sheath and took a step toward Mateo.

"It was the black bitch. From what I could see, she took one in the shoulder," Mateo said, staring at Ronnie.

"You are all the same. I could shoot every one of your boys in the head out there and you would stonewall me, but when the violence comes to you, your pussy ass always talks."

"You would too," Mateo replied.

"Some of us know the difference between what is right and what is wrong. Men like me would die before we betrayed the people that we love, but that's something that you can't understand."

"We all die. Just not me today, and I will take extra pleasure in the fact it's eating you up inside." Mateo laughed.

Ronnie flicked the knife across his face from above his left eye down past his mouth. Blood spilled from the man's face. He didn't scream. He didn't cry. He just stared at Ronnie. Luke pulled Ronnie back, and Ronnie put his knife back in its sheath.

"That is for Becky. Every time your pathetic ass looks

in the mirror, I want you to remember my face. I don't know how, but one day I'm going to choke the life out of you." Ronnie growled as Luke held him back. Mateo sat and looked at him, then cocked his head to the side.

"I'm going to burn everything and everyone you love to the ground. I promise you that," Mateo said with no emotion as Ronnie turned and exited the tent.

CHAPTER 29

Kenny and Marco heard the screams before they could see anything. They had been walking all night, and daybreak was just around the corner. The night was pitch black, and the clouds in the sky blocked out the moon.

The screams broke the quiet of the night, and they were creeping toward what they thought was the direction of the source. They had made good progress that day, covering several miles. They were tired as they moved to investigate, and this made Kenny nervous that they would make a mistake that would give away their position.

Eventually they grew close enough to see the glow of a campfire set up just outside of the woods. The closer they got, they picked up another sound: a baby crying. This caused them both to stop and look at each other. Fear grew in the boys about what they were about to walk into.

They squatted about thirty yards away from the scene. The fire illuminated the night, painting a clear picture of what was going on. A truck was parked, and the camp was set up behind it. There were two men sitting by the campfire, cooking what looked to be a can of chili. Both men had pump-action shotguns lying next to them in the dirt. Everything about that looked fairly normal, just like two guys out camping.

What didn't look normal was the teenage girl tied to a tree. A baby maybe about a year old rolled around in the leaves, screaming and scared. Unbound, a woman lay next to the fire. She was beaten badly and trying to crawl to the screaming child, her efforts slow-going. One of the men stood and walked over, giving her a kick to the ribs and evoking a shriek of pain from her.

"You ready now, bitch. Just give us what we want," the man shouted as the woman rolled onto her back.

"Please let me get my baby," the woman cried.

"Bitch, if you don't give us what you want, you ain't going to have a baby no more."

Kenny looked to Marco and could tell from Marco's face he was filled with as much anger as Kenny felt. He silently nodded, and the two of them fanned out. Kenny white-knuckled the machete as he crept toward the man still fiddling with the beans.

Kenny was filled with fear. What the hell was he doing? He wasn't Rambo. Could he really get up there and take a man's life? He inched closer. He had lost track of Marco. The man harassing the woman had left his gun sitting on the ground. Kenny was almost there. Only a little farther.

When he was right behind the man, he stood up. The man must have sensed him and turned around in a jerking motion. The man reached for his gun, but it wasn't there. They both looked over to Marco, who had snuck over and picked up the shotgun. He racked the slide.

"I know what you are thinking: pretty sneaky for a big boy. Grandpa was in Vietnam, and he taught me a few things. Now, I would suggest, unless you want me to turn that ugly face into hamburger, you get up real slow like and go stand next to your friend," Marco said.

"God damn, son. Take it easy. We ain't got no beef with you," the man said, putting his hands up and standing next to his friend, who remained silent.

"Kenny, take that duct tape out of your pack and tape these two pricks together," Marco said, taking control of the situation.

"You ain't going to tie us up. Now, we will get in our truck and leave, and you will never see us again. Hell, I ain't even sure that you know how to use that thing," the man who had been silent said, pointing to the shotgun.

"Mister, I was born with a shotgun in my hands. Not that it matters at this range, but I could shoot the asshole out of a duck from thirty yards. So shut the hell up and do what I say," Marco said, holding steadfast with the shotgun.

Kenny squatted down, digging through his pack. Sorting the contents, he found the large roll of tape and pulled it out. He cautiously walked over to the men, and Marco told them to get back-to-back as he stepped closer with the gun on them. The men hesitantly obliged and got in position. Kenny wrapped the tape around in a large circle. He tied at their elbows, hands and knees, making the men unable to move in any direction.

When he was done, Marco walked over and handed the gun to him. Kenny took the gun hesitantly. He had never even seen a gun in real life, let alone touched one. It was heavier than he would have thought. He looked up to Marco with a nervous eye.

"Man, I ain't never held a gun before. I don't even know what to do with it."

"It isn't hard, bud. They do some bullshit, you point and pull the trigger," Marco said forcing a nervous laugh.

The first thing Marco did was walk over and pick up the baby. He cooed and rocked the child in his arms and gave it a kiss on its forehead. The baby stopped crying and looked at him with eyes red from the fit. Marco had helped raise his younger siblings and was good with small children.

Next, he walked over to where the girl was tied to the tree. He pulled out his folding knife and, with one swift motion, cut the rope that was binding her. She instantly ran to her mother, leaving Marco holding the child. The men were silent, watching their work being undone.

"Momma, are you okay?" the girl cried as she helped her mom to her feet.

The woman could barely walk, and she spit blood from her mouth. She was probably around fifty, Kenny thought. She was short and had long blond hair that her daughter sported as well. He thought from looking at the daughter that if her face wasn't so badly beaten, she would probably be a very pretty woman.

"I will be okay," she whispered as the two of them stumbled toward Marco.

"Thank you. I'm Kate. This is my mom Annie, and that is my little brother, Nate," the girl said as she sat her mom into one of the folding chairs next to the fire.

"I'm Marco, and that is Kenny. No need for the thanks. People have to look out for each other," he said, still holding the baby.

"Thank you anyhow. Do me a favor and cover that baby's ears, would you?" Kate said.

"Why?" Marco asked.

She didn't respond to him. She walked over and picked up the other shotgun. She pulled back the slide, making sure that the chamber was loaded. Moving quickly, before anyone could figure out what was about to happen, she made her way in front of her captors. In a blaze so fast that Marco almost didn't get the child's ears covered in time, she unloaded the six shells into the men. It had happened quickly and they didn't even have time to react.

Smoke poured out of the barrel. The girl's mom was in so much pain and the onset of shock that she hadn't even flinched. The baby was crying and moving all around in Marco's arms. The girl dropped the shotgun and took her brother from him. Marco and Kenny stood with their mouths open.

"They killed my daddy on the road. Were gonna do unspeakable things to my mom. They killed him and laughed about it as they tied us up and threw us in the back of that truck like cattle. They can burn in hell. They deserve it," she said as she bounced around, trying to soothe the child.

"Man, they sure did. Just wish you would have given us a heads up. My ears are ringing," Kenny replied, still holding the gun.

"What now?" Kate asked.

Emory's family sat around the table in the kitchen. Debbie had poured them all a heaping portion of chicken stew that she had put on hours ago. She also had served them some homemade bread that she had baked in the giant wood stove that sat in the corner of the kitchen. They each had a glass of milk, and there was even a chocolate cake for dessert.

It seemed like a typical old lady kitchen, adorned with various knickknacks and kooky signs. It definitely had a country theme, all the way to the cast-iron pots and pans that hung above the stove. Eugene had eaten his bowl faster than Emory had ever seen him eat before. Emory looked down at the empty bowl in front of him. It had been the best thing that he had eaten in weeks, let alone the last few days.

"Thank you, ma'am," Margot said with her mouth half-full of bread. The meal was starting to lift her spirits, it seemed.

"It's quite all right, sweetheart," replied Debbie.

"I have to admit, you scared me a little bit when we first met." Margot smiled.

"A woman has to be twice as fierce as a man to make it in this world. The way things are now, make that four times as fierce," Debbie declared.

"I guess that's right," Margot said with the slightest glimmer of worry in her eye.

"Dear, it's better to die fighting than it is to be someone's slave. That's something that you should carry with you. No man has been my master or ever will be," Debbie said.

"Yes, ma'am."

"Now, let's clean up these dishes and get some food out to the clinic," she ordered as she pushed a tray of food into Emory's hands.

Emory exited the kitchen and made his way to the clinic. The night sky was crystal-clear, and the stars were shining brightly. It had been a long time since he had been out in the countryside. Out here, you could really see the sky. They had gone camping a lot when he was a boy, and he always loved it. Being out here reminded him of a simpler time. A time when everything still felt right in the world. Looking at the stars above, he thought of his mother. Emory had struggled with his relationship with God ever since he lost his mother, but he hoped, if there was a heaven, that she was looking after them.

Would she even know him if she saw him today? Could she recognize her little boy after watching him sink a tomahawk into a man's skull? Entering the door to the clinic, he made his way to the exam room. Becky was asleep with an IV in her arm. For the first time that day, she finally looked like she was at peace. Hearing the whispers from the side of the room, he turned in that direction. Jennifer and Emily sat in chairs, looking at the back of Emily's hand.

"Hey, I brought you guys dinner. Em, you okay? What's up with your hand?"

"What? Oh, nothing. Becky asked me to marry her," she said, turning her hand so that he could see the ring. The news caught Emory off guard, and he didn't really know how to respond.

"Oh wow. That's great," Emory finally replied.

"I know. She found the ring in that last house we were at, and she asked me right before she fell asleep tonight. I'm so excited." Emily was radiant with happiness.

"How is she?" Emory asked.

"She is doing pretty good," Jennifer explained through bites of stew.

"Lost a lot of blood and fluids. I'm going to keep her here overnight and through tomorrow, and then she should be strong enough to travel." Jennifer said as she chewed.

"Then what? We go on foot?" Emory said, turning to Emily.

"Nope. Jennifer said she's got an old farm truck that still runs. The saint she is, she told me that her and her momma would drive us the rest of the way. Should only be a couple hours."

"Thank you, ma'am. Your generosity knows no bounds," Emory said as he breathed a sigh of relief.

"It's alright. We were wanting to poke around a bit and see what is going on around here anyways. You look tired, son. Why don't you go inside and get some sleep? You have a big day of chores around here tomorrow to help pay for your future sister-in-law's treatment, so go get some rest."

"Yes, ma'am, I will. Thank you. Night, Em," he said as he walked back outside.

Halfway back to the house, he stopped. He looked around and lay on his back on the ground. He stared straight up into the night sky. It had been so long since he had seen it so boldly. He laid there enjoying the night. He didn't know how long it would be before he felt at peace like this again. The screen door shut, and footsteps came in his direction. Still he just lay there, staring up into the sky and someone cuddled up and put their head on his chest.

"Debbie, I think I may be a little young for you, but I'm game if you are."

"Shut up," Margot said with a giggle as she playfully slapped his face.

"Oh, it's you."

"Yeah, it's me, dork. I got Eugene in bed and saw you lying out here. I decided to crash your party."

"Well, I enjoy the company. Especially from a pretty girl."

"You're sweet. You didn't say much at dinner. Are you okay?"

"I don't really know how to answer that."

"Try."

"Well, it's hard to explain. Two days ago, I was a lost teenager, and to be honest, swallowed by sadness. I spent my days brooding, trying to push anybody that was close to me away. I was selfish, and I can see that now. The darkness in me I thought couldn't be any deeper, but after what I did to Scott, and after killing that man, I'm kind of afraid that I don't even know who I am anymore."

"Emory, you did what you had to do, for us," she said as she took his hand.

"It's just... I don't know. If my mother could see what I've done and who I am becoming, I think she would be ashamed of me."

"Emily told me about your mom, and I'm so sorry you had to go through that. I'm sure she would be proud of you for protecting your family."

"The last thing my mom told me was..." Emory tried to choke the words out.

"It's okay."

"She told me that I needed to look after my brother and sister. Made me swear to hell and back that no matter what, I wouldn't forget blood is thicker than water."

"That's what you are doing."

"I've never told anyone that before. Not even Emily. I don't know what it is about you, but I feel safe when you're around. Like you understand somehow."

"Yeah, I know. I get it. I feel the same."

"It scares me. If I lose you, I don't think I can..."

"I'm not going anywhere," she said, lifting her head to look into his eyes.

CHAPTER 30

"This looks like as good a spot as any," Hank said, taking the last drag of his cigar and flicking it in the woods.

"Natural choke point. People coming around that bend in the road ain't going to see it coming," Cecil chimed in.

"Damn straight," Hank said, pacing next to the road.

"We get a chainsaw and drop a few trees across the road. Set up a blind over here to hide in. Hell, boys, we is about to be rich as kings."

Emory woke with sunlight peeking in through the windows and illuminating the walls. It felt good to be sleeping in a real bed. He had slept soundly and risen feeling a lot better than he had the evening before. He turned with Margot cuddled up under his left arm. She had tried to hide it last night, but she was really sad about losing Lola. To be honest, so was he. He had built an attachment to the dog and it was like the group had lost a friend. Hell, a family member. He was also thankful that the dog had been filled with so much love for them that she had attacked to protect their little group.

It was a shame that they would have to leave this place. Getting up slowly so as not to wake Margot, he crawled out of bed and gave her a kiss on the top of her head. He made his way down the stairs and to the kitchen where he found Emily drinking a cup of coffee. Debbie was cooking a pan full of scrambled eggs and singing an old church hymn that Emory couldn't put his finger on.

"Go on, sit down. These eggs will be ready in a minute," Debbie said, breaking tune.

"Thank you." Emory sat down and looked around. "Where is Eugene?" he asked.

"Still sleeping. I didn't have the heart to wake him. For the first time in three days, he looks peaceful. I'm kinda worried about how he will adapt to this new world."

"He will adapt. We all have to adapt. If you told me three days ago that I would be fighting and sinking tomahawks into people's heads, I would have said you were crazy," Emory replied.

"Yeah, about that. You okay?" Emily said, peering over her coffee cup.

"I guess. I mean, he was going to hurt us, but still, I feel quite a bit of remorse over it. I don't think that I will ever forget the look in his eyes. Pretty sure it will haunt me until the day I die," Emory said, staring off into the distance. Debbie stopped what she was doing, came over and sat in the chair next to him. She took his hands and looked him in the eyes.

"There is evil in this world, boy. I have seen it. I was a nurse in the emergency room for thirty long, ugly, bloody years. I have seen the violence that people do to each other on a daily basis. There ain't nothing wrong with protecting yourself, and there damn sure ain't nothing wrong with protecting the people you love. You understand what I'm telling you, son? You ain't got a thing to be ashamed of."

"I guess, but I still feel..."

"No 'I guess' about it. Some people are evil turds, and they just need a flushing back to Hell," she retorted, standing back up and going over to the stove blazing in the corner.

"I like her," Emily said, laughing as she stood and made her way back to the coffee press.

"I'm sure you do. How's Becks? Is she okay?" Emory asked, eager about the news.

"She's good. We can move on tomorrow. Jennifer and Debbie are going to give us a ride. Shouldn't be but a couple hours," Emily stated.

"I know. I was there when she told us that. Said I'm gonna pay for it in chores, remember?"

"Oh yeah. Shit, I'm so damn tired I can't really keep anything straight. Even this coffee isn't helping," she said, putting the cup down.

"Go to bed, nerd. I'm gonna go check on Becky," he said with a smile, standing and headed toward the door.

"Take this out with you," Debbie said, handing him a tray full of toast, coffee, and eggs.

"Sure thing," Emory said as he took the tray and started out the door.

The short walk to the clinic was nice, and the farm was alive with activity. Chickens chirping, goat bleating, and dogs barking could be heard all around. Probably not a good thing, Emory thought as he entered the front door of the clinic. They were a loud advertisement to passersby that this place had food.

It warmed his heart to see Becky sitting in a chair, alert and talking to Jennifer. He knocked and entered, setting the food down on the examination table.

"Brought you breakfast," he stated.

"Thanks. We were just talking about the wedding," Jennifer told Emory.

"I never took you as the wedding type, Becks," Emory teased.

"Hey, I'm gonna look badass in a dress, rocking this scar on my shoulder."

"I'm sure you will. All joking aside, Becky, I'm really happy for you guys. I mean, I already think of you as a sister; now we are just making it official. For real, though, I love you," Emory said, walking over and giving her a hug.

"I love you too, bud. Hey, I guess getting shot at and almost dying has taught us to spill emotion while we can." Becky laughed.

"If you two are done with all the mushy stuff, I have a huge pile of wood that needs cutting, and I know a man who owes me a favor," Jennifer said, turning to look at Emory.

"Okay let's get to it. Show me where the axe is."

After John and Hank had dropped the trees and set up the blind, they just sat by the road in the hidden spot, watching and waiting. It had been a few hours, and they were starting to run out of beers. John sat with his back to a tree, whittling away at a tiny stick with his old pocketknife. He wondered if people could smell the men and were running the other direction. He chuckled in his head at the thought and kept at the stick. He was having a hard time staying drunk enough to keep the ugly visions out of his head. He knew he was wrong. He knew somebody was going to make them pay for what they had done, but at this moment he didn't really care.

Voices were coming around the bend, and he bent down in the shrubs, dropping the stick. He was about thirty yards behind where Hank and Cecil were hiding. His job was to stop people when they tried to make a break for it. He peeked out to see a man and two young boys walking down the road. Father and sons, he figured. They seemed oblivious to what was going on around them. The boys were running around their father and seemed to be in good spirits. They had no idea what was about to happen to them. They kept walking until Hank and Cecil stepped out from where they were hiding.

"There's a toll for this road, mister," Cecil snarled at the man.

"What?" the man asked, thoroughly confused.

"Toll. What you got to give us to pass?" Hank replied forcefully.

"I don't really have much of anything, gentlemen. We are just trying to make our way to one of those FEMA camps," the man replied as he took a step back.

"What's in the backpack, asshole?" Cecil said, taking a step toward the family.

"A couple bottles of water and some granola bars," the man's tone started to show fear.

"Good, that will work. Hand it over," Hank demanded.

"It's for the boys. You surely aren't going to steal from children, are you?" The man was growing angry.

"I don't give a damn about those little bastards. Now give it over," Hank said impatiently.

"NO!" the man said, scooping up the smaller boy as they turned and ran as fast as they could back up the road.

Hank and Cecil didn't make an effort to pursue the fleeing man. They figured that John would jump out and stop them. They figured wrong. The father and sons ran past John's position and made a hasty getaway. Hank was full of fury as he stomped down the road toward John. John stood, made his way into the road and met Hank.

"What the hell was that? You let them get away," Hank exploded.

"We ain't messing with no children, are we?" John said

weakly.

"I don't care about no kids."

"It ain't right."

"Look, you been my friend, hell, a brother, for years but if you do that shit again, I'm gonna shoot you myself. Quit being a goddamn pussy and do what's right," Hank said, slapping John across his face.

John stood stunned for a moment before he hid back in the shrubs. He was in shock that Hank had struck him, and his face burned from the impact. Reaching into his coat pocket, he pulled out the bottle of whiskey he had brought with him. He didn't know if was going to be enough, but he was going to try. He was going to have to be good and numb to get through what they were doing today.

CHAPTER 32

Marco and Kenny stood, looking at the girl who had just blasted away two men. She bounced around, trying to get the baby to stop crying and trying to talk to her mother. She had asked them what came next, then stepped away, assumedly to give them space to discuss it. Neither one of them really knew.

"So, I assume the truck runs?" Kenny said, pointing at the rust bucket.

"Yeah, more than likely," Marco said, his eyes fixated on the carnage.

"You see that coming?" Kenny said, forcing himself to look at the bodies.

"Hell no, but I get where she is coming from," Marco said, looking at Kate.

"Strong girl," Kenny replied.

"No shit. I would be a damn mess if I saw all of that."

"Yeah, me too," Kenny agreed.

"Well, I figure it wouldn't be right to leave them out here. We can take them with us. Mom will be thrilled to have a baby at the farm again," Marco said, turning his head to spit.

"Should we load up the truck and get going, then?" Kenny asked.

"Safer to wait until nighttime. Lots of people are going to want that truck."

"If we camp here, what the hell are we going to do with the bodies?" Kenny asked, fearing the answer.

"I'm gonna attach a rope to them. Gotta pull them down the road a ways. Leave them in a ditch," Marco said like it was a normal thing to do.

"Is that right? Should we bury them?" Kenny asked, not feeling right about throwing them on the side of the road like trash.

"They are murderers and rapists. Let the coyotes get 'em," Marco said as he turned and walked toward the truck.

Marco got in the front seat of the beat-up old truck and looked in the ignition. He was relieved to see the keys dangling. He really didn't want to go digging through the dead man's pockets. He turned the key, and the truck fired to life. It may have looked like junk, but it was clear that the pair had kept it in operating condition.

He looked around the cabin of the truck. It was jammed full of things. There were four packs that he assumed were plunder from attacking the family. On the floorboard of the passenger side were scattered boxes of shotgun shells.

Something else caught his attention, though. In the mix of shotgun shells was a box of .44 Magnum rounds. He hadn't seen either of the men wearing a pistol. He ran his hands under the seat but found nothing. Leaning over, he opened the glove box. There it was: a .44 Magnum Smith and Wesson with a six-inch barrel.

He pulled the revolver out and looked it over. It was in good shape, and he assumed that the men had kept it as a backup to their shotguns. Having a handgun made him feel better for some reason. He got out and walked back over to Kenny.

"I'm going to take out the trash. You go over and tell Kate and her family the plan," he said as he went over and looked for rope in the back of the truck.

Seeing the bodies made Kenny feel a little ill, so he put his attention back on Kate. She was a pretty girl, he thought. He also was a little afraid of her. Seeing the way she put down the two men made him nervous about being around her. Letting out a sigh, he walked over and sat down next to her in one of the camp chairs.

"Hope he ain't leaving without us," she said as she watched Marco work.

"Nah. He is a good dude. He is just dragging that mess out of here," Kenny replied awkwardly.

"What's the plan now? Are you two moving on? If you are, can we at least split the gear and weapons?" she said, shifting the baby to her other arm.

"We are leaving, but we would like you to come with us."

"To where?"

"Marco's family has a farm. He thinks it will be safe there."

"Are we going to be welcome?"

"He says his parents will be thrilled to have a baby there again."

"Well, shit, let's get going. Anywhere has to be better than here."

The pile of split wood was growing with each stroke, as was the pain in Emory's shoulders. This was hard work. At first, he thought it would be fun to play with an axe, but now he wasn't so sure. He had been at it for a solid two hours and was making some good headway. The mindless manual labor helped him to escape from his problems for a while.

He wasn't used to hard work like this. Growing up, he had lived in a world of video games and a full refrigerator. He wondered if this was the new normal. Working hard and earning a chance at survival. He also wondered why his father had been so lax on them. He never gave them rules or chores. Maybe it was because he was deprived of his childhood and wanted them to enjoy theirs, he thought to himself. Wiping his brow, he looked up at Margot walking toward him with two glasses in her hands.

"Thought you might be thirsty, Paul Bunyan," she said as she gave him a kiss and handed him the glass. He took a long swig before answering.

"Man, that's good."

"Jennifer told me that you could be done with this. It's time for lunch," Margot informed him.

"Thank God," he said, taking her hand and walking toward the house.

They walked and drank their lemonade, laughing and teasing each other. Emily and Becky were sitting on the swing on the front porch, watching as Eugene ran around playing near the house. This was a good day, Emory thought to himself, soaking it all in. Who knew how long it would be before they had another day of peace. He had a lot of anxiety about what was going to happen when they got to his grandfather's house. Did he even know that they existed? How the hell was he going to prove who they were? What if, in some messed-up way, their grandfather didn't believe them and hurt them? His mind was on fire with these questions.

"Hey, guys, go on in. I'm pretty sure they are about ready," Emily said from the swing.

The two entered the house and made their way to the table. It was the same thing that they had seen this morning with Debbie flying around the kitchen, except this time she had a big platter full of sandwiches she was putting on the table.

The sandwiches were all produced on the homemade bread. What he assumed was handmade jam spilling out the sides. The sight of the platter made his mouth water. Realizing how much energy he had spent on the wood pile; he was suddenly very hungry. Jennifer carried a big bowl of what looked like pasta salad and set it on the table, followed by a big pitcher of lemonade and another of sweet tea. At this point, the three from outside came in and took seats around the table.

"Hope you all are in the mood for some peanut butter and jelly and pasta salad. Options are pretty limited around here right now," Jennifer said.

"I love peanut butter and jelly," Eugene said excitedly as he reached onto the table, grabbing a sandwich.

"Me too, little man," Becky said, tousling his hair and grabbing a sandwich.

They laughed and ate like a big family. For some reason, sitting here like this, at this moment, made Emory sad more than anything else. He tried to fake a smile, but he knew everyone could see it. He missed his mom. He missed his dad. It felt a little empty without them at the table. Margot squeezed his hand under the table, and he turned and gave her a smile. He excused himself, made his way out to the back porch, and sat looking off into the woods.

"I miss them too, you know," Emily said as she sat next to him.

"Do you think Dad is still alive?" Emory asked.

"I hope so. I'm not going to sugar coat it. We may never see him again. After losing Ronnie, I don't know. Grandpa is really the only hope we have left."

"I mean, this is crazy. We don't even know the man. He doesn't know us. What happens when we get there?"

"Uncle Moose knows us."

"How?"

"Mom used to email back and forth with him. She kept it a secret from Dad. Sent him pictures of us and tried to keep him in the loop. She said he liked watching us grow up, even if it was on a computer screen."

"Sounds like Mom. The woman was a saint. I miss her."

"Me too. At weird times especially. A certain smell. A certain song. I catch glimpses of her in everyday things. I think she would like it like that. I know she is watching over us," Emily said, trying her best to be optimistic.

"I know what you mean. You know, Mom would be proud of you, Em. Keeping us together like this and all. I see a lot of her in you."

"Thanks. That means a lot. Now, come on. Jennifer has a pig pen for you to muck out."

"Ugh. Hope I don't lose everything I just ate."

CHAPTER 33

Ronnie walked into the medics' tent and breathed a sigh of relief when he saw the dog up on all fours and walking around. She looked a little shaky and was moving slowly. That being said, the fierceness had returned to her eyes. Seeing the vast improvement lifted his spirits. The medic sat on the ground, petting the dog and feeding it out of an MRE. Seeing Ronnie, he stood and walked over to him.

"I thought you said this dog was a warrior. Seems like a big baby to me," he said, laughing.

"I watched that big baby lacerate somebody's throat once," Ronnie said, deadpan.

"Gross. She was licking my face," the medic said, his smile fading.

"Gross, indeed. What's up with her? She was on death's doorstep when I brought her in here. What did you do?" He raised an eyebrow.

"Shot wasn't as bad as we thought. The bullet was a through-and-through. The wound was not really a big deal. She lost a lot of blood and fluids. She was very dehydrated and hungry. She is still weak, and I patched the wound, but I'm pretty sure after resting tonight she will be ready to roll out in the morning."

"Good. Tomorrow I'm going to go look for my family. I will welcome the company."

"You going by yourself?"

"Yeah. I'll be fine. Not going to risk any of the boys so I can go find my family. They are my responsibility. I will find them."

"You are not going out there alone," Luke said, overhearing him as he walked into the tent.

"Yes, I am."

"So, you expect me to let one of the men in my command go off to a militia camp full of paranoid nutjobs by himself? Forget the fact that he is a good friend. Hell no. I will go with you, at least," Luke said, shaking his head.

"Fine, it can be just the two of us. Maybe we can do some bonding," Ronnie said, annoyed.

"Three if you take the beast," the medic said, pointing at the dog.

"The beast. I like that," Ronnie said, laughing.

The pile of loot was more than Hank and his boys thought they would be able to obtain in one day. It was impressive, really. They had hit eight traveling groups, all of them small. They just kept coming, one after the other. Nobody even had the foresight to pay attention to what was going on around them. They just strolled on their merry way until it was too late. Some of them were even carrying guns, but, from lack of attention, didn't even get a chance to raise them. Now they sat in the pile of looted bootie the men had stolen.

The crown jewel was a four-wheeler that sat next to the pile. Most people had willingly given over their stuff at the threat of violence, but four-wheeler man had not. When they had ambushed him, he had skidded to a stop. He never said a word, just looked at them through the helmet, apparently weighing his options. When he made his mind up, he had fired ignition on the quad and tried to make a break for it. Hank had shot him right off the ATV as the man tried to ride off. He had gotten some blood on the ATV, but Hank didn't really seem to mind.

The man had fallen to the ground and was rolling around in agony. Reaching into his coat, he had pulled a small semi-automatic pistol and tried to aim it at a slowly-advancing John. John had panicked and pulled the trigger on the new 870 shotgun they had acquired earlier. The blast took the man out of his misery and he finally laid still.

This was the first person that John had ever killed. It made him feel sick. What was worse was the way Hank and Cecil had been so congratulatory to him. He had just murdered some poor man who probably had somebody somewhere depending on him. It was all too much to take. After the other two's chorus of laughter had died down, Hank had ordered him to get rid of the body. He had kicked the man in the ditch, and John covered him with limbs off a pine tree.

John was out of his mind by this point. Barely able to function, so consumed with drink. He felt nothing. He thought nothing. He sat in his hiding spot, holding his revolver in his hand, wondering if he should just put it to his head and end this nightmare for good. Cecil was so jacked up on crystal meth that he had beaten one of the travelers damn near to death over nothing.

They packed everything they had obtained in the back of the truck and made their way toward the house. Cecil followed them on the four-wheeler.

Hank thought of the young woman he had raped and tied to the bed. After a hard day of pillaging, he was ready for a long night of depravity. He first noticed something was wrong as he pulled up to the house and the front door was open. He pushed the gas pedal down a little harder as they pulled up to the house. He got out of his truck and made his way to the front door. Upon entering, he went to the stairs to his new room and opened the door. The bitch was gone, he muttered to himself. He slammed the door and thundered his way downstairs, his blood boiling.

"Hey, she's gone," he yelled at Cecil.

"Mine's here, but we got a problem," Cecil replied as Hank walked toward him.

Hank entered the room and the woman was hanging from what looked like a blanket tied to the ceiling fan. Her eyes bulged and her tongue slightly hung from her mouth. John, upon entering the room and seeing her, puked all over the floor.

"Damn it, Johnny, you got it on my boots," Hank yelled.

"Oh, sorry, man."

"You better sober up, asshole," Hank scolded.

"What you think happened here?" Cecil asked.

"I'm guessing the daughter saw an opening to get away and took it. Momma got loose later and couldn't find her and assumed the worse. There was a fair amount of blood on the bed. She must have thought I killed her and got rid of the body. Decided to check out early," Hank said with no remorse.

"What a waste of a woman," Cecil said, disappointed.

"Oh, hell, we will get us some more. Dime a dozen. John, clean this puke up and help Cecil get this bitch out of here," Hank ordered.

"What if the young one goes and finds her some help?" John asked.

"Then we kill them too."

The rest of the day had been a blur to Emory. From mucking out pig pens to moving feed bags, all he knew now was he was more tired than he had been when they arrived. After the communal dinner, he went outside with Eugene, who wanted to catch fireflies. He laughed as the boy ran around with a jar that

Debbie had given him, attempting to catch the elusive bugs. Emory wondered how long the boy could keep his youthful exuberance with all the bad things he had already seen. But in this moment, he seemed to let the past two days' experiences melt away from him. Kids were resilient like that, Emory guessed, but who knew the lasting impact.

"Come here, bud. I want to talk to for a minute," he said as he patted the swing next to him. The boy obliged him.

"I got ten of 'em," he said, proudly displaying the jar for inspection.

"That's great. Maybe we can poke some holes in the top and you can keep them next to you tonight."

"Wow, that would be great. Like nature's night light."

"Yeah, never thought of it that way. How are you doing, bud? Are you okay? I know that you have seen some bad stuff the last few days."

"I'm okay. I miss Mom and Dad," the boy said, his mood shifting to sullen.

"Me too, bud. Me too. We have been up against some bad guys lately. Does that scare you?"

"A little, I guess. But I have you and Emily to protect me, and that makes me feel better."

"Yes, you do, and I will always try to protect you. You are a tough little booger, aren't you?" Emory said as he stood from the swing.

"Don't forget it," the boy said as he ran off in pursuit of more bugs.

Emory sat down, feeling a little better. Eugene was what reminded him of the good and pure in the world. The boy was still innocent and hopeful. As Emory watched him run and jump, a smile crept across his face. He would do what it took to protect Eugene. He would do whatever it took to protect his group. He knew that without a doubt. He knew his purpose in life now. It was to fight for the things and people he loved. Next time he was forced to commit an act of violence to keep them safe, he would be unfaltering. Those who meant to hurt them, he would do his best to put in the dirt.

Emily came out back and yelled for Eugene to come inside and get ready for bed. He protested but eventually caved to her demands, giving Emory a high five as he went inside. Emory sat and enjoyed the quiet until Margot came out and snuggled up next to him. They sat like that for a while, not speaking, just enjoying the night together. Eventually she broke the silence.

"I miss Lola."

"I know. Me too. Brave little bear, standing up to protect us like that."

"She was a good dog. Always there for me. My parents were gone a lot. They traveled all the time. She was my closest friend." Margot's eyes teared up as she spoke.

"I'm sorry for your loss."

"I feel silly for crying about a dog. You have lost more than I can imagine, watching your mom die. I think I'm being selfish." She lost control and sobbed into Emory's shoulder.

"No, it's okay. The dog loved you, and so do I. Just let it all out," he said, embracing her and realizing he had just declared his love for her. He had thought it, but this was the first time he had verbalized it. Normally, saying something this personal would mortify him. With her, it just came out naturally, and he had no regrets.

"I love you too. Does it ever get any easier?"

"No. It hurts less with time, but they are always with you everywhere you go," he said, stroking her long black hair.

They sat there until she regained her composure. He took her hand, and they walked to their bedroom, and he tucked her into bed. He kissed her on the forehead and walked to his side of the bed. He was worried about running into that group from the farm again in the morning. But now he was ready. His head was in the game. It was time to be a warrior, and this time he would be ready for them.

CHAPTER 34

Kenny and Marco had spent the time waiting for night to come, getting ready for departure. They had done a thorough inspection of the truck. It turned out only two of the packs in the truck were from Kate's family. A shiver ran up his spine as he thought about how the bandits had done this to somebody else. Somebody not lucky enough to find help.

They had heated up four of the dehydrated meals salvaged from Kenny's basement. Kate ate hers quickly. It had been a while since she had eaten anything. The baby took a few bites of the scrambled egg pouch they had heated up. Kate's mom refused to eat anything and sat quietly, staring off into the distance. She was in shock. Kenny didn't blame her; he felt that way too.

"Thanks. It's been a long time since we ate," Kate said as she stood and stretched.

"No problem. We have plenty," Marco replied to the girl.

"Hey I was wondering... My dad died a little up the road. Could one of you help me go back and bury him? It tears me up thinking about him lying in the road like a piece of trash," Kate said, her eyes welling with tears.

"Yeah, for sure," Kenny answered, seeing the sadness in her eyes.

"How about I look after little man here, and the two of you make your way out there?" Marco said, taking the baby from Kate's arms.

"I don't know how to drive," Kenny answered, embarrassed.

"I do," Kate replied.

"I'm good with kids. Got three little siblings at the farm. We will have a good time, won't we, bud?" Marco said, bouncing the child in his arms.

"Okay," Kenny said, apprehensive about leaving.

"Come on, let's get this done," Kate said, kissing the baby on his head and heading to truck.

Kenny followed and climbed into the cab. Kate fired up the old truck, and Kenny watched as the camp disappeared in the rearview mirror. He studied Kate's expression of determination as they sped down the road. She was a brave young woman. Strong. Stronger than he was. If it had been him who saw his father murdered in front of him, he would be a mess.

"We only drove ten minutes down the road after they did it," Kate said, not diverting her eyes from the road.

"I'm sorry this happened to you," Kenny replied.

"Yeah. Me too."

"This shit is crazy."

"I know. A couple of days ago I was worried about passing an English exam. Seems pretty stupid now."

"Yeah," Kenny said, not knowing how to respond.

"Thank God you and Marco showed up. I don't know what would have happened otherwise."

"I'm happy we got there in time to help."

After a few minutes of silence, the truck came to a stop.

"We're here."

Kenny looked out the front of the windshield at the body of a man lying on the ground. It was an ugly sight. Animals had gotten to the body, and nature was taking its course. Worried, he looked at Kate. She was frozen, staring at her father. A few tears ran down her face, but for the most part, she was staying put together.

"I saw a shovel in the mess of tools in the back. I'm going to get it and start," Kenny said, getting out of the truck and looking for the shovel.

Kenny started digging a hole on the side of the road close to where the man lay. He dug for a long while. The whole time, Kate sat in the truck with her eyes transfixed on her father. As strong as she was, she didn't have the strength to get out and see him in that manner.

When the hole was four feet deep, Kenny stopped. Kate showed no signs of moving. He was going to have to do this himself. He was okay with that, if it helped Kate. He went to the back of the truck and pulled out an old blue tarp from the mess. He walked to the body and laid the tarp next to it.

He lined the edge as close to the body that was lying face-down on the pavement. He was glad that he didn't have to look at the man's face. Somehow it made it easier. He closed his eyes and rolled the man up in the tarp. When he had the man completely wrapped, he dragged him over and put him in the hole in the ground. Kenny stood, stretched his back, and grabbed his shovel. He started to put back the disturbed earth as Kate finally got out and walked over.

"Thank you. I don't think I could have done that," Kate said as she watched the blue tarp disappear in a cascade of dirt.

"It's okay. I understand."

"Just all seems so unreal," she said, unable to break her gaze from the hole.

"Do you want to say something?"

"Yeah. Do you mind if I say it in private?" She looked up at him.

"I will give you space. I'm almost done with this," Kenny said, putting the last few clumps of dirt on the mound.

Kenny walked away with the shovel, leaving Kate to make her peace. He stood at the truck and drank a bottle of water. He watched as Kate spoke, but he couldn't understand what she was saying. She fell to her knees, crying and pounding her fist into the dirt. She stayed on her knees crying for about ten minutes.

She then rose slowly. She kissed the palm of her hand and placed it on the makeshift grave. Slowly she walked back to the truck and climbed into the driver's seat next to Kenny. She was able to regain control of her emotions after a short while. Looking over to Kenny, she took his hand and looked into his eyes.

"He was a good man. Thank you for this."

Emory woke to Margot packing their things into bags. It was time to go. He stood and walked to the gear in the chair in the corner of the room. He slipped on his clothes and put the stiff gun belt around his waist. He pulled out the Glock 19 and looked in the chamber to make sure it was loaded. Sliding it back into his holster, he adjusted the Gerber knife on his belt. Last but not least, he picked up his father's tomahawk. It made him feel strong to think of his dad, and this reminder gave him hope somehow. The blade still had blood on it from his last encounter, and he thought about washing it off but decided against it. He would leave it there as a reminder to himself of what he was capable of in the face of those who wished to inflict evil.

He and Margot went downstairs to find Eugene on the front step, egg sandwich in one hand and the jar of fireflies in the other. Emily and Becky were right behind them with all their gear. Becky looked so much better. The color was running back into her checks. Her eyes were more alert, and she sat up on her own. Still not one hundred percent, but much better. Jennifer pulled up in the old truck and parked in front of the steps. Without any more words, they loaded all their gear in the back and climbed in. Jennifer slid open the back window. The loaded revolver was in her lap and the side-by-side shotgun sat next to Debbie.

"Alright, you hooligans, ready to hit the road? Emily, sit close to the window in case I have any questions about directions, and be ready to use them rifles if we get ourselves into any trouble," she said as she got the truck moving.

There were three extra gas cans riding in the back with them. More than enough to get there and back, Emory thought as he scanned the road, looking for signs of trouble. His hand was on his pistol as the truck bumped over the old country roads. It was going to be a long, uncomfortable ride, but it sure beat walking.

The old truck was audible before he could see it. This was the score that Hank had been waiting on. John just hoped that nobody got killed during it. He fiddled with the safety on the shotgun Hank had forced him to take. If he messed up this time, Hank would kill him for sure. The truck whizzed past him, and it slammed on the brakes. It came to a sudden stop, and Hank was clapping and laughing at the sight of his new trophy. He stood and blocked the path of the vehicle, raising the riot gun. Seeing the three young girls, John knew this was about to go very, very badly. Holding the gun with one hand, he pulled out his flask and took a long draw. He was not going to be numb enough for this one.

When the truck slammed to a stop, Emory's head bounced off the back window, and he caught Eugene, who slid into him. Dazed, a ragged old man stepped out of the bushes, raised a shotgun, and pointed it at them. The man looked like hell and could barely walk a straight line. He was clearly intoxicated, and that was not a good thing. Emory reached for his weapon, but Emily put her hand on his and shook her head. With a matter of pumps, that gun could put a lot of hurt on them.

"Put yer guns on the ground and get out of the truck real calm-like, and nobody is going to get hurt," a voice yelled from the front of the truck.

"Alright, mister. Just don't shoot us," Emily yelled back. Everyone threw the guns out of the truck, and they all got out with their hands held high.

"Everyone over here on their knees. John, get your stinking ass up here. Keep your gun on them in case they try to get cute," the man said, laughing.

They all did as they were told, lining up and getting on their knees. Emory studied the faces of the men. They looked old, beaten, and broken. They looked like they had nothing to lose. This was not good. Not good at all.

"If you want the truck and the gear, it's all yours. Just let us go," Jennifer offered.

"Why in the hell would I do that? You all got something I need, and so many flavors to choose from. Which one should I taste first, Cecil?" he said, licking his lips and staring at the girls.

"Damn, Hank, they all look pretty tasty to me," he said, laughing and adjusting the crotch of his pants.

"Gross," Margot snickered.

"You're first, then, buttercup," Hank said, picking her up by her hair and dragging her toward the bushes. "Been a long while since I had some Chinese."

Emory jumped to his feet without even thinking. He rushed the man, delivering a low shoulder blow and taking them both to the ground. He attacked like he was feral, and any thoughts fled his mind. He didn't even see the knife coming. Cecil sank the four-inch stag-handled knife from his belt into Emory's shoulder. Emory's adrenaline was pumping so hard he didn't even feel it. The assault didn't stop until the butt of Cecil's shotgun smashed into Emory's face, sending him flat on his back. Hank stood and spit on Emory.

"I'm gonna kill your ass, but first I'm going to make you watch me rape your girl," he said with a sick smile as blood ran from his nose.

Hank got on his knees and started to rip off Margot's pants. Emory lay in a fog, unable to move. Was this how it ended? It seemed like a cruel joke. He had found love for the first time in his life, and now it was being stripped away. Was his sister next? As the blood pooled under him from his shoulder, he tried to will himself to move. Nothing. He looked over at his family. Emily was screaming something, but he couldn't make it out over the ringing in his ears.

The man called Cecil was making his way toward Becky. He grabbed her by her hair, and that was when it happened. The shot penetrated the scene and the back of Cecil's head exploded. He stood there for a second with a confused look on his face, then fell to the ground. Hank turned from trying to get Margot's shirt off and stood, scanning the tree-line. He had let his guard down, and some kind of primitive darkness came over Emory, powering him to get up.

With a primordial scream, Emory charged Hank. Hank raised his pistol from his belt but was too slow. For the second time, Emory tackled him to the ground and started pummeling Hank's face with his fist. Margot, in shock, slid back to watch Emory proceed to smash Hank's face.

Three men dressed in woodland camo came out of the

woods, and Emory stopped to look at the new threat. All the men's faces were covered with black masks that hid the lower halves of their faces. The two men in the back looked tiny in comparison to the man in the front. He was huge, at least six-foot-six. He had a belly and had to be every part of three hundred pounds. Still, he didn't look out of shape. He looked scary. Long, matted dreadlocks protruded down his back. His thick, bushy beard flowed from under the concealment of the mask. The rifle he carried in his arms was a Heckler and Kock G3. Emory recognized it from some of the video games he played. Even it looked small in the man's hands. They stood there with their rifles raised, trying to assess the situation.

The man named John had scooped up Emily and was holding a small nickel-plated revolver to her head. They both swayed with the man's drunken movements. The man had tears streaming down his face, which was struck with fear. He looked like he had no idea what he was doing. He also looked like he had nothing to lose. A man with nothing to lose holding a gun to his sister's head was something that filled Emory with panic.

"Easy, fella. I'm pretty sure that's my niece you're holding a gun to," the huge man said in a booming voice. The leader pointed a rifle at the man.

"I didn't do nothing. It was all these two. Tell 'em, Hank," John yelled as he dragged Emily backward, struggling to stay on his feet. Emily's face didn't show any fear as she was pulled all over the place.

"Let the girl go and we can talk about it," the man commanded in the booming voice.

"I don't deserve this," the man said, letting Emily go. He stood there for a second, then put the revolver to his head and pulled the trigger, falling to the ground as a small flask slid from his pocket. Emily turned around and stared at the man as he lay there, blood pumping out of his head.

"Emily? Is that really you?" the man asked, lowering his

rifle and trying to break her trance.

"Uncle Moose?" she said, confused.

"My name is Reginald, but you can call me Moose if you prefer. I'm glad I finally get to meet you. Just wish it was under better circumstances," the man said, wrapping her in a bear hug.

"You must be Eugene. You are the spitting image of your mother. Come on up and give me a hug."

Eugene stood and attached himself to his uncle's leg.

"And you must be Emory. My god, you look just like your daddy. You poor bastard," he said to Emory, who was still frozen in place on top of a barely-moving Hank.

"God damn, boy, you got a pig sticker popping out of your shoulder and you are still handing out an ass whooping. You really are your daddy's son," the man said with concern in his eyes.

"They tried to hurt us," Emory said, getting to his feet shakily. Margot came over and put his arm over her shoulder to stabilize him.

"I know they did, son. Don't you worry. This piece of shit ain't gonna hurt nobody ever again," the big man said as he walked over and shot Hank twice in the chest with the big rifle.

"Come on, you all, we are going home," he said as he led them toward the woods.

CHAPTER 35

Ronnie was packed and ready to roll at daylight. The big dog had woken him with kisses before the sun was up. She looked much better and was walking and running around the camp as he found his way to Luke, who was standing by the Hummer with two cups of coffee.

"You ready to roll?" Luke asked, handing him a travel mug.

"Hell yes."

"How do you even know that they will be at that camp?"

"I don't, but I'm damn sure gonna see for myself. They are out there somewhere," Ronnie said as he opened the door and the dog jumped into the back.

"I hope they are, buddy, because we are being recalled to Texas to re-format and bring in the prisoner. I'm pretty sure we are going to war. Your family is going to be smack dab in the middle of it if we don't find them," Luke said, starting up the Humvee.

"Well, shit."

After everyone had regained their senses, they retrieved their collective weapons. Emory lay in the back of the truck while Jennifer pulled out the knife and started to patch up the wound. Moose and his men had combed the area, finding the body of what he assumed had been a previous victim. They had buried the body of the man on the side of the road and put a makeshift cross made from cut tree limbs as an epitaph to the man with no name.

Then they dragged the other three men into a small clearing on the side of the road. There they had collected as much wood as they could find and covered them. Next, they poured the extra gasoline from Jennifer's truck on the bodies. They had waited until everyone was ready to move, and they set the makeshift funeral pyre ablaze with the flick of a match.

Jennifer and Debbie had opted to go with them to the camp so that they could look after Emory's wound. Moose told them that he appreciated it, and, after Emory was better, he and his men would give them an escort home. Moose seemed to be a happy man, and when he spoke, his words came out soft and tender. A soft contrast to the man they had met a few hours ago who had just killed the two monsters.

Moose led them through the woods to a small clearing that bore three small pickup trucks. They were all what looked like four-wheel-drive Ford Rangers with extended cabs. They had been painted camo, and one had what looked like a machine gun mounted to the top. They laid Emory in the back, and Margot got in with him. The others piled into the other two truck beds.

A teenage Arab girl sat quietly in the back of one of the trucks, and Becky sat next to her. She was hugging her knees to her chin and rocking back and forth. She was dirty, and her body and face were covered in injuries and caked-on dried blood. Becky gently touched her hand to ask her if she was okay. Before she could get any words out, the girl jumped away from her. Her face was covered in terror. Her eyes darted around to all the people around her, yet she wouldn't look anybody in the eye. Becky wondered what had happened to this poor girl as Emily got in the cab of the truck with Moose. The trucks rolled out.

"Uncle Moose, what's with the girl in the back?" Emily asked, confused about why she was sitting there all alone and looked so troubled.

"We found her in the woods while we were out on patrol. She was hysterical. Said those men back there had killed her mother and father. It's a pretty grisly story, one I don't know if you should hear," Moose said as he drove, trying to avoid eye contact.

"They raped her, didn't they?"

"Yeah."

"I can't imagine. I'm glad they are dead. At least they can't hurt anybody else." Emily was searching to find a positive in this messed-up scenario.

"There are more like them. People are nasty creatures."

"Will she be okay?"

"I don't know. Probably not. That's a lot to be put through," he said. The sadness in his voice spoke volumes.

"Em, there is something else we need to talk about."

"That's not good."

"No, it is not. The men I am with... They are not very good men. Dad kept them in line when he was around. Problem is, he was in the city with half of our guys when this happened. I'm losing control."

"Is it a good idea that we are going here? What kind of men have you surrounded yourself with? What kind of man are you?" she said, fearful to hear his response.

"We don't really have a choice. The other two guys with me would have killed me if I had tried to make a break for it with you guys. The type of men willing to give up society and live in the woods are not usually stable men."

"You did."

"Didn't have a choice. I was born into it."

"That's an excuse. Dad left."

"Your father was a much stronger man than me. I couldn't bear the thought of leaving our father behind. Some chains are hard to break."

"Are we going to be safe there?"

"I don't think that they would try anything with me around. They fear me, but they don't respect me. There is a man named Tony who is causing most of the trouble. He wants to be in charge. Hell, I would love if we could just get my stuff and leave. They won't let me."

"Why don't you just tell them that we are going to look for Grandpa?"

"They would make us leave a couple behind as insurance we were returning."

"Well, let's go meet this Tony, then."

The ride back to their small camp had been quiet and awkward. Kenny tried his best to avoid eye contact and looked out the window. Luckily for him, Kate was not in a talking mood. As they drove, night set in. The darkness overtook them as they slowed to adjust to the night.

When they arrived back at camp, Kate left the motor running and stepped out without a word. Kenny followed as she took her baby brother back from Marco.

"He was a good boy while you were gone. You are about out of diapers in that bag, though. Gonna have to figure something else out." Marco said as he picked up their packs and tossed them in the truck.

"I hadn't even thought about that," Kate answered, her voice barely higher than a hushed whisper.

"I'm sure my mom has something that will work. We were too poor to buy disposable diapers for our family. I'm sure she has some cloth ones put back," Marco explained.

"Thanks. That would be really helpful. What's the plan now?" Kate asked, finding her voice again.

"Gonna be slow going. Probably another night or two. Figure the baby and your mom will ride with me in the cab. I'm gonna keep the old wheel gun up here with me. You and Kenny ride in the bed with the shotguns, watching our backend. Wish the boy had a car seat."

"Yeah, he used to. Not that it helps any now."

"Okay let's get this merry band of misfits on the road," Marco said as he clapped and rubbed his hands together.

Kenny and Kate helped Kate's mother get into the truck. She was still unresponsive and in a state of shock. Kate hoped she would regain her senses soon. She was having a hard time being the one to keep it together.

Next, they secured the child the best that they could in the middle seat. They ran the seatbelt over the boy, who was squirming to explore the cabin. Marco placed the revolver on the small shelf in the driver's-side door, out of reach of the boy. He jumped into the running truck and adjusted the mirrors from Kate's previous trip.

Kenny and Kate hopped in the bed of the truck. They sat with their backs to the rear window. The window had a small sliding door in it. Marco reached back and pushed it open.

"Here's hoping for a quiet night. Be ready with those guns anyhow."

Tony sat with the other man around a blazing fire pit. The man was about average height. He was muscular but sported a beer belly and had a bald head and a thick mustache. When someone thought of what kind of man would be in a militia, he was a perfect poster child.

Tony had been a member for eight years. When he arrived, he had been an angry, drunk man. He had just lost his house to the bank and was searching for someone to blame. Instead of looking at himself and the fact he drank the mortgage away, he blamed the financial collapse of 2008. The government was at fault for that. So, full of hate and booze, he packed up his truck and made his way south. He had met Neil Ellison at a local gun show previously. They had hit it off, and Neil told him he should make his way down south.

When Tony hit rock bottom, he decided to take Neil up on that offer. He packed his truck full of as many guns and as much booze as he could and made his way there. When he arrived at the camp, he was met with armed guards. Upon becoming a member of the little community, he had learned to love the place. When the booze ran out, he had a very rough transition. Neil had held his hand through the detox and helped him transition into smoking weed. This was something of abundance they had on site.

Tony looked up to Neil, who was like the father he had never had. He was jealous of Moose. Moose was Neil's son and the second-in-command. Tony had sat up at night obsessing about how to get that coveted spot next to Neil's throne. He wanted the power. He was a true believer, and he knew that at times Moose's faith in his father's teaching waivered. He didn't deserve it. Tony did.

With Neil in the city and the lights going out, Tony was finally going to have his chance. There were only six men here, including Moose. The other four men Tony had been pursuing for months to help him cook up a plan to get rid of Moose. The time was finally here, and the arrival of the EMP gave them the perfect setting. One night very soon, they would simply wait for Moose to fall asleep. Then they would shoot him in the face. It was as simple as that. In times like these, when Neil returned, they could simply tell the old man that a marauder had penetrated their lines and done the deed himself.

Sitting next to him was Dan. Dan was a very small man. He barely came up to five-foot-three. Dan was skinny with no muscle mass. He followed Tony around like a lost puppy. Dan was an annoying person to be around. He was the type of guy who was always telling stories about all the fights he had been in and all of the girls he had made love to. But in reality, he had never raised his fist once in his life and had only been with two girls. Nobody, not even here, really took him seriously. He was the butt of many jokes and hated it. He longed to be the third spot from the top, and Tony had promised him it was all his as soon as Moose was dead. As he packed his pipe full, he peered into the fire, fantasizing about what would be happening soon.

The other two men that had gone out with Moose on the patrol were named Jeremy and Kevin. The two were nothing more than barely functioning morons. They were wild like animals, and when Tony had told them of how they would live like kings in this new world, they had agreed to be a part of the plan. They were out on patrol with Moose to make sure that he didn't flee.

Tony was sure that the man felt the especially heavy tension in camp in the last few days. The last thing Tony needed was for Moose to up and run off and come back after his father's return. It was a battle of wits, and Tony was pretty sure that he was winning. He sat back, took a long drag of marijuana and stared into the sky. The time was near, and he was ready.

Moose had shifted the subject on the rest of the ride home to asking about Emily's life. He asked as many questions as he could get out, and she could tell he was relishing the details of their upbringing. The sadness in his eyes mirrored her own. It bothered him that he had not been a part of their life. He really did seem to care about them. She watched as the happy, big man shed a tear when she spoke of her mother's last days. For as scary and foreboding as he looked, he was surprisingly in touch with his emotions. He told her about his relationship with their mother. He loved her like a sister, she could tell. He may have been up on the side of a mountain, but her death had still affected him.

She watched as the trees whipped past on the old mountain road. They were going deeper and deeper into the woods. Finally pulling to a stop, she stood up and took a look at the surroundings around her. The woods had been cleared in a huge circle where the camp lay. Ten small cabins were lined up in a row, with a large cabin on the other side of the camp. In the middle sat a huge fire pit and an outdoor kitchen. Directly behind of all of that sat a small lake with a fleet of small rowboats of an old dock. It was like something she had seen in history books that reminded her of settler times in the new world. Everyone else had been set back by a hundred years, but she imagined that this place didn't so much as blink.

The other two trucks pulled up, and Emily turned to see Margot and Jennifer helping Emory out of the back of the vehicle. He was pale and sweating and didn't look good at all. Moose excused himself from Emily, walked over and picked up Emory. Margot and Jennifer were taken aback for a moment.

"It's okay, bud, I got you. I know just the place you can rest. Is there anything that you need?" he said, directing his attention to Jennifer.

"Some clean bandages and rubbing alcohol would be nice. I don't suppose you have antibiotics, do you?" she said, joking.

"What kind do you want? I have 500mg Amoxicillin. Will that work?" he said as he strode toward the cabin closest to the water.

"Uh, yeah. Why do you have that? Just curious."

"Crazy survivalist, remember?"

"You don't seem that crazy to me. You seem sweet," she said, half-blushing.

"Well, hold out your opinion on survivalists till you meet the rest of these assholes," he said as he gently opened the door.

CHAPTER 36

The inside of the cabin was dark and a bit dreary. Moose carefully lead Emory to the bed. Walking to a wardrobe on the adjacent wall, he pulled out two pillows and a blanket. He propped the pillows under Emory and covered him with a blanket.

"I'm feeling much better after the pain killers. I can take care of myself now." Emory protested.

"It's all right. I don't mind." Moose said with a smile.

Moose pulled a lighter from his front pocket and lit the oil lamp that was hanging from the ceiling. The room was mostly bare. Emory looked around, seeing a small desk with some papers on it, the wardrobe and a footlocker by the bottom of the bed. The big man pulled over the desk chair and sat down.

"This was your daddy's room growing up. When he went away, my dad left it just the way it was. He didn't move a thing."

"Wow," was all Emory could get out, most of his energy drained from the fight and his wound.

"You get some rest. I will be back to check on you after a little while," Jennifer said from behind Moose.

"Yes, ma'am."

"Reginald, could you escort me out there to check on the others? I would like to take a look at the girl from the back of the truck's injuries," Jennifer said.

"Yes, ma'am, and you can call me Moose. Everyone else does."

"I'm not everyone else and I will never call you that," she said as they walked out the door.

Margot stood there at the end of the bed, looking at Emory. He didn't know how to take it; they had barely spoken for the whole ride to this place. She paced back and forth, running her hands through her hair and shaking her head. Eventually she stopped and crawled into bed with Emory. She laid her head on his bare chest. He gently brushed the hair from her face.

"Hey, what's wrong? Besides the obvious," Emory said with a little chuckle to himself.

"Were you going to kill that man today?" she asked, her voice barely audible.

"Yes."

"Were you going to kill him because of me?"

"I would do anything to protect you."

"You could have been killed."

"That's the theme of this new world."

"When I saw you there, lying in all of that blood, the only thing I could think about was how I would feel if I lost you," she said with tears in her eyes.

"I'm not going anywhere."

"You can't promise that. None of us can."

"I can promise you that I will love you until the moment that I take my last breath," he said as he lifted her chin to see her face.

"That could be tomorrow. I'm realizing how short life is. I don't want to miss anything with you. I wanted to wait, but after today I think I am ready now," she said, getting up and taking off her shirt and walking over to the oil lamp.

"Ready for what?" Emory blurted at the sight of her with no shirt.

"Ready to take our relationship to the next level. I wanted my first time to be with somebody I loved, and I love you. Are you ready?" she said, giving him a wink and sly smile as she blew out the lamp.

"Don't worry. I will be gentle."

The Humvee made slow process down the congested roads. More than once, Ronnie had to get out and put the vehicle in neutral so they could push it out of the way. It would be nightfall before they got there at this pace. At least they would have the cover of night to survey and assess the situation, he thought as he looked out the window.

They had passed many small groups of people on the side of the road. Families mostly, it looked like. Ronnie had insisted that they bring as many MREs as they could fit into the back of the truck. When they pulled up and saw people walking, he would get out of the vehicle and give them each two meals. It broke his heart to see the kids especially. He had brought along a few cases of candy bars that they had stored in the mess tent. He gave each child one, the smile on their faces furthering his sorrow. It was slowing the process, but it was the right thing to do. These people needed help, and more than that, they needed hope. He hoped the small act of kindness would lift their spirits and show them that there were still good people in this world.

"This is going to take forever," he grunted at Luke, growing ever more annoyed.

"We will get there. I'm sure they are safe with their grandpa," Luke said, trying to reassure him.

"Yeah, I sure hope so. For his sake. How the hell are we going to make it to Texas in this shit?"

"We are getting a ride."

"From?"

"Air Force is sending Blackhawks with Apache support."

"Really? That's VIP treatment. I feel like the belle of the ball," he said, giving Luke a wink.

"Well, we caught a VIP. They want him bad. Most of the groups scattered around the country are staying in place, keeping an eye on the camps they are attached to."

"They okay with civilian passengers?"

"No, not really, but I told them the score. If they want Mateo, then they are taking us all. It took some convincing."

"Thanks man, that really means a lot. Guess I owe you a beer," Ronnie said with a chuckle.

"Brothers look out for each other."

"Yes, we do," Ronnie said, trying to hold back a tear.

The road took a sharp ninety-degree turn, and Luke slowed to a crawl. After spending so much time in Afghanistan, he saw a potential ambush from a mile away. Both men held their breath as they passed and let out a sigh of relief when they came around. Lola sat up, and a low growl rumbled in her stomach. Before the men could say a word, gunfire erupted from both sides of the street. The rounds crashed into the armored vehicle, and Luke slammed the pedal to the floor. They were a half mile down the road before the firing seized. He slowed to a stop and turned to Ronnie.

"Jesus," he said, looking around the vehicle to see if there was any damage.

"Just like old times," Ronnie said as he stood and looked out the back of the vehicle.

Ronnie pulled a pair of binoculars out of the dash and climbed out the gunner port. Standing behind the fifty-caliber machine gun mounted to the roof, he looked down the road. Four men stood in the middle of the street, one of them looking back at him through his own binoculars. Two of the men had shotguns, and the other two had semi-auto rifles of some kind. Ronnie's mind thought back to all the families they had passed on the way here. If it were any of them walking through the trap, he knew what that meant. His head filled with white-hot rage as he looked at these opportunistic vultures. He racked a round into the fifty.

"Put it in reverse, and I mean slam it."

"We don't need to mess with this. Let's go on our way."

"I'm not leaving these shit stains to hurt somebody else. You either put it in reverse or I'm going at it on foot." Ronnie demanded, making himself clear.

"Okay, hold on."

As the truck blasted backward as fast as it could go, Ronnie opened up with the big gun on top. The men were frozen in their tracks like deer in headlights. He was all over the place, spraying bullets everywhere. Eventually, as they moved closer, the men woke and tried to take cover. It was too late. The gun made short work of the crew, and the scene was a grizzly one. Luke slammed on the brakes, and Ronnie almost flew out of the top, losing his footing. Both men got out of the vehicle, and both took a side of the road. When they were sure nobody else was coming, they lowered their rifles.

"Hey, Ronnie, you better come take a look at this," Luke yelled from the other side of the road, his head still ringing from the blast of the gun.

Ronnie jogged his way over to where Luke stood. In front of him was a mountain of what he assumed were stolen backpacks and gear. Sitting back-to-back were an older man and a young boy. Their hands were bound to each other. The older man looked like he had taken a beating, and the boy had a black eye and a split lip. They sat in shock. It was a miracle that they were not hit. Ronnie walked over and pulled his knife from his sheath, causing the older man to flinch.

"I'm not going to hurt you. We are the good guys," Ronnie said as he helped the man to his feet.

"Thanks," the man mustered.

"What happened here?" Luke asked in a calm tone, trying not to upset the boy.

"My grandson and I were coming down this road, and they jumped out and demanded our packs. I gave them what they wanted, and they beat us anyway. My grandson was visiting for the weekend when this all happened. I was trying to get him home to my son," the man said with shame in his eyes.

"This isn't your fault. Why were you tied up here? Why didn't they let you on your way?" Ronnie asked as Lola finally trotted up beside him, catching the boy's interest.

"Can I pet your dog?" the boy said, perking up.

"Absolutely, buddy. Here, why don't you go over by our truck and enjoy this candy bar?" Ronnie said as he tussled the boy's hair.

"Thanks, mister," he said as he ran to the truck.

"They were going to kill us. I could see it in their eyes. I was in Vietnam, and I know when somebody has killer intent. I told them my son was a survivalist and had lots of stuff. He isn't, but I thought it would buy us some time," the man said, raising his sleeve on his left arm to reveal a Marine Corps emblem on his skin.

"Well, I will be damned. Where the hell you heading, you crusty old grunt?" Ronnie said, smiling and giving him a pat on the back.

"Brookshire, Kentucky."

"That's on our way to our destination. If you don't mind the smell of the beast in the back, we would be glad to give you an escort," Luke offered, slapping the man on the back.

"Hell yeah, we will take a ride. I will tell you the story about how I took shrapnel in the ass in '68. Makes it a real bitch to walk. You boys just made my day."

"Brothers look out for each other. Once a Marine, always a Marine," Ronnie said, looking at Luke.

They gathered up the man's possessions out of the pile and walked over to the Hummer. The boy's eyes were as big as saucers when they told him he was going to ride in the truck. They all piled in, and Ronnie pulled out two MREs for them. From how fast they ate, he figured it had been a lean few days. After they were finished, the old man stretched out the best he could in the back and fell asleep in minutes. Soldiers could sleep anywhere, and Ronnie figured that was something that didn't change with age. The boy leaned between them as they drove.

"Thanks for helping us. Hey, I was wondering: can I maybe shoot that gun up top?"

CHAPTER 37

They lay under the covers, their bodies pressed together. Margot had fallen asleep with her arms around Emory. Emory held her, looking at the ceiling of the small cabin. He had always thought that his first time having sex would be awkward and that he would be nervous. Neither of those things had applied. The two had become one, and it felt natural. More than natural, it felt like fate. As he gently rolled out of bed, he put his boxers back on.

Looking at her sleep, he reaffirmed to himself that he would do what it took to keep her safe. He knew that she would do the same for him. He looked for his shirt and then he remembered that it was covered in blood and torn up. He walked over to the wardrobe in the corner of the room and opened it. The clothes were old and musty, and he hesitated to pull one out to wear. Eventually he found an old Pink Floyd tee shirt and slipped it on.

Looking through the rest of the closet, he chuckled at the 1980's selection in front of him. Then something else caught his eye. Pushing the hangers aside, he pulled out a green military-style coat. "Ellison" was embroidered over the left pocket. The right pocket had an American flag hand-drawn onto it. He thought back to how his father must have looked in the jacket. He pulled the coat on. Perfect fit.

He decided to further investigate and moved over to the footlocker by the bed. Opening it slowly so as not to wake Margot, he peered inside. It was about half full of his father's possessions.

On top of the small pile of items was a black canvas backpack. It was in good shape for being over thirty years old. Nothing was inside. He removed it and set it beside him. Underneath that was an old 1911 handgun. It had been greased up for storage, and he pulled it out and wiped away at it with the rag it was wrapped in. The nickel plating was flawless even after all these years. He wiped it clean the best he could. Finding an old leather holster, he loaded the weapon with some bullets that were stored in an old ammo can that sat next to it and put it on his belt.

The next item he found was an old kabar fighting knife. This was the kind of knife that soldiers had used in World War II and Vietnam. He assumed from the shape that it was in that his father had inherited it. He removed the knife from its sheath and touched his thumb to the blade. It was still razor-sharp after all these years. He decided that he would put this on his belt as well.

The last major item in the bottom was a leather-bound journal. He picked it up and opened the cover, and a photo fell to the floor. He picked it up. It was a picture of his mom and dad. They were at a dance of some kind that his father had no doubt snuck off to with her. They looked so young. After losing everything in the house fire, this was the only picture Emory had of either of them. It felt good to see their faces again. He gently placed the photo back in the journal and placed it in the canvas bag.

Walking on tiptoe as not to wake Margot, he left the cabin, shutting the door softly. It was dusk by this point, and the sun was setting. He spotted Emily sitting with Becky, Jennifer and Moose by the campfire. He walked over and sat down next to Emily.

"Holy shit. Seeing you in those clothes is like seeing a ghost of your father's past, boy," Moose said as he took a long drag off a cigar.

"Found all of this stuff in the cabin," Emory said, confused whether he should have taken it or not.

"It's fine; your dad would want you to have it," Moose said, reaching over and giving him a pat on the back.

"Hey, Em, look what I found," he said as he pulled out the old photo and handed it to her.

"Oh my god. I never thought I would see them again," she said, her eyes welling with tears.

"Come with me," Moose said.

They stood and followed him to his cabin. They all piled in, and he lit two lamps, illuminating the room. It was pretty sparse. In one corner sat an old acoustic guitar. It had the same wardrobe and footlocker set-up as Emory's dad's old room. The only difference was that in this room there was also a rack filled with guns. Emory counted two shotguns and three rifles, plus a few random pistols. That was not what Moose wanted to show them. He opened his footlocker and pulled out the contents, placing them on the bed.

Next, he pulled out a false bottom, revealing a hidden compartment that he must have installed very carefully. He pulled out an old photo album and set it on the bed.

"Go on, open it. Take a look," Moose said as they gathered around the bed.

The first few pages of the book were all photos of their father and uncle as children. Random pictures of them playing with their grandparents. As they turned the pages, they watched their father turn into a young man right in front of their eyes. As they continued to flip the pages, pictures of their family appeared. The collection of family photos filled the rest of the book. There was not a dry eye in the room by the end.

"How do you have all of these?" Emily asked as she wiped her face with her sleeve.

"Your mom used to send them to me. She would post me letters in the mail sometimes," Moose said as he leaned back in the chair.

"Why were they hidden?" Becky asked, confused.

"Your grandfather didn't want reminders of him around. If he had found them, there would have been hell to pay. I loved your daddy and your mom. I'm sad that I missed out on so much of your lives, but thanks to your mom, I feel like I know you. And when we find your dad, I'm going to make up for lost time." Moose was very close to losing his composure, and it was clear how awful he felt about all of this.

"It's okay, Reginald," Jennifer said as she put her hand on his.

"If you are going to use my real name, can you at least call me Reggie?" he said, forcing a smile.

"You think Dad is alive?" Emory asked.

"Your dad was one of the toughest son-of-a-bitches that has ever walked this godforsaken shithole of a planet. Let me tell you this, son. You may not know it, but he is too goddamn stubborn to die. We will see him again. I can bet my life on it." Moose stood and walked over to the gun rack.

"This was your dad's shotgun. He loved this thing. Many a quail and duck fell by it." He handed the gun to Emory.

Emory inspected it. It was an old Remington 870 pump-action shotgun. The wood was polished, Moose must have taken good care of it.

"It nice," he said as he tried to hand it back to Moose.

"You hang on to that until we find your Dad. You can give it back to him. Careful, it's loaded." He gave Emory a wink.

"Thanks," was all Emory could say before the camp was filled with a woman's panicked screams.

CHAPTER 38

Marco drove the truck slowly in the middle of the road. He didn't use headlights, really bringing their progress to a crawl. Still beat walking, Kate thought as she snacked on a granola bar from Marco's pack.

The baby was asleep with his head on Kate's mother's shoulder. Kate's mother just watched out the window and every now and again let out a low sob. She was getting better, though. Kate hoped that after a full meal and a night's rest she would be closer to her old self.

Though she would never again be like the woman who raised her. Her mother had always been sweet and a bit naive about how the world really was. Now she would be permanently changed forever. They all would. Kate didn't feel sorry for herself, though. She felt sorry that her baby brother would have to grow up in this horrible new existence. They would re-build their lives without their father. They had no other choice.

Kate had always been a tough cookie. She was headstrong and very intelligent. In the running for valedictorian at her school. This was a blessing and a curse for her. Sometimes she wished that she were dumb. It was so easy for her to get wrapped up in her thoughts and block out the rest of the world. This is where she was now, so she didn't hear most of what Kenny said to her.

"I'm sorry, I didn't catch that," she replied, glad it was dark so he couldn't see her blush.

"I asked if you were okay. Pretty dumb question considering what you have just been through." Kenny ran his hand through his hair, avoiding eye contact.

"I'd be lying if I said yeah. I don't really know what I am other than lost and confused."

"Yeah, me too."

"Where are your parents at, Ken?"

"They were out of town at a medical convention. My dad is a doctor." He wished he hadn't brought up fathers.

"Oh, wow. I'm sure he is fine, then. Everybody needs a doctor."

"Yeah, that's what I told Marco."

"My dad was a professor. He taught American history," she said, eyes fading into the distance.

"I always loved history. It was one of my favorite classes," Kenny replied, unsure of what to say.

"He was good at it. Had a passion for it. We spent many nights talking about American politics of the past and present."

"What do you think will happen next? I mean, for the country."

"People will fight. Armies will rise. Hopefully the good guys win. Otherwise, we are in for some pretty bleak times," she said.

"Are these not bleak times? Seems pretty harsh out here now."

"Right now, it's just a cluster of people roaming around doing whatever they want. Imagine the same thing, but with a dictator chasing you too. Things can become much worse."

"What can we do about that, though? We are just a group of mostly teenagers?" Kenny said.

"We learn how to fight, and we pick the right side."

"I'm not much of a fighter. Throwing a few punches is one

thing. Shooting at someone I don't know is something I can't do."

"Then you can learn to be a medic. You can help people. You can help win the war."

"Seems like a rush to think we are at war. How do you know that?" Kenny asked, confused.

"Trust me. In a time like this. We are at war. Most likely with each other. If you can cover this, I'm going to lay back and take a little nap," she said, trying her best to get comfortable in to bed of the old truck.

Kenny sat back and thought about what she had just told him. She was smart, he could see that. If she said they were at war, then he believed her. It felt strange to him to talk about fighting. Maybe she was right. Maybe he could become a medic. He had another day before they were at the farm. Getting there was first priority. He didn't even really know what to expect about the farm. Part of him thought it was going to be great. The pessimistic side of him wondered if anyone was even there.

The old man slept for most of the trip to his son's house. Ronnie and Luke figured that it had been a good long while since he had a rest, so they let the boy sit up front and took turns driving. The boy had told them that his name was Liam and that his grandpa was Jimmy. That was when they realized that, in all that confusion, they had not even asked their names before giving them a ride.

The boy was ten. They learned a lot about him and his grandfather. After he was comfortable around them, he was a chatter box, but Ronnie didn't mind. Having the boy around lifted his foul mood and made him remember why he did this. It was not about the fighting. It was about keeping people like Liam safe. He gave the boy his helmet and sunglasses and told him to keep watch while he rested in the back. He lay down and eventually fell asleep.

"Yo, wake up. We are about there," he said as he slapped Ronnie's boot, stirring him awake.

Ronnie sat up and leaned against his rifle, looking out the window. They were on an old dirt road heading for a farmhouse. They passed cattle and sheep as they made their way down the lane. Pulling to a stop, they sat around for a second looking for any signs of life. They told Liam to stay in the car and got out and made their way to the house. Nothing was stirring. On the front porch sat two old hound dogs, not even bothering to lift their heads as they made their way to the door.

Ronnie opened the screen door, but before he could raise his hand to knock, the door opened, and a double-barreled shotgun pointed at his face. He took a step back and raised his hands. Looking out the corner of his eye, a man with an old lever-action rifle was pointing his gun, keeping Luke from reacting.

"You guys are on private property. We will not be going to any camp," the man said as he slowly made his way up to them. "Get in your vehicle and leave. We don't want to hurt nobody, but we will defend ourselves," said a woman, revealing herself as the bearer of the shotgun.

"MOM. DAD," Liam said, getting out of the truck and running up on the porch.

They both dropped their weapons at the sign of the boy and ran up and wrapped him in an embrace. Two more children appeared in the doorway and ran to join the family hug. After a long while, the man stood and walked over to Ronnie and Luke.

"Is my dad dead?" he asked with a tremble in his voice.

"Hell no. That old badger is sleeping in the back of our truck," Luke said with a smile.

"Sounds like him. I don't know how I can repay you for bringing them home."

"How you set up on food?"

"Okay, I guess. Not great, but we will manage." He ran his hands through his hair.

"Come with us to the truck," Ronnie said.

"Um, sure."

They walked to the truck, and Luke opened the back. The old man was still sound asleep, using a few MREs as pillows. Ronnie and Luke pulled out all the food and water that remained in the back, save what they needed for themselves to finish the mission. The man was confused as he looked at the supplies.

"You take these things for your family. Next time we come out this way, we will try to bring more," Luke said, patting the man on the shoulder.

"Thank you," the man said in disbelief.

"How are you on weapons? You got anything better than them relics you pulled on us?" Ronnie asked.

"No, sir, this is what we got, and not many shells at that," the man replied.

Ronnie looked at Luke. Luke silently nodded, and Ronnie reached in and pulled out the weapons that were still intact from their run in with the bandits. One SKS rifle and one shotgun were still intact. In the waistband of one of the bandits they had found a cheap nine-millimeter, and he threw that on the pile. Their truck had been outfitted with a rack in the back that held six M4 military assault rifles and six Beretta M9 pistols. Leaving a backup for both of them, he pulled out four rifles and four pistols and put them on the pile.

The man's eyes went wide at the sight. They also had six ammo cans with them. Three cans of 9mm and three cans of .223. Each of the cans held a thousand rounds of ammo. He left them a can of each and pulled out the other cans and set them on the ground. Next, opening a box, he pulled out a pile of magazines for each of the rifles and pistols.

"I don't even know how to use a rifle like that, but thank you. Don't you need them?"

"We have enough. Besides, we are going to Texas for a while, and we can get more. These are extras anyways, and we have a shit load at the camp. Your pop will know how to use them and can teach you. You need to protect those youngins, and these are going to help," Ronnie said as he stretched in the sunlight.

"God bless you," the man said, a tear rolling down his cheek.

"We will do anything we can to help. We will check on you all next time we are back around. I would suggest next time a Hummer rolls up and it's not military, you open fire on them. You don't want those kids in a camp," Luke said as he made his way back to the driver-side door.

"Is there anything that I can do for you?" the man pleaded.

"Yeah, wake your daddy up. It's never a good idea to wake up a sleeping Marine," Ronnie said with a smile.

Emory and Moose burst out of the cabin toward the sound of the screams, now attempting to be muffled. In the dark, it was hard to see, and they couldn't pinpoint the direction. Emory's heart froze when he thought of Margot. He hoped that those screams were not coming from her. Moose made his way to the front and cupped his hand to his ear.

"You three ladies get Eugene and go in the cabin with Margot. If anybody who isn't me comes in, shoot them. Take the safety off that gun, boy. I'm pretty sure these animals just crossed a line," he said as he racked a round into the big rifle that he was carrying.

They ran toward the cabin that Eugene was sleeping in, and Moose took a step toward the water. Emory really hoped that Margot had woken up and put clothes on before they went rushing in there. Debbie was watching over Eugene as he slept. Moose waited to see them collect the boy and the old woman and secure themselves in the cabin.

"Pretty sure it's coming from down here," Moose said, pointing to the water.

They crept toward the sound. Moving closer and closer, the noise became louder and louder. As they walked, their eyes adjusted to the darkness. They could make out the shapes of two people. They were both on the ground, one on top of the other. When Emory crept closer, Dan came into his line of sight. He was on top of the girl that had lead Moose to finding them. They both knew what was going on. What happened next was something that Emory wasn't ready for.

Moose charged the little man and picked him up by the neck with one hand. The man hadn't seen it coming and let out a scream of shock. Moose threw him against a tree, and the man bounced off with a thud. He stood on shaky legs, and blood poured out of a wound that had opened up on his forehead. Dazed and confused, the man pulled out his pistol and tried to raise it.

Moose slapped it out of his hand like he was scolding a small child. The gun went off, breaking the silence of the night. Moose landed a solid blow to the man's nose, and he fell to the ground. Moose straddled the man and wrapped his giant hands around his neck. The man clawed at his grip, but he didn't let up. The man shook hard, and Moose pressed on. The girl, by this point, was sitting with her back against the tree, her knees pulled up to her chin.

Out of the corner of Emory's eye, one of the men who had been with Moose on patrol was stepping up to the scene with his gun raised, pointing at the back of Moose's head. Without thinking or hesitation, Emory pulled the trigger. Two things happened. Having never shot a shotgun before, the force took Emory by surprise, and he dropped the weapon. The other was the impact of the 00 buckshot ripping into the man. It took him completely off his feet in a cascade of blood and gore as he spun to the ground. Emory stood there in shock, watching the man take his final breaths.

The roar of the shotgun had snapped the girl out of her catatonic state. She got to her feet and ran into the woods. Emory watched as she disappeared into the blackness of the night. That was the last thing he saw before the world went to black and the rifle butt impacted on the back of his head.

CHAPTER 39

Ronnie and Luke crept through the woods with Lola behind them. They had parked the truck about two clicks back and decided to take the rest of the journey on foot. They moved slowly, not seeing anybody. Twice they had to stop to avoid setting off homemade claymores that had been set up in the woods. This was not their first time around improvised explosives, but the threat had slowed them down substantially.

When they heard a shot from a shotgun explode in the night air, Ronnie stood straight up, ready to bolt toward it. Luke grabbed him by the arm and pointed to the ground, kicking the leaves off a dug-out spike trap in the ground. He didn't say a word, but in his eyes, they needed to keep moving slow. The dog on their heels stuck close, like she knew the score and was only walking where they did.

Ronnie feared what they were going to find but kept moving forward. How stupid had he been to let them come here? If anything happened to them, he would blame himself for the rest of his life. They were getting close, and he could just make out the outline of the camp. Muffled voices broke the silence of the night. The outlines of figures moving around danced in the shadows. He couldn't tell what was going on, but something felt off as they moved in. Something in his gut was telling him that the situation was not a good one.

Emory woke with his head throbbing. Taking a minute to collect his surroundings, he looked at was going on around him. He tried to lift his hand to touch his throbbing head but couldn't. Looking down, he was duct-taped onto an old wooden chair. He was in front of the cabin that held his family. Looking to his side, a half-awake Moose was bound to a chair in a similar fashion. His face was swollen and bruised from taking a beating.

"Welcome back," Tony said as he stepped up and slapped Emory as hard as he could across the face, setting his head on fire again. Looking to his side, David was holding a shotgun on him.

"Yeah, I'm still alive, asshole," Dan said, seeing the surprise in his eyes.

"Not for long," Moose said, regaining his senses.

"I'm the one holding the gun, big man," Dan said, giving Moose the finger.

"You will both burn for this," Moose said, seeing the third man standing next to him.

"Shut up," the man said as he stood impatiently with his rifle slung.

"Enough. Let's get on with this," Tony said as he walked over to a position in front of the cabin.

"Let them go," Emily said as she stepped out to negotiate with Tony.

"Sorry. I'm afraid I can't do that." Tony took a seat in a chair in front of Emory and Moose.

"Yeah, you can. We will take Moose's truck and leave this place. You will never see us again," Emily pleaded with the man.

"They both broke the rules. Hell, your brother here killed one of us tonight."

"Rape is against the rules too," Moose spat with bile and contempt.

"I didn't do nothing," Dan snickered.

"You tried," Moose said as he spat blood out of his mouth.

"This is a long time coming. I would be lying if I said I didn't enjoy what happens next," Tony whispered in Moose's ear.

"Eat it, you pussy," Moose said as he turned his head and glared at Tony's face.

"I'm going to wash any trace of your brother's family off the face of this earth. Best part is you are going to watch me do it. I will save you for last," he whispered again.

"Why do all of you assholes always have the same plan?" Emory grunted, pulling at the straps of duct tape confining him.

"Here is the deal I will make you. All of you come out with your hands in the air and your weapons on the ground. I will let you take his truck and leave. Simple as that," Tony said in a sickly-sweet voice.

"Don't do it, Em..." Moose commanded as Tony silenced him with a swift punch to thc mouth.

This blow sent Moose over the edge. Emory thought he had seen the man's rage before. He hadn't seen anything yet. He watched as the sweet man from the cabin turned into an animal. He stood up in the rickety old chair and jumped on his back, sending the chair shattering in a million splinters. Before anyone could react, he rolled to his left, into the legs of the man who was supposed to be guarding him, toppling him to the ground.

Dan raised the gun and pointed it at Moose. With all his force, Emory rocketed himself in the chair, making impact with Dan, who swung the gun wildly away from Moose, setting the gun off in the air. At this point, Emory toppled over face-first into the ground. Turning his head, his uncle picked up a rock and smash it into the struggling man's head, making his body limp.

Emory about had a heart attack when the guns opened

up from the cabin on Dan. The man had lifted his gun at Moose again. Before he could pull the trigger, he was impacted by Becky, Margot, Jennifer and Emily all at once. He danced around like a rag doll until falling into a bloody heap on the ground. The shotgun miraculously was not hit. Emory stared at it. He took it as a sign that maybe his dad was still alive and, like the gun, hard to hit.

Tony stood with his hands held high in the air. Moose stood and silently walked over to him.

"Let me leave, and you will never see me again," Tony pleaded with him.

Moose didn't respond. He just stood looked at Tony with fire burning in his eyes. With one hard blow, he punched the man with every ounce of force that he carried in his big body. The blow crushed the man's windpipe, and he fell to the ground, grasping at his neck. Moose pulled back his boot and kicked him with as much force as he could muster, sending the man into the next life.

Margot rushed out and pulled her knife from her belt, cutting Emory free from the chair.

"Are you okay?" she asked as she helped him to his feet.

"Yeah, I think so," he said, rubbing his pounding head.

"Thank God," she said, wrapping him in a tight embrace.

"We aren't alone," Moose said, pointing to the two men breaking the tree line with rifles raised.

"Holy shit, it's Ronnie," Emily screamed as she ran up and gave him a hug.

"Uh, hi, Em. We are here to, uh, rescue you?" he said, looking over at the bodies on the ground.

"LOLA," Margot said as the dog ran up and crashed into her and Emory.

"How?" Emory asked, confused as could be.

"Let's get this mess cleaned up and I can explain everything."

◆ ◆ ◆

After they threw the bodies in the woods, they all had gathered in the big cabin across from the small ones. Emory helped Moose, who was still on shaky feet from the beating that he had endured. He told Emory that after he heard the shotgun blast, he had turned just in time to see Tony hit him in the back of the head and he release David. At gunpoint, they had taken turns pounding on him until he lost the will to struggle against them.

When they entered the cabin, Emory took a look around. Photos of Moose and who he assumed was his grandfather lined the walls. He figured this was his grandfather's cabin, and it made sense. The cabin was wired with power from solar chargers that were located outside. Unlike the other cabins, this one was furnished lavishly. They walked into a room that had enough couches to seat the big group. He figured this was where they had held meetings previously. They all sat down, with even Lola finding a seat. They all took a second to lavish in the luxury of sitting on something that was not hard.

Emily was the first to speak. "I thought you were dead, Ronnie."

"Would have been. Except I ran into an old friend," he said, pointing to Luke.

"Hi, I'm Luke. Ronnie and I served together in Afghanistan."

"What are the chances of that?" Becky asked, dumbfounded.

"Slim. I assumed that my sister was looking out for me," Ronnie replied.

"I watched Lola get shot and not have the strength to get up. How is she alive?" Margot asked Ronnie.

"She is tough as hell, for starters. She was in bad shape. We showed up right after you left. I found her and forced the medic to take care of her. She still isn't one hundred percent yet."

"Doc was real happy about it too." Luke laughed.

"You were at that farm?" Emily asked, confused.

"Yeah, that bastard who was trying to kill you was a high value target for the joint chiefs. His dumb ass stole a government truck that was low jacked with a satellite feed. Followed him there."

"Wow," Emily said.

"Yeah, Charger's back at the base. I want to thank you for helping the kids out, ladies," Ronnie said, looking at Jennifer and Debbie.

"It was the right thing to do. No thanks required. Plus, I got to meet this little rascal," Debbie said as she rubbed Eugene's head.

"Stop it," Eugene said as he squirmed, giggling.

"The joint chiefs? Are they in charge?" Jennifer asked, confused.

"Sort of. It's a long story," Luke replied.

Luke explained the state of the country. Everyone listened in shock and horror as he told them about the division of the country and the path leading to a civil war.

"What's that mean for us?" Jennifer responded after digesting the information.

"Well, Luke and I are taking the prisoner to Texas. There is a spot for everyone in this room at the camp. Luke made sure of that. It's safe there. As safe as anywhere can be at this point."

"How long will it take to drive to Texas? What are the chances of us making there in one piece?" Moose asked, speaking for the first time.

"We are going by helicopter. The Air Force is sending two Blackhawks with Apache support to pick us up tomorrow," Luke answered.

"COOL," Eugene said excitedly.

"Very cool. We need to leave this place soon," Luke said, smiling at the boy.

"Moose, there is something I wanted to talk to you about," Ronnie said.

"Go for it."

"How much food, water, medicine and guns are here?"

"A metric shit ton. Why?"

"If you are going to roll with us, how would you feel about donating that stuff to a family in need? We met some fine folks on our way down here."

"Fine with me. We have an underground storehouse located right under our feet here. I don't know how much help I will be loading it in my current state, but you can take it all."

"Thanks, that's great."

"Speaking of your current state, let's go take a look at you," Jennifer said, standing.

"I'm fine," Moose argued.

"Looks like it. Now, come on, Reggie, I won't ask again," she said, snapping her fingers and pointing to the door.

"I think you better do what she says," Becky said, laughing.

"I think you are right. The door to the storage is under this rug," he said, standing and walking to the door like a scolded puppy.

◆ ◆ ◆

What they found in the storage room blew Emory's mind. It was more like a warehouse than a room. It stretched a long way and was more than they could move in a couple hours. There was row after row of freeze-dried food. Every kind that he could imagine. The next few rows contained hundreds if not thousands of cases of bottled water. There were whole sections containing any medication that one could think of, from Advil to antibiotics. The weapons were ridiculous, and way more than their small group could utilize. They even found grenades and belt-fed machine guns. Then they found the explosives. Enough to level a small town. From the look on Ronnie and Luke's faces, Emory imagined they didn't want to breath near it, let alone try to move it.

"What should we load the trucks with?" Becky asked as she skimmed the rows.

"Food, water and medicine first. As many guns and bullets as we can fit in last," Luke ordered.

"I saw a trailer up there behind the cabins with a huge diesel tank on it behind the cabins. We are going to take that too." Ronnie said to Luke, who nodded.

They formed a line up the stairs and out the front door of the house. Everyone helped, even little Eugene. Ronnie and Luke backed the trucks up to the cabin and took positions to load the beds. They found four trucks in total: the three that they had seen when they were rescued earlier, and they found an old deuce and a half in a spot hidden in the woods. Their plan was to fit as much as they could in the next two hours, and with the line they moved quickly. They took every scrap of food, water and medicine from the house. They were packed to the gills with supplies. They fit most of the weapons and ammo into the back of the deuce and a half.

The plan was for them to be a five-car caravan on the way back, with Luke manning the Hummer and Jennifer, Becky and Emily taking a truck each. Ronnie would drive the deuce and a half. Luke didn't like leaving the explosives for someone to find. Ronnie told him that they could destroy them, but he liked that plan even less. Ronnie said he read about Viet Cong in the Vietnam War putting rubber bands around live grenades and dropping them in GI gas tanks. The gas ate away at the rubber, and when the bands failed, the explosive detonated. It took a lot of convincing, but Luke finally agreed.

After getting with Moose on the locations off all the homemade claymores, Ronnie and Luke got to work. They couldn't in good conscience leave them lying around for some innocent person to stumble into. They moved quickly and retrieved them in less than an hour. After defusing the bombs, they stacked them with the others in storehouse. Standing back, Ronnie looked at the pile of explosives, and a shiver ran through him. At least these men couldn't hurt anyone else, he thought as he carried the five-gallon bucket of fuel down the steps.

Moose and Jennifer entered his cabin, and she walked over and lit the old lamp. The low glow illuminated the room. Moose walked to the bed and lay down, letting out an exalted groan as he lay his head on the pillow.

"I feel like hell," he declared.

"You look like hell," Jennifer retorted.

"Thanks. I know I've always been an ugly fella." He chuckled.

"I didn't say that. Honestly, I want to know what's under all that hair," she said with a smile.

"Nothing good." He laughed.

"Hopefully I can be the judge of that on my own one day," she said with a wink.

"Oh," Moose said, taken aback.

They laughed and joked as Jennifer cleaned his face and bandaged the wounds. She ordered him to try to get some rest. His body must have been feeling drained, because within ten minutes he was out. His snores were loud, probably from the damage he took to his nose.

Jennifer sat in the chair at the desk and looked for something to occupy her time while she let the big man sleep. A small stack of books in the corner caught her eye and she decided to investigate. Pulling the stack close, she examined the titles. The books took her by surprise: all classic pieces of literature. She had expected to find books on guns and history, but his small collection was devoid of that. She turned, puzzled at the complexities of the man. Most people would think he was a big Neanderthal by the way he looked. But there was more to him, and she could see that even if others couldn't.

On the back corner of the desk was a small leather-bound notebook. She shouldn't open it, as it was probably personal, but temptation proved to be too much. Opening it, her jaw dropped slightly. Where she had expected to find a journal or notes about the place, she found poems. Handwritten poems that covered a variety of subjects. But most of all, what surprised her was how good they were. She turned as Moose was sitting up in the bed, half-awake.

"Sometimes writing my emotions is easier for me than speaking them," the man said in a soft voice.

"I understand. Sometimes I can come across as stern. It's how I protect myself," she replied in an equally soft tone.

Before they could exchange any more words, there was a light knock on the door. Jennifer opened it, and Ronnie made his way inside. He walked over to the empty chair and sat across from Moose.

"Them are some damn fine kids your brother and my sister made out there," Ronnie said, leaning back in the chair.

"That's for sure. Hey, man, I never got to tell you how sorry I was for what happened to her. She was a good woman. Talking to her was one of the few things that kept me sane in this freak show," Moose said sadly.

"She damn sure was. I miss her every day, but I see her in those kids. I came here to ask you two things, Moose."

"Okay, go for it."

"Number one is have you ever taken a man's life before today?"

"No."

"How are you handling that?"

"I'm not really sure the full weight of it has hit me yet."

"It will. Trust me. I have taken more souls off this planet than I care to think about. At the end of the day, you have to trust the fact that those who did evil got what they deserved."

"I guess. I can't get their faces out of my head."

"You never will. After a while, they will fade, but they will always be there, haunting your dreams. Maybe that's a good thing. I tell myself the day it doesn't weigh heavy on me is the day I have lost myself for good."

"Makes sense."

"The second thing I wanted to ask you was..."

"If you can blow up the camp?"

"Uh, well, yeah."

"I don't want any innocent people to get hurt either. So yeah, blow this shithole to pieces. I'm ready to start a new chapter in my life. Away from this place and all of the bad memories it holds for me."

"Good. I was really hoping you would say yes."

"I would be a fool not to."

"Why don't you get some stuff together, and we will move on in about an hour."

"No problem."

"Thanks, Moose." Ronnie stood and shook the man's hand.

Ronnie left, and Jennifer stood next to the man on the bed. Sensitive, compassionate, fierce and not afraid to show his emotions. She had not had any feelings toward a man since her Paul had died. She felt like she was betraying him now with the emotions that were creeping around inside of her. She was a cautious person, and she was going to move slowly, but she wasn't sure that she wanted to explore these feelings.

"I can pack your bag for you," she offered gently.

"It's okay. I can do it," he said stiffly, getting off the bed and retrieving an old army duffle bag from the footlocker.

She watched as he went to the wardrobe and carefully packed the clothes he was going to take with him. They were all normal. No more camo, it seemed. He laid an outfit on the bed and walked over to the gun rack. They had already put most of the guns from the rack on the truck. He had picked three handguns and the big rifle to keep. Everything else was donated. He laid the rifle and one of the pistols on the bed. He wrapped the other two up in tee shirts and packed into his rucksack. Last he walked over to the footlocker to pull out a holster for the pistol. He placed a large sheathed knife and a large folding knife on the bed.

"If you would excuse me, ma'am, I need to change."

"Okay, sorry. I didn't mean to linger," she said as she made her way to the door.

"It's okay. To tell you the truth, I can't remember such

good company," he said, giving her a wink.

"I enjoyed myself too," she said with a slight blush as she hurried out the door.

Standing in front of the cabin, she watched as people moved all around her. It was amazing to her. These new people in her life. They felt like a team. More than a team, she thought. Family. She pulled up one of the chairs outside the cabin and took a seat. After a few minutes, Moose crashed out of the room. He was dressed in jeans and a black flannel shirt. Seeing him out of the camo made him a bit less scary looking. His long, matted hair was pulled behind him, and he wore a set of thick black glasses. With an outfit change, he had gone from wild woods man to a hipster who could blend into any Seattle coffee shop. Seeing her, he set his bag down and took a seat next to her.

"What are you doing?" he asked as he pulled out a cigar and lit it.

"Do I know you?" she said, looking him up and down.

"Yeah, I know. I'm ready to leave all of this behind and start a new life. If I ever have to put on a uniform again, it will be only too soon," he said as he took a puff off the cigar.

"That's a bad habit, you know," she said, scolding him.

"I know. You never answered what you were doing out here."

"Just taking it all in," she said as she watched the activity fluttering about her.

"I know what you mean. Having these kids in my life is something I'm really looking forward to. Even though I was surrounded by people up here, I was lonely. Really lonely. Nobody here understood me." He cast his eyes to the ground.

"You are not alone anymore," she said, gently placing her hand on his.

CHAPTER 41

They all loaded into the fleet of vehicles. The Hummer was in the lead. It was followed by the three small trucks, with the deuce and a half in the back. Luke was in the Humvee. Becky and Emily were in the next truck. They were followed by Jennifer, Eugene and Debbie. Moose and Emory were the last small truck. Margot and Ronnie were the caboose of the convoy with the deuce and half and the diesel trailer. All the engines were running, and they were just waiting on Ronnie to come back out before putting the grenade in the diesel.

They watched as Ronnie sprinted out of the house. He was frantically waving his arms for them to move. Moose laughed as he put the truck into gear and started to move. Ronnie was in a full sprint and practically lunged into the truck. Emory and Moose rolled down the road silently, both of them holding their breath, waiting for an explosion.

"How many explosives were down there?" Emory asked, looking at his uncle.

"Enough that when that it goes off, people all around the mountain will hear it." He chuckled to himself.

"It's a shame that we couldn't help the girl who ran into the woods. What was her name?"

"Don't know; she never gave it to me. People up here are hard, but they are good folks. Hopefully she finds someone and they take her in," Moose said, his eyes on the road.

The boom was so loud that it shook the windows on the old truck. Moose came to a stop, as did all the other vehicles. Everyone got out and looked at the mushroom cloud that was billowing up into the air. Ronnie looked at Luke and shook his head.

"Alright everybody, back in. Let's get this show on the road," Luke commanded from the front of the convoy.

Getting back in, they made their way down the road. Moose peppered Emory with questions like he had with Emily. They were making good time. It didn't seem like anyone wanted to mess with a military-looking convoy. Emory looked out the window and a small family was walking down the road. They looked exhausted. A husband and wife pulled two small children in a wagon behind them. The kids looked tired. Their faces were covered in what appeared to be soot from a fire. The convoy stopped, and Luke and Ronnie got out and walked to the family.

"We don't want any trouble, sir," the woman said fearfully, stepping between the wagon and the two men.

"Ma'am, we are here to help," Ronnie said as he jogged over to the deuce and half.

"We don't want to go to no god damn camp," the man said, looking Luke in the eyes.

"We are not going to make you go anywhere," Luke replied.

Ronnie jogged back with some water and a few MREs. He opened the water bottles and handed one to each of them. They chugged them down so fast it made Ronnie wonder when the last time they had something to drink was. Next, he pulled out two candy bars and handed them to the two little boys in the wagon. Their faces lit up, and they ripped into the packages like wild animals.

"Thank you," the couple said in unison.

"We are going to a place with good folks. You would be safe there if they let you stay. I think they will," Ronnie said, taking a sip of his own water.

"No offense, but I don't think we can trust government people right now," the man said with cold eyes.

"Hold on," Ronnie said as he ran back to the truck.

Pulling out two assault rifles, he ran back over to them. The man's hands curled into fists, ready for a fight. He had a wild look in his eyes.

"Easy there. Here, take these." Ronnie handed the guns to the very surprised couple.

"Uh, why?" the man said, looking at the guns in his hands.

"I want to prove we don't want to hurt you. Sir, the United States military are the good guys in all of this. I know it's a hard pill to swallow, but nobody who wanted to control you would give you an AK47." He smiled.

"I guess that's true," the man said as he removed the magazine and checked to make sure it was loaded.

"Plus, you can watch out the back of the deuce. Another pair of eyes never hurts," Luke added.

The man looked at them for a moment. Then he decided to trust them. They walked to the back of the truck, and he helped his sons up into the back. After he helped his wife in, he picked up the wagon, and they loaded it in. He turned back to the two men.

"Thank you. We would have died out here."

"In times like these, we have to look out for each other. That's what America is about, man. Somewhere we lost sight of that. Now it's time to relearn," Ronnie said, shaking the man's hand and helping him climb into the truck.

They picked up one other family on their journey back to the farm. This time it was a mother and two teenage girls. They had been apprehensive to believe that they were there to help. When Ronnie had approached them, the mother had pulled out a small .38 revolver. Ronnie put his hands in the air after putting his weapons on the ground. He introduced her to the other family in the back of the truck. Eventually, after some persuading, she agreed to join them. Ronnie telling her she could keep her weapon helped.

The rest of the journey was quiet. For the most part, they didn't see anybody else. They passed a few random people on the road, but all they seemed interested in was getting out of the way. The roads on the mountain were winding and had some sharp ninety-degree turns, so it was a slow process.

Moose had run out of questions, it seemed. He and Emory were both content to ride in silence. Emory stared out the window, reflecting on what had happened at the militia camp. He had lost his virginity and killed a man within an hour of each other. Gone from cloud nine to that familiar sinking, sick feeling in his stomach. He was learning that in this new world, nothing was certain. He hoped Margot was okay. They hadn't had much time to talk after they had made love.

They finally started to pull down the long dirt road to the farm. Nobody was outside, and this put Emory on edge. Luke pulled the convoy to a stop and stepped out of the vehicle. One by one, the family popped out of where they were hiding. Emory spotted three adults and three children walking up to Luke.

"Hello again," Luke said with a smile and a wave.

"Hello. I realized last time that we were so shocked by you bringing Dad and Liam home, I never even told you our names. I'm Bobby, and this is Lisa. The other two children are Reba and Steven." He chuckled.

"Well, it's officially a pleasure to meet all of you again," Ronnie said, jogging up to the group.

"We were worried about you all. Heard a massive blast," Jimmy said, walking up and shaking the men's hands.

"Had some ugliness at the camp," Luke responded.

"You find your family?" Lisa asked.

"Yes. Thank you for asking," Ronnie responded.

"What brings you all back?" Bobby asked.

"There ain't nobody left at the camp. Brought you some supplies," Luke answered.

"Oh, I see. We will be appreciative of anything you would like to share with us," Jimmy said.

"Well, here's the thing. It's all for you," Luke answered to three blank stares.

"There are strings attached. We picked up two families on the way here. We want you to let them join you. There are plenty of supplies here for you and them to live off of for a long while," Ronnie explained.

"I don't know about letting strangers around our children," Lisa protested.

"They seem like good people. I told them I would try to persuade you to give them a two-week trial. They can help build this place up," Luke answered.

"After what these men have done for this family, I think we owe it to them to pay it forward and at least give it a shot," Bobby interjected.

They introduced the two families to Jimmy's family. The small boys ran off, playing with Bobby and Lisa's kids. Even Eugene got in on the action. Bobby suggested that they store all the food and water in the barn. The convoy pulled up to the large old barn, and with everybody joining in, they had it unloaded in forty-five minutes. It was a mess, but Lisa insisted that they could organize it later.

Next, they formed a line and passed all the guns, bullets and medicine into the home. Luke said that the medicine should be stored in the basement for the best consistent temperature so that it would last longer.

It was a good afternoon. Spirits were high. People joked and laughed. Moose and Jennifer mixed up pitcher after pitcher of Kool-Aid, sending the kids into a sugar-induced frenzy. Eventually it was time to go, to everybody's dismay. Eugene protested adamantly about staying the night while they loaded him up into the deuce and a half. The families gathered around them as everyone else made their way outside.

"Thanks for everything. We will never be able to repay you for the kindness you have shown us here today," Bobby said, walking up and shaking Ronnie and Luke's hands.

"It's the right thing to do," Luke said with a smile, winking at the kids still bouncing around.

"One last thing," Ronnie said, walking up and pulling a key from his pocket and handing it to Jimmy.

"We are all taking the deuce back. The rest of the trucks and the Hummer are yours to keep. We filled up the deuce out of the diesel tank, but we are leaving the rest with you," Ronnie explained while everyone stared at him in shock.

"Well, I don't really know what to say about this that can do it justice. Thank you," Jimmy said, looking at the keys in his hands in disbelief.

"That Hummer is special. It's armored. You get these people trained how to look out for each other. If some heavy crazy stuff goes down, pack the kids in that truck and take off. It should stop common rifle and pistol rounds," Luke said, slapping the old man on the back.

"Been a long time since I was a Marine," Jimmy responded, doubt in his voice.

"Marines are Marines for life. Now, do your duty, devil

dog, and hopefully we will see each other again," Ronnie said as he climbed up into the truck.

"Yes, sir," Jimmy said giving them a salute as they fired up the truck and made their way down the road.

CHAPTER 42

Emory sat in the back of the loud truck with his hand in Margot's. Emily gave him an accusatory smile, sitting across from him and raising an eyebrow. He wondered if she knew. How could she? Was she messing with him? Didn't matter much to him anyhow. Looking over at Margot, he smiled and leaned in close, brushing the hair from her ear.

"We never really got a chance to talk about what happened," he whispered in her ear.

"Not much to talk about. What we did was natural. It was right. I hope you feel it too."

"I do. I love you. Funny thing is, I don't cvcn know your last name," he said, looking into her eyes.

"Well, let's keep some mystery in this relationship, Mr. Ellison. I will tell you later," she whispered, giggling.

"Hey, that's not fair. You know mine. Are you really going to keep it a secret? Secrets aren't nice," he said, giving her a playful shove.

"Well, in that case, I will reveal my deepest, darkest one to you," she said, turning stone-faced and serious, causing Emory to worry.

"Yeah?" he said, afraid of what he was about to hear.

"I really miss that kitten shirt." She burst out laughing loudly enough to make everyone look at them.

Kenny's group had made the choice to drive through the day. They were close to Marco's family's farm, and they didn't want to spend another night in the woods. The drive was quiet. Nobody spoke. They saw no people moving around. They didn't even see much wildlife.

The group was weary and exhausted as they pulled up to the long dirt lane that lay off the road. Marco reached back and slapped Kenny to make sure he was awake. Kenny was too nervous to sleep, and he stood and leaned on the cab of the truck to see what they were walking into.

His eyes went wide with fear when he saw the row of trucks and military Humvee that were parked next to the barn. Marco slammed on the brakes, nearly sending Kenny spiraling off the top of the truck. The sudden jolt woke everybody else, and the baby started to wail.

Kenny jumped off the back of the truck and walked to the window. No one had seen their approach, and only a couple of people were milling around the front yard.

"You know them?" Kenny asked as he pulled the shotgun out of the back of the truck.

"Never seen 'em before."

"What do we do now?" Kenny asked, afraid to know the answer.

"Hell, I don't know, go and meet them," Marco said, annoyed at his homecoming.

"Is that our best option?"

"It's our only option. Unless you want to live out of this shit box."

"Good point."

"Kate, me and Kenny are going to walk up there and see what's going on. You get in the driver's seat. If something goes down, you get your family and get gone. Don't worry about us,"

Marco explained.

"I'm not going to leave you behind," Kate said as she hopped down and made her way to the driver's side.

"Take a good look at that baby. That sweet little boy is worth more than me and Kenny combined. If it goes sideways, you need to get him to safety. Understand?" Marco said in a firm tone.

"I agree with Marco. Ain't nothing more important than you guys' safety," Kenny said as he put on his pack.

"Thank you," Kate's mom muttered.

She looked up at the boys just in time to see a man emerge from the woods. The man was old and holding a rifle on the group. Seeing the fear in his eyes, Kenny and Marco both turned at once. The man looked at them and dropped his rifle, which swayed at his side.

"Grandpa?" Marco asked, confused.

"My god, boy, it is good to see your face. Your parents have been worried sick about you."

Marco walked up and embraced his grandfather. Both of their eyes were misty, but no tears fell. The two stayed like that for a long while. It made Kenny miss his parents. He prayed that wherever they were, they were safe.

"Grandpa, let me introduce you to my little band of misfits here. The other fella is Kenny."

"Pleasure to meet you, sir," Kenny said, shaking the man's hand.

"This is Kate and her mother and baby brother."

"Pleasure is all mine, miss," the old man said, waving to the group.

"Grandpa, I have about a million questions about what went on while I was gone."

"Well, I will try my best to answer them."

"First off, is everyone okay?"

"For the most part, all in one piece. Maybe some emotional scars."

"Thank god. Second: How the hell are you here, and what the hell happened to your face?"

"Ran into some unsavory men on the way here. Caught a beating. Thank god that was all it was. Some Marines came through and saved the day. Got a ride back with them. Good men."

"Is that why the Hummer is here? What the hell were they doing way out here in the sticks?"

"They left it for us. With about enough supplies to make your head spin. They saved all our lives. They were out here looking for one of the men's families up the mountain in some crazy survivalist camp."

This set off alarm bells in Kenny's head. It couldn't be them. What would be the chances of that?

"Did they find his family?" Kenny said, butting his way into the conversation.

"Yeah, sure did. Met them when they came back through."

"Was there a boy named Emory in the group?"

"Yeah, there was."

"With a sister named Emily and a boy named Eugene?"

"Yeah, how do you know that?"

"Emory is my best friend," Kenny said in shock.

"Well, that hurts. I thought we did some bonding on this trip," Marco said, laughing.

"I can't believe that we missed them," Kenny said, shaking his head.

"They are with the military now, going to Texas."

"Texas?"

"It's too much to explain here in one sitting. Let's go the house and introduce you to everyone. Marco, be ready; they may explode with happiness," the old man said with a chuckle.

"One last thing. Are they coming back?" Kenny asked hopefully.

"They said they would come back through at some point. Now, come on, let's get rolling. I'm going to catch a ride in the back of your truck," the old man said, hopping into the bed.

With that, they rolled toward the house. Kenny was too lost in thought to notice the people pouring out of the house at their arrival. Maybe this was a bigger part of the universe's plan. Maybe he was meant to get out of the car on that day. Maybe it was so he could meet Marco and help save Kate and her family. Still, he looked forward to the day when he could see the Ellison family again. For now, he would help make this place work. He was lucky that he had found a place where he felt like he belonged.

CHAPTER 43

After a long and bumpy ride, they eventually found their way back to the small camp that the Marines were calling home. They were met with raised and cautious rifles at the sight of the unfamiliar vehicle. After Ronnie and Luke stepped out, they were met with a chorus of hoots and hollers. They had barely made it. The chopper was due to land in the hour. After they all piled out of the truck, they made their way to the improvised chow tent. They were met with a round of MREs, which made everybody groan. They sat around the table, eating the pre-packaged food and enjoying each other's company. They even opened up a package for Lola. The dog sat at Margot's feet, enjoying the spoils of the camp.

"Uncle Ronnie, I have a question for you." Emily spoke.

"Shoot."

"Do you think when we get to Texas, we can find a preacher to marry Becky and me?" she asked cautiously.

"Baby girl, I will find a preacher for you even if he has to deliver the ceremony at gunpoint." They all laughed.

"Do you really think it's safe there?" Moose asked, wiping food debris from his beard.

"Yes, I do," Ronnie answered.

"Good. Because after we take the children and these fine ladies there, I'm coming back," Moose answered.

"Why would you do something like that?" Jennifer said, looking up out of concern.

"Two reasons, really. One: I'm not going to rest until I find my brother."

"We don't even know if he is alive or where he is," Ronnie interjected.

"He is alive. I know he is. I can feel it, and I will find him," Moose said.

"What is the other reason?" Emory said, his interest piqued.

"Well, I don't really know how to say it. I'm not the kind of man who can sit back with his feet kicked up when all this suffering is going on. I want to help people. Even if it does put me in the face of danger," he said, looking at Ronnie.

"I know the feeling. I think that after they secure the prize, we will be sent back here to our unit. I have no problem with you hitching a ride," Ronnie said as he crumpled the wrappers from his meal and tossed them in the trash can.

Before anybody else could speak, the whooshing blade of a helicopter cut in. Looking up, they watched as two of the biggest helicopters Emory had ever seen landed in the field beside the camp. They cut their engines, and the crews hopped out with their weapons, securing the area. Ronnie and Luke got up and walked toward them. After speaking with them for a moment, they watched as giant relief skids were pushed out of the cargo areas into the grass.

They got up and made their way to the chopper. They all looked over what was delivered. It was skid after skid of food, water and medicine. After the choppers were emptied, Ronnie split them into two groups. Becky, Emily, Eugene, Debbie and Luke got into one chopper. Margot, Emory, Moose and Jennifer got in the other. Ronnie told them he would be back in a minute.

Emory looked around the inside of the helicopter, and they all found seats. It was apparent that this machine was built for efficiency and not comfort. The seats didn't have any cusions and the walls were metal and lined in gear. It was going to be a long ride to Texas. Lola was curled up on the floor by Margot's feet. He took notice as the big dog put back her ears and let out a low grumble.

Ronnie made his way back into the chopper, pushing a man with an orange jumpsuit on. He had a hood over his face. His hands and feet were shackled together, and he clanked as he shuffled. Ronnie took him to a seat far away from the rest of them, pulled out more cuffs and cuffed him to the side. Then he removed the man's hood. It was the man who had tried to kill them at the farm. The man whose men had shot Becky. The anger swelled in him for a moment as he started to get up. Margot put her hand on his and shook her head.

"Ronnie has this under control," she whispered to him.

They watched as the man sat there, looking like something out of a horror movie. His face had been cut badly and poorly stitched together. There was no effort in the medical care, just enough to get the job done. The man sat there with his eyes affixed to Ronnie. The two were having a staring match that Emory was happy he wasn't a part of.

"You talk and I'm gonna make you wish that you didn't. You try to get away, I'm going to hurt you so bad that you won't try twice. You understand me?" Ronnie said, his words cold as ice.

"Yes, sir," the man said with all the contempt he could muster.

"Good," Ronnie said as he turned away from the man.

"Just one thing there, old pal. When I said I was going to burn everything you loved, I just wanted you to know I meant it," he said calmly, looking at everyone in the helicopter. "Even the dog." He spat in Ronnie's direction.

"I said no talking," Ronnie said as he delivered a vicious blow to the side of the man's head, rendering him unconscious.

Ronnie walked over and sat in his seat. The pilot poked his head in and told them it was time. They all put on their seat belts, and the chopper lifted off the ground. Looking out the window, Emory was struck with a fear of the unknown. Leaving behind his town was something he had wanted to do his whole life. Now that he was actually doing it, he felt wrong in a way. He wondered if he would ever see Kenny again.

Watching as the FEMA camp became a small dot on the ground, he sat back and put his arm around Margot. He reflected on what Moose had said. He knew he was right. He knew his place was here, looking for his father and trying to help people. He knew he was coming back, and he hoped that Margot understood why.

He laid his head on her shoulder, his eyes becoming heavy. Before he passed into slumber, his last thought was of his mother. He hoped that she could see him and that she would look over them all in Texas. Sound asleep in the arms of the woman he loved, they made their way near their new future in a world that was uncertain. He wondered to himself what life they could make out of the ashes of the old.

ABOUT THE AUTHOR

Paul Mcvay

Paul McVay lives in the midwest with his wife and three children.

Made in the USA
Coppell, TX
23 January 2021